*Praise for A Map of Her Own*

"The juxtaposition of two women's stories provides an American tale that's been in the shadows far too long. Montgomery has a gift for capturing the raw yearnings of women in search of identity, purpose, and meaning. Their voices spoke to me." — Rosalind Noonan, New York Times Bestselling author of *And Then She Was Gone*

"Montgomery has created a well-written, engrossing, dual-time novel with a strong sense of setting. The story offers a detailed and compassionate exploration of two women's internal conflicts as they navigate strikingly similar challenges of womanhood, economic realities, and healing, though separated by generations. Highly recommend *A Map of Her Own*, especially for readers interested in labor history and the history of working women." — S.L. Stoner, author, Sage Adair, Historical Mysteries

"*A Map of Her Own* is an exploration of resilience and connection across generations. Blending past and present, it illuminates how women's struggles for dignity and meaning echo across time." — Marianne Monson, USA Today best-selling author of *Frontier Grit* and *The Opera Sisters*

*Other books by Dede Montgomery*

My Music Man
Beyond the Ripples
Humanity's Grace
From First Breath to Last

# A Map of Her Own

# A Map of Her Own

## Dede Montgomery

*Bink Books*
Bedazzled Ink Publishing • Fairfield, California

Disclaimer
This is a work of historical fiction. The story is set in a real historical
period and may include references to actual events, locations, and people.
However, the protagonists and most supporting characters are fictional. This
book should not be interpreted as a definitive account of historical events.

978-1-960373-77-9 paperback

Cover Design
by
Sapling
Studio

Bink Books
Bedazzled Ink Publishing
Fairfield, California
http://www.bedazzledink.com

*For my daughters*

# Chapter One
## Celia
### December 9, 2024, Astoria, Oregon

WHEN SHE LOOKED out to sea, Celia felt the past and future collide in a shock that excited and frightened her. Yet, her own existence had begun to feel ho hum. There must be something exciting hiding deep within her. After all, what else was life about? You were born, got a few birthday cakes when you were lucky, maybe had a good friend and good sex, caved and had a kid or two, and then what? Wait to get sick or die suddenly?

"Hey, Celia! You joinin' me?" Ed called from his boat. "Get the ropes and pots organized, and the guys will load the bait and everything else later." He gave her that stern you're late, weird uncle-like smile. Occasionally she could stomach the expression while other times it bugged her, making her feel young and insignificant. She knew she should feel lucky to be accepted by her boss, not an easy feat for a woman in the fishing industry. She pulled her backpack higher on one shoulder and picked up her pace along the dock.

Their crew was scheduled to head out across the bar to dump the crab pots for their pre-soak at eight o'clock the next morning. The boat, *High Hopes*, would join a parade of hundreds of other fishing boats permitted to commercially crab off Oregon's coast. The day would begin early in the dark and stay busy. It would lack the intensity of pulling up pots laden with crab and slinging them into holding bins, even though each empty pot weighed nearly as much as Celia. Might it be the pride she felt to hold her own that was keeping her from moving on?

Celia took her final steps along the weathered wooden dock and peered at Ed's boat as she climbed aboard. It was beaten down from seasons of pelting storms and crashing waves, and she was certain he no longer treated it with the care he had when new. She could barely read the lettering of *High Hopes*. Although crab yields and prices were predicted to be as high as seven dollars a pound, she knew she'd be smart to look elsewhere for work. She'd heard some guys boast about making as much as forty grand in a season, but she'd never cleared more than fifteen. Most of the guys she knew moved on from crabs to other fish to make a decent annual income. In the beginning, Celia liked the idea of sharing catch profits. Kind of a "one for all and all for one" philosophy. But recently she admitted Ed's boat was never going to be a high profit earner. Her actual take plus restaurant paychecks was barely enough to make rent and essentials while living in Astoria, especially as city folks from Portland and Seattle discovered the town and drove up rent. She worried she'd have to move further out to a smaller town or worse, ask her mom to bail her out. She knew, though, her increasing discontent was about more than making enough money.

"Headin' over to the marina office for a bit." Ed climbed off the boat, his body wearing the hunched curve of old age. Even though she was no youngster at thirty-seven, she retained the muscle strength of her late twenties. Use it or lose it, she figured. Ed had recently celebrated his seventy-eighth birthday, and his body looked the part; his muscles weaker, hair gray and receding and his skin like dried-out jerky. He wore his usual navy captain cap that was so drab and ancient she had no idea if it once had an insignia or logo. "Justin and Trevor won't be here till tonight." He signed off with a head nod, turned, and plodded down the dock.

Celia inhaled the fishiness of the brackish water as she climbed onboard and stepped toward the pots Ed had loaded by crane earlier. She pulled off her ball cap, tied back her curly black hair, and fastened it with a hair tie from her wrist. After tucking her short ponytail under the collar of her jacket she replaced the cap. Although she never hit six feet, once she grew out of the embarrassed teen years, she appreciated the gains achieved with extra height, longer arms, and legs. In the years since, she recognized she had better coordination than some her size. Seagulls called out their hahas while she pulled on her leather gloves, as if they were laughing at her taking on another season. Celia coiled and organized ropes and buoys to make the next day's crab pot drop speedy and efficient but was distracted as her recent phone call with her mom replayed in her head. They spoke every week or two, following a usual script and this call had been no different.

"Hey, Mom." Celia had tried to make herself comfortable on her couch.

"Hi, Celia, how's it going?" Celia knew this was rhetorical, and she stayed silent. "I've been swamped trying to finish all the end of year work, you know, waiting for the slowpokes to get me their financial details." Her mom liked to remind her how busy she was. "But how about you? Anything new on the work front?"

Celia sucked in a snarl and was grateful her mom couldn't see her roll her eyes. This question came up each time they spoke, her mom eager for her to find something better to do with her life. Celia had learned to fake it, yet this time was bothered her mom might be right. "All is good, Mom. You know, the season opens next week, and we have a lot to do." She didn't want to give her mom the benefit of hearing her doubts; they'd never had that kind of relationship, although it had improved as they spent less time together.

Even now, as she coiled the last of the ropes and buoys, she could imagine her mom biting her lip to stop nagging. "Oh, yes," she offered instead. "Well, you be safe out there." There was silence. "How is your friend, uh, Kate?"

Yes, she was trying. "She's fine." Celia felt mean stonewalling her again but could not seem to break their communication pattern. So instead, her mom went on about her parents' health and how they'd like a visit sometime since Celia didn't plan to join them for Christmas. Celia felt a twinge of guilt, knowing she was delinquent for not visiting. It was all pretty routine.

Now, these few days later, Celia tried to immerse herself in the Zen of the moment like Kate suggested. Yet she could not stop her brain from rehashing the phone conversation or ignore a new prickly warning that trickled from her brain to her scalp. She stretched back and reached her arms to the sky. "Fuck, fuck, fuck!" she shouted at the seagulls. Maybe it was her subconscious trying to urge her to complete this chapter of her life; or might it be more than that? A premonition? It reminded her of the feeling she'd once had her first season fishing when she worked on a charter boat. The crew was knowledgeable, but the captain lacked people skills, and she knew she needed to leave it. She worried then something terrible might happen before the end of the season. The captain told her once some believed women were considered bad luck onboard. His quick laugh didn't convince Celia that he didn't believe the old saying.

Now as she moved the metal pots and plastic totes, and allocated coils of ropes and buoys—her mind spun with memories back to that first summer of fishing. The naivety and pretentiousness of customers annoyed her. Once in a while, the clients were a bunch of guys celebrating a bachelor party or reunion, acting like royal assholes.

"Welcome Aboard!" the charter captain offered new guests wearing rubber-soled shoes and life preservers on a day trip toward the end of the season. He nodded sternly to Celia, meaning, "be friendly." Celia forced a fake smile to the ten guys climbing aboard, some making their way up to the bow and others claiming spots at the back of the boat. The guys swaggered their energy, boasting about catching their dozen crabs. A couple of them had sweatshirts with a logo with a KA and a pitchfork, while others had beaver ball caps. Celia didn't have anything against Oregon State, but pompous frat guys annoyed her.

"Hey, hey, here we go!" one of them yelled, jostling another with his elbow.

"Gonna impress Sandra with your crabs?" one fraternity brother chided to the other, shimmying his hips.

Celia muffled a groan; wondering how they'd behave if they didn't haul in their limit.

"Don't sit next to Evan," another guy continued, nodding at a man who looked green, probably having chugged too many beers the night before. "A hundred bucks he'll heave before we see a crab."

Captain laughed with them.

One of the crew passed Celia and mumbled, "He'll probably be begging us to leave him on a buoy." Celia groaned as she noticed another guy in the party pull two six packs out of his insulated bag.

A bit later as the boat navigated toward the pots, the loud guy ranted on about a round of golf they'd played the day before and some hot chick they saw in the bar. Celia focused on her boat responsibilities but knew then she didn't earn enough to put up with this shit. She felt delirious with relief later that afternoon when the boat returned to dock, the only issues being a few faulty crab pots and the guy Evan barfing over the gunwale. At least she hadn't had to clean off globs of yellow puke from the deck. She finished working the season but didn't reach out again to the captain, knowing the feeling was mutual.

Celia slowly exhaled. At least she wasn't working on a charter boat anymore. She focused on the grass green Megler Bridge as it crossed the nearby mouth of the Columbia River. It was easy to be mesmerized by cars as they circled from the main road upward to the top span of the bridge. She had crossed it several times but still found it hard to believe it was nearly five miles long. What a feat it must have been to build. She imagined those early years when people paid a toll to cross. Or even earlier when the choice was to cross by ferry. Maybe those olden times were when she should have had her shot at living.

She coiled the final rope and buoy and set them inside the pot. In addition to being distracted these days, she admitted only to herself feeling lonely. She had prided herself on being independent, not needing to rely on anyone. Her mom's voice rang again in her ear: "Celia, you have to actually try. Pick yourself up and take care of yourself, dress to fit the part. Nobody will want to hang out with you if they think you don't care much about yourself. Or how you look." When her mom said this to her back in her teens and early twenties, Celia did the opposite. Occasionally she'd meet up with other women. The ones she met in school and during work, cafes, the cannery. To her then, so much of the circling inane chatter and worries seemed stupid and irrelevant. Yet she couldn't pinpoint what it was she craved and needed now.

Celia stood up and surveyed the boat. Although she could hear voices and folks moving equipment around in the harbor, *High Hopes* felt oddly peaceful. She preferred how December at the marina was quieter than the height of the summer. She pulled her water bottle from her pack and took a long drink. Her toes felt cramped inside her size ten boots, and she was tempted to take off the extra pair of socks she'd thrown on. She wanted to feel happy and excited to be moving into the season of crabbing. But now the hard labor of pulling up crab pots and braving morning cold no longer challenged or satisfied her. Back when she had begun fishing four years prior, she could not imagine finding any other work as fulfilling. She had echoed what other fisherfolks said; it's hard work but the beauty of a sunrise and the freedom of being on the water beat all else. But now, the intensity and competition of the catch competed with the peace she sought, making her question its merits. Yet, she could not rouse herself to grow the seed into any different course.

"Hey, Celia!" Justin yelled as he neared the boat from the dock. She turned toward him in surprise. "Ed wonders if you've got everything ready for me and Trevor for later?" She didn't know why he was checking up on her. She had swapped her time so she could work a restaurant shift before they headed out in the morning.

"Good Lord, think I'm an idiot?" she asked under her breath, but nodded.

"Ed told me to ask, you know. I mean, I'd just stopped by," he said as if reading her mind.

"Yeah. I get it," she replied louder, turning toward him. She shouldn't take her frustration out on Justin. He was barely more than a kid only trying to earn a living. She forced a smile as he grabbed his phone.

Celia felt gloomy. How could the ocean be so alive, yet these days she felt nearly dead? Once she was working on the water she'd look out over the boat bow into the water's choppiness in wonder. Amazed by its seeming ability to keep going; its energy spinning as it did. At least so far. She heard voices warning about the oceans dying, coral and starfish disappearing, waters warming. Others pushed back, arguing how fishing was becoming more sustainable, and crab fishing always had been. She couldn't help but assume some of the climate deniers were the same ones who claimed life was perfect for women today. Maybe that was part of it. Back then she imagined working on a boat captained by a woman, or eventually even getting her own. Years ago, that might have seemed the solution to her discontent. Now she knew that wasn't the gist of it.

Several years before, her friend Kate had asked about her fascination with the ocean. After a beer one night Celia admitted it might go back to her love of Pippi Longstocking.

"Pippi Longstocking?" Kate laughed. "You mean the girl with the red braids who lived in a house with her horse?"

Celia's cheeks warmed and she tried to explain. "You know, the book about the South Seas?" How silly to remember details from a kid's book. She had imagined back then what it might be to have the freedom to simply escape. Crab fishing in the freezing waters of the Pacific Ocean was a far cry from her childhood longing of warm water, tropical islands, and freedom. But then, soon after the Pippi Longstocking conversation she was downtown the evening the cops apprehended a guy accused of murdering a man. From the start she hadn't been able to figure out why she was compelled to first attend the memorial service for the dead guy and then visit the man's old buddy. The dead guy's old buddy's colorful tales about working on the docks and the thrill of crossing the bar stayed with her, even if she could tell he fabricated some. Those stories, in part, propelled her on this strange and now seemingly unrealistic dream to claim that calling for herself.

Celia peeked at her phone in her pocket. She had half an hour to finish work, clean up, and get to the cafe. She stood, stretching her arms above her head, and looked out toward the ocean. She shook her head and groaned, knowing she was as fictional as Pippi. All the love in the world for the ocean didn't make her feel satisfied spending her remaining working days fishing like she thought it would.

Justin was still talking on his phone. She nodded to him and climbed off the boat. "See you at six tomorrow," she mouthed, pasting another fake smile on her face. "Text me, I guess, if you have questions."

Justin nodded but kept his mouth to his phone as he moved away from her toward the parking lot.

Celia walked to the end of the dock and peered out. In front of her, nothing but docks, fishing boats, dilapidated piers, and water melding into the seemingly infinite Pacific Ocean. In the beginning, she understood the gig would be seasonal, and although she hoped she'd make enough to take her through each year, everyone warned her not to have pie in the sky dreams. She was exhilarated then to believe she had punched through the glass ceiling and was intent on finding a place to explore this new passion. How cool to be paid to spend the day on the water, she had thought. She liked being one of the few women to prove some wrong to think she couldn't keep up, even though she was as strong and big as most of the men. In her first seasons, when she had to overnight on the water, she felt as though the ocean was rocking her to sleep. Celia knew she was tougher and more resilient in the cold than many, regardless of gender. She wasn't one of those tiny women who were always cold, complaining about blue fingers and toes. Not her. She had wanted to shout out across the breaking waves: *hey, Dad, whoever you are. Look at me! The good for nothing kid you abandoned is good at this!*

These days, though, this contention no longer fed her spirit. Each night as she put her feet up on her shabby fake leather couch, scrolling through news and social media on her phone, she nearly felt desperate. She had thought things would change once she was more adept at crabbing. But after several seasons of chasing the job, the seasons, and waiting tables, she felt worse not better. It was as if her soul was waiting for a cosmic message to guide her forward. She would never admit to anyone this yearning that a message would pop, fizz, and sparkle, inviting her to move toward it. Like the light in *The Shining* but not scary or creepy.

*It's going to be a banner season*, Ed had texted his crew the day before. *The crab quality looks good!* The season opened in a few days and folks were hoping it to be a success.

Celia didn't thrive on the competition of the harvest like some. You had to be smart and work your tail off to succeed. That's what troubled her. Even with the storms and cold, the shoreline and ocean were beautiful. The power and energy of the storms added to its allure, even if they also made it terrifying. How could she be bothered by such minor stuff onboard when she was surrounded by this wondrous beauty? Why did she keep circling back to this existential thought about there being something more for her?

She once loved crossing the bar, first thinking the "Graveyard of the Pacific" to be a book title, naïve she was in the beginning. This past year she learned another fishing boat was out at the wrong time and place, and two of the crew drowned. As she listened to news reports she developed an obsessive need to learn more. She began to feel fatalistic. As if with each trip over the bar she moved that tiny bit closer to the last one that would end in chaos. She even had a dream about it happening but tried to tell herself it wasn't cautionary. She's sure that's what provoked her most recent anxiety. Too, she had begun to wonder if Ed was still up to the work, even though she envied him for giving his life to what he knew he loved. She suspected his body hurt and worried his reflexes had slowed. The push to do more wasn't helped by a fish distributor pushing to get more crab faster.

Celia checked her phone again and picked up her pace toward her car. Just then she overheard Ed and his wife talking near the dock. "Enough is enough, Ed."

Celia ducked behind a shed, within earshot, knowing she shouldn't eavesdrop.

"Seriously, Ed," his wife added, exasperated. She pulled her fleece jacket tightly as she hugged her arms together. Her canvas narrow-brimmed hat blocked her face from Celia's view. "This isn't what I bargained for in old age." She hesitated. "Yes, you are old," she said more quietly. "We both are." She dropped her hands and pointed first to Ed and then herself. "And we should be doing other things. What are you still trying to prove?" Her voice was shaky, and she brought her hands to her cheeks.

"I'm not proving nothing." Ed's voice rose in frustration. "This is my life, Janet. My whole life." He hesitated before moving closer to her. "This is what I do."

Celia hurried to her car. Although she knew some fishermen wives loved time apart when their spouses were at sea, even if they also worried, it didn't sound like Janet felt that way.

Celia hadn't left enough time to clean up at home so she headed on to the café to help with the late lunch shift. She kept spare clothes in her car and hadn't handled bait, so she probably smelled okay, giving herself the sniff test. The marina parking lot was quiet, and she knew it would be busier in the early hours the next morning. She turned on the radio, hoping music would help her feel upbeat, but wishing she could forget her responsibilities and continue over the bridge and to the far northern tip of the Long Beach Peninsula. The prickle in her scalp returned, upping her anxiety, as she continued to the cafe. She caught herself—how many times had she told herself this? It was time. Yes, it was time. This season would be her last, she promised herself.

# Chapter 2
## Emma
### October 15, 1912, Camas, Washington

"EMMA! EMMA, WHERE are you? I need your help. Please," Emma's younger sister Mary called.

Emma stopped cleaning the kitchen and rubbed her temples, unable to stop thinking about her co-worker Cassie since the day before. Her family's house sat alongside other stick frame homes near the banks of the Columbia River, built to house workers lured to the town's paper mill in days that felt long ago, even to Emma. Her family's structure was one of the original homes, far too small to house a family of six even without the extra space taken up during visits by her older sister and family.

Emma knew she must attend to the children and retreat from thoughts flooding her mind that morning. She fiddled with bunched hair strands falling out of her bun. She did not dare imagine being as brave, bold, or strong as Cassie, and was intimidated by her. Even though she was nineteen, she knew a few men thought it silly to have what they called "girls" work in the factory, with some younger than her. Emma took precious time each morning to put her long brown hair into an updo. At the factory, she tied a cloth around it, hoping to protect the hair from grime or getting get caught in one of the bag-cutting machines.

It was important to Emma to convince others she could complete daily tasks at the bag factory with ease, even if she was exhausted by the end of the day. She thought calling it a factory was silly. As if factory made it fancier than what she knew it was inside, even if the making of paper bags intrigued her. Many evenings she fretted her pointed-toe boot clad feet would not be able to walk the half mile along rough Sixth Avenue, over the steel trussed bridge, and finally home. When she started working at the mill she had thought, because she was slim and small busted, she would not wear her corset to work. After all, her petticoat was cumbersome enough. This would have shocked Mother if she knew. The first week, however, she learned the supporting corset made her back ache less, although it became less effective as it softened with use. At the same time, she discarded the petticoat during work hours as she became wiser to the challenges of the job.

She had now worked at the mill a full year, following Father's demand to finish high school first. Back then he insisted she take full advantage of education unknown in other smaller towns. Camas benefited by the town's high school expansion with three fulltime teachers her final year of school, and Father was proud the mill provided funds for their town's schools. In the beginning, Mother insisted she not work there at all, but Emma's insistence and the extra dollar a day wage to put more food on the table quieted her in the end.

But Cassie. She admired Cassie more than any woman she had met, nearly to the point of feeling infatuated at first. Cassie was smart and strong, and the only female machine operator in the bag factory. She was not spending her day running errands and packaging bags like the other women. She seemed proficient at everything and widely respected, not seeming to look to men for approval. Once Emma even heard Cassie denigrate a man who made an inappropriate comment to a girl Emma's age. Emma might redden, but she knew better and tried to ignore it. Sometimes she blushed because they told her she was pretty—something she had never heard from boys her age. She felt mixed up; comments like that made her feel more like a woman rather than infuriated as Cassie. Emma nodded or issued a nearly inaudible *yes* anytime Cassie asked something of her.

"Yes, I am coming." Emma tensed her shoulders as she slurped her final sip of tepid tea. She rinsed and dried the cup before hurriedly setting it in the dish cupboard her father had built. Their house was shabbier than many, especially the ones built recently to house more workers in the growing community, or those owned by mill managers higher on the hill above town.

"Oh my." She sighed and glanced out the kitchen window. Her one day off was filled with chores, church, and children. She forced a smile, feeling unusually grumpy. Yet if Mother heard her complain, she would insist she leave the mill regardless of her earnings. Emma knew her job was more to her than only the pay or escaping responsibility for her siblings all day. As difficult as the work might be, she prided herself on how it made her feel independent.

"Shall we go outside for a breath of fresh air?" Emma asked Mary, forcing her voice to be light. She bent down and stroked Mary's blonde hair. "We have perhaps an hour before I need to help make supper." She glanced at the cotton towels and shirts drying near the fireplace, knowing she should fold them first. She shook her head, deciding she would deal with Mother's disapproval later. Lately their mother seemed exhausted, and Emma tried to feel sympathetic. At church she prayed to find more room in her heart for compassion.

"Yes!" Mary cried with a smile, reaching her hands up.

Emma gathered Mary's coat and two others. "Helen and John. Come, get your coats. We're going for a walk." She wanted this to go smoothly, forcing herself to inhale Mary's joy as she helped her put her arms into the sleeves of her woolen coat and gently straightened her bib collar and skirt. She sighed, knowing she would rather slowly stroll the main street free of both work and sibling responsibilities.

"Let's see Father!" Emma's siblings cried out in chorus. Rarely were they allowed to visit him at the Pioneer Store.

Emma didn't care where they went if they could be outside in the fresh air. Or as fresh as it seemed to get while living near a paper-making plant, the plume from its stacks darkly colored and often smelled like rotten eggs. She would rather walk the other direction toward her special spot on the banks of the Columbia River and gaze across to snow-topped Mount Hood, but Mother would scold her if the children snitched. Mother worried needlessly about the children being near that sometimes-swollen river. Emma consoled herself, knowing she would rather savor river time to daydream by herself as the ships passed by, like she had when she was younger with her oldest sister Martha. Back in those days before Martha began her own family and moved away.

"Yes, we can. Now, none of your complaining about the walk coming home." Emma pulled up her stockings and drew her cardigan tighter to her body.

"A is for apple," Helen sang quietly to Mary. The two sang the A, B, C song while John hit his stick on the ground in time with each additional letter. The younger children were delighted that a few of the streets like Burton and Clara began with letters they now knew how to draw. Once on a walk, Emma agreed to let them follow Columbia Street past the mill nearly all the way to the Columbia Slough.

"John, no throwing now. We have just enough time to get to the store for a short visit and return home." Emma regretted the sharpness of her voice and patted John on the shoulder as he dropped the rocks.

His knickers were pushed above his knees; Emma knew he wanted to wear long pants like the bigger boys. He loved to spend as many minutes as he could dropping stones into the Washougal River as they crossed it from their home in Oak Park. Oak Park might just as well be called Camas, as life seemed indistinguishable between the two. This place was all Emma and her siblings had known, lending the town a comfortable familiarity. She was grateful their home, even as simple and outgrown as it was, was closer to the wild Columbia River than the slough.

Their parents left the nearby city of Portland, joining others by steamboat soon after Mr. Pittock opened the mill. Emma wished to know more about her parents' early days in Portland, and she suspected some days Mother regretted their decision to leave the city. Father once said he might have liked to stay in Portland. Yet Mother became pregnant with Martha and Father lost his job as business owners became increasingly worried about an economic downturn. It was Mother's final insistence, that the gatherings of single men looking for work created an unsafe and immoral atmosphere for families. She wanted her growing family to find a small town to establish roots. Although Father had been born in Portland, and Mother in Salem to the south, worries about an economic crash were what finally made Father agree to seek work opportunities in Camas. He had mistakenly thought he would be hired on in an office job at the mill.

Emma had not yet traveled to Portland, even though a few of her friends' families had taken the steamboat there to see friends or even visit the theater. What a wonderful treat that might be.

Emma cleared her throat. "Now, children." She stopped and pulled the three of them near, her hands gently curved around the two youngest's shoulders. "You must not call out or in any way disrupt Father from work. This will be a surprise, as you know I normally work on Friday, and you would be home with Mother."

She dropped her chin and pressed her lips together before waving her hand and signaling they walk toward Sixth Avenue. She had been sent home from work that morning after two of the bag machines had broken down. She felt pleased to have a few extra hours, even though her wages would be less.

The downtown had grown to hold three hotels, a post office, and a few stores including Pioneer General. A few blocks down the hill sprawled the Columbia River Paper Company, emanating the sounds of noisy papermaking, and its stacks reaching toward the sky. Wooden troughed log flumes stretched downward, some were elevated on trestles. Emma was uncertain as to the location or exact functions of each mill operation, but never tired of knowing how it used logs to create first pulp, and then paper.

"And no begging for a treat. You know Father can't give you something without it being taken from his pay." Emma tugged her tan kid gloves at her wrists, as if to remind them of her adult responsibilities, even if one of the seams needed mending. "And, John, no handling the merchandise."

The children looked at her seriously and nodded. Mary hung her head.

"It is still nice, Mary, to have a special visit with him." Emma touched Mary's cheek.

Mary smiled and nodded.

Emma adored her siblings even if she sometimes grew frustrated. She did look forward to having her own children someday. Not soon, though. She wished she was bold enough to tell Mother, "All in good time." She knew this might be the only time in her life to be free from responsibilities required by a husband and family of her own.

After climbing up the hill past the mill, Emma nodded respectably to Mr. Smith as he stood outside the Camas Hotel. The two-story hotel was newly finished and although she was curious to see the inside, Emma knew better than to dare a peek now with the children. She did believe most of the local folks, Mr. Smith included, understood the need for the mill to employ women. She guessed they weren't as critical of women working there as was Mother. The local merchants relied on the mill for their own business success, and women helped keep it running. Their town was all about the success of the mill.

The children quieted as they reached the store. Their feet thumped on the stairs and along the porch. Emma put up her hand for them to stop and wait, and she opened the wooden door to peek inside. She let out a sigh of relief as she spotted Father alone crouching in front of a shelf that held potatoes, his back to the door.

Emma backed away and put her finger to her lips. "Remember your manners."

The children followed her into the shop, immediately forgetting her command. "Father!" they each called out, thumping across the pine planked floor toward him.

He looked up and smiled. "Emma. Children. What a surprise." His smile disappeared. "Is everything alright?" He straightened, rubbing his lower back, before pulling his long white cotton apron down over his trousers. He unrolled his shirt sleeves and buttoned them at his wrists, blinking back pain as he stood upright.

"Oh, yes, Father. We thought we'd take a short stroll and enjoy a few minutes of fresh air before I begin supper." Emma ran her hand along the smooth counter next to the cash register.

Their father gave each of the children a pat on the head. He limped as he always did now, a hobble that had lessened but not fully healed even four years after suffering a mill accident. If the injury had happened a few years later, he might have received compensation from the company. While he couldn't move well enough to take on the physical mill work and was unable to gain an office job, Emma knew working in the store was hard for him some days.

She ran her fingers over the small bundle of newspapers stacked on the counter next to her, newly delivered by steamboat and not yet unpacked. Behind Father were shelves of glass jars and baskets containing supplies required by townsfolks, everything from spices and flour to hardware. All of it lent an air of festivity to the otherwise simple shop. She loved the smell emanating from the wares, spices mixed with vegetables and textiles; it reminded her of Christmas.

"Did you notice the chill in the air?" he asked. He tussled John's hair. "We're in for a weekend storm, they say. Good thing they got that big paper shipment out on the water before the storm comes or they might have had a major loss. That Columbia River is wild during weather like that. Must be a fright to captains when it tosses so." He grinned.

"I'd like to be a river captain, Father." John clapped his hands and beamed.

Father would be surprised to know Emma had only recently found news about the mill's production compelling. She knew others didn't understand why she felt proud to work at this first mill in all the west to make paper from wood pulp, and that soon would use electricity. But now, with production worries and unfulfilled demands secretly discussed by workers, she found it particularly important to pay attention. She felt uneasy about what might happen next and worried that as a woman she might learn less than the men. After all, she was paid less and considered bottom of the heap of workers. She drummed her fingers on the counter softly and strained to read the newspaper headlines.

"Children, come here." Father took out a small handful of taffy from the taffy barrel and put one piece in each  youngster's hand. "But no eating them until after supper." His sparkling eyes contradicted the seriousness of his voice.

John made a face and began to protest.

Emma shook his shoulder and reached out her hand. "Why don't you all let me hold them." The children reluctantly handed her their taffy. Mary began to cry but she shushed her.

"Emma?" Father asked, holding a piece toward her.

"Oh, no thank you. Father." Emma shook her head and placed the children's taffy in her bag. Any free treats must be for the children. "We will be off," she added, ensuring they did not overstay. "We will see you at supper, Father?"

Father nodded and smiled, briefly touching Mary's head. "Thank you for your visit." He rolled up his sleeves.

Emma knew better than to kiss him in public. His comment signaled their visit had been long enough: she was certain he hoped to finish his reshelving early so he could be home in time for supper. The Pioneer Store was open parts of both Saturday and Sunday to allow single mill workers to shop, given their six-day, and occasionally when demanded, seven-day schedules. She was grateful the shop owner provided occasional relief for Father on the weekends.

"Come, children." She grabbed John's hand to pull him away from a barrel of nails. She knew he was only curious, wishing he could stay to explore large barrels and tubs holding staples, usually gravitating toward the hardware. "Come along." She ensured Helen gently closed the door behind them.

She looked wistfully toward the end of the road, wishing she could stay out longer but knowing better. Instead, she confirmed Helen was closely behind her before picking up her pace. She had come to expect Helen, as the middle sister, to do as she was told, already understanding her role. She and Helen looked alike, both smaller and wispier than average, Helen's brown hair plaited into two long braids. She hadn't changed from her cotton work dress. No matter how hard she tried to clean it, the dress held dust and grime from the bag factory, even though she covered it with an apron most days. One of the women at work had advised her to replace it, but Mother had only recently made her a new summer dress for church.

They passed the mill, and she pushed back her thoughts about work and Cassie.

"Emma." John tugged on her hand after crossing the bridge back to Oak Park. She felt badly for daydreaming again and ignoring the children.

"Yes, John? What is it?" She smiled at her active eight-year-old brother with the dimples, his twinkling smile sometimes excusing his naughtiness. How could anyone not give in to his delightful face?

"Father said you made paper bags at work. But Mary said that is what the men do, not you."

Emma glared at Mary, wondering why either of them were talking about her job. Mary must have overheard Mother talking to someone.

Emma crouched down and steadied her voice. She looked intently at both Mary and John, ensuring she had Helen's attention too. The least she could do was give her siblings a lesson. "I do help make bags, John. It is very important work."

John nodded solemnly. He was already interested in the mill's operations.

Emma folded her arms, narrowed her eyes, and looked at Mary. "And women help make them too. In fact, if women were not there to help there would not be enough bags."

Mary looked at the ground, put her fingers over her eyes, and peeked through them at Emma. Helen nodded enthusiastically and smiled. Helen was a smart girl. Emma knew she kept many of her insights to herself, carrying herself quietly with an elegant knowingness.

"Would you children like to know how the bags are made?" All three nodded. Emma had never been asked by anyone in her family, and while she felt empowered to explain the process, she teased herself for getting satisfaction talking about it to three small children. She pulled them close to her, huddled along the roadside. "First, the paper mill brings over sheets of paper. You know that is what is made in the mill, correct? Especially newsprint, or the paper newspapers are made from. And, of course, the paper is all made from trees, from the pulp of trees." She released her arm and gestured first toward town and then from west to east. "Although long ago it was made from rags and other things."

"Of course, silly," John said as he nodded authoritatively to Mary.

"In the old days the bags were all made by hand. Cutting and glueing the paper together; oh my, that would be so much work." The children's eyes grew wide. "But now we use machines. In fact"—she glared at Mary—"a woman invented the type of machine we use." Emma was glad she had paid attention to stories she heard at the factory. "This machine can cut, fold, and glue the pieces of the bag together, if you can believe that."

The children nodded enthusiastically.

She stood up and dusted her hands together.

"I want to do that," John said.

Emma laughed. "Maybe you'll work at the mill too someday." She touched his head. "Now, you know the bags that have the flat bottoms?" She brought her hands together, palms up.

The children nodded.

Emma grabbed John and Mary's hands and smiled at Helen. "That is how bags are made." She clapped her hands together and stood up straighter. "And now, we best be getting home."

Emma felt more spring in her step from the simple gesture of her siblings appreciating how she spent her days. This boost was a needed remedy to recent concerns about work and the rumors flying around the mill. She also tired of men telling her over and over how to do things, even though she was more experienced than a few of them. She wanted them to understand how much even a girl could do. It confused her. She tried to pray about it on Sunday, but her prayers some days contradicted the sermons she heard only moments earlier about the husband being the sole decision-maker of the family.

"Home!" Mary shrieked as they approached their front door.

The children continued to chatter, and only then did Emma hear the calls of the chickadees. Enough daydreaming. She had more to do before the end of the day.

"Yes, come, children." Emma opened the door. "Time to clean up and finish your chores."

# Chapter 3
## Celia
### December 9, 2024

LATER THAT AFTERNOON, Celia wiped down the last of the tables, relieved the cafe served only breakfast and lunch in winter. Earlier shifts best suited her morning person preference, and she doubted she'd win many tips if she had to pretend to care serving food into the evening.

"Thanks, Cee," she heard from the kitchen. Kate popped her head out the doorway. "I do appreciate you picking up shifts when days get busier. I don't know what I'd do without you." They were nearly the same age, but Kate's face was more lined; maybe paler skin wrinkled more. While her own body looked capable of pulling up crab pots, her face did not yet show much sign of sun and wind. Kate moved her wiry body with simple efficiency and speed as she worked but rarely seemed to eat. Celia wondered how she ever got enough calories to sustain the energy she exuded.

"Of course." Celia nodded and threw the rag in the dirty laundry bag as she entered the kitchen. She removed her denim jacket from the hook near the office door and pulled her arms through. She felt bad occasionally, dreading parts of this job and knowing how she depended on it to stay afloat financially. Not every employer would support her irregular schedule, and she was glad they could help each other out. She liked Kate, her only friend to have created a nickname for her. Even though their lives felt worlds apart as Kate somehow managed both a business and navigated a complicated relationship.

"Do you have time to sit for coffee? I could use a break, but I'm not ready yet for the chaos at home." Kate put her hands to either side of her face, pushing her fingertips into her scalp as shook her head. She lived with her partner who shared custody of his two young kids.

Celia hesitated. She had an early morning ahead, but Kate was one of few friends she trusted. She knew she should appreciate invitations to share time alone together. "Sure." She attempted a smile. She knew she couldn't hide how drawn and tired she felt. "But no coffee for me, I'll grab tea."

Kate already had poured a cup of coffee for herself into the plain white standard issue ceramic cup, probably the pot's dregs. Celia needed to fall asleep earlier not later that evening and poured the last of the hot water over a tea bag before turning the burner off and setting the pot on the counter.

They slumped into the tan cheap vinyl back booth. Celia pulled off her jacket and tucked it behind her on the cushion. Her back ached from moving pots earlier. The blinds were partially drawn, door locked, and only the emergency lighting reflected out into the darkening streets. Celia was surprised to feel cozy, this little hole in the wall tucked down a quiet block from the river shoreline. Kate was lucky to host many regulars, as the place was hidden from Astoria's Broadway Street thoroughfare. All she needed were a few scented candles and a cozy fleece blanket and she could fall asleep.

Celia dipped her peppermint tea bag a few times into her cup, mesmerized for a moment by the hot water ripples. Up and down, up and down, like the buoys in the waves. She had read peppermint was good for depression, alcohol bad. As she dealt with existential questions about her life, she was trying to identify ways to be better to herself, even if she didn't always follow through.

Kate slipped her shoes off and pulled her legs onto the booth cushion. The vinyl squeaked in protest, as she rubbed the soles of her socks and groaned. "Kids soccer tomorrow." She made a face and took a drink of her coffee before pushing her hands through her short hair.

Celia laughed, surprised to find energy to respond. "Is it that bad? And does that make you one of those soccer moms? I never thought my hip friend would ever fall into that suburban mom category." She clapped her hands over her mouth, but a snicker escaped.

Without trying, Kate looked like a hip not yet forty-something; usually outfitted in jeans and a fitted shirt, beach sandals or sneakers, and a chic short haircut. Celia knew she must wear makeup, her complexion was too perfect, but she did it in a way that you couldn't tell. The last time Celia remembered wearing makeup was to her high school graduation.

Kate rolled her eyes and waved her hand as if throwing a ball to Celia. "You've got it wrong. I think kids in every community everywhere play this game at some point in their lives till they get burned out or turn to drugs or are forced to work. Or who knows what else?" She fidgeted in her seat. "Sometimes I look across at the other parents as their eight-year-olds ravage each other on the field and think, I bet they all wonder how they got here too." She stretched her arms over her head and closed her eyes. Yes, Celia knew she was seeking her personal Zen space.

"Yeah, you're a good stepmom. Or whatever you call yourself." Celia took a deep breath and let it out. She could not imagine regularly taking half a day to go watch little kids run around in the winter mist and on muddy fields. She'd walked by kids playing soccer the week before and it looked more like a competition to see who could get the muddiest. She had no intention of ever having kids.

"The thing is," Kate continued, opening her eyes and sitting straighter. "I hate to admit it but I kind of get it. I mean these kids have so much energy and if the alternative is to find other activities all weekend to tire them out, I'm not sure I could handle it. Gone are the days when kids just take off on their own to build forts or whatever, only returning in time for dinner. I guess I shouldn't complain and instead feel lucky we can afford the fees." She took a drink of coffee before resting her elbows on the table.

Celia smiled and sipped her tea. Kate adored her partner's kids Jack and Addie. She had known them since just after Addie's birth, and when the kids' parents split up, they took to her well. But everyone seemed to like Kate. She too had contended how she didn't want kids, but having them in their lives half the time was perfect.

Kate's phone buzzed. She seemed to have it tethered to her body, and Celia bet she took it with her into the shower. She recognized the ring tone.

"I'm sorry but can you hang on for a few?" Kate asked.

Celia nodded, and Kate slowly stretched out of her comfiness to pad toward the kitchen in her socks for privacy.

Celia placed her cup on the table and traced and retraced a scratch in the wood with her finger. She closed her eyes, the peppermint soothing as advertised, crisp but invigorating, smooth but not sweet. She wondered if appreciating sipping tea meant she was getting old. It felt like some old lady thing. Whatever, she replied to her inner voice, enjoying the calmness while it lasted. She opened her eyes to the rattle of the front door and was glad when they figured out the café was closed. She could see the lower half of a raincoat head back toward Broadway.

Celia tried to appreciate Kate's point of view, but soccer was something she had hated as a kid. She too was of a generation whose parents thought their kid had to participate in any popular thing that came their way. Maybe it was still that way. As if it was a childhood milestone to get one of the "every player deserves a trophy" at the season's end. Soccer's only redeeming feature for her back then was that boys and girls were grouped together, maybe to be able to fill teams. Back then she preferred to hang out with boys, which was ironic to her now. "Yes, Celia, you must," Mom had said that first day all those decades ago.

She looked up to see Kate's shadow behind the kitchen pass still talking with the phone in one hand and twirling short strands of her hair with the other. Celia's back felt stiff, and she pulled herself out of the booth. She wandered toward the door and stopped to peer at the local kids' sports team pictures on the wall. Mostly white kids smiling, looking up, wearing t shirts, some with local business names she couldn't make out. Someone paused again outside the door, and Celia went back to the table. She sat down, slouched into the cushion, then turned and drew her knees up to rest her feet on the backside of the booth. She closed her eyes. Occasional cars passing outside and the alternating swishing and humming of the dishwasher allowed her mind to retreat, as if a lullaby. The smell of grilled ham and cheese lingered as if baked into the upholstery.

Celia had thought she'd get out of soccer since she hid the paperwork when she was in the second grade, and it was too late to join by the time her mom caught wind of it. She hoped her mom would realize she was behind other kids in understanding soccer, and since she liked her daughter to be a winner, maybe she'd back off. Her mom was too busy with work to volunteer in the classroom, which relieved Celia back then, although she still hammered her with questions at dinner about school. She tried a newer tactic the next fall.

"But, Mom, since I didn't play last year, I'll be behind. Let me do something else on my own if you're worried about me getting fat or something." Celia knew that would shut her mom up. Her mom never bought women's magazines and made a point to tell Celia she was more than her looks, or ask why advertisers should decide what was most important anyway?

"Ceee-lia." Mom held her hand with the pen in the air, drew an exaggerated invisible circle before signing on the dotted line. "Please make sure to turn this in at school tomorrow." Matter closed.

"Hey Cee." Kate peeked through the kitchen pass, her hand over her phone. Celia opened her eyes. "I'm so sorry—it'll just be a few more minutes. Are you okay? I understand if you need to take off." She shrugged and gave an apologetic smile.

Celia nodded, making no effort to move from her comfy position, thoughts from her past still circling inside. She closed her eyes again.

She remembered how she felt when she learned that fall soccer season would last six weeks. She wasn't certain whether to complain about how much of her life would be ruined or to breathe a sigh of relief it wouldn't last longer. It was a warm September and most of the kids showed up at Portland's Grant Park in shorts and tennis shoes. She identified the kids whose parents were already banking on soccer scholarships. They were wearing shiny new cleats and jerseys with names on them like Mia and Ronaldo. Names she assumed were famous players somewhere. The best kid on the team was a girl who impressed Celia. But not impressed enough to try harder. She lagged behind the other kids jogging on the field and kicked the ball when it came to her. But as soon as practice was over, she was the first kid to head to the parking lot.

Three weeks in—halfway she reminded herself jubilantly—her coach called her as she headed to the parking lot. Celia thought it was funny they called their leader "Coach," since all she did was try to keep a bunch of third graders in line, sometimes asking the show-offs to demonstrate how to do things.

"Celia," Coach called again. "Can you come over for a minute?"

Celia was surprised the coach knew her name; she thought she was staying under the radar.

"Thanks," Coach said as Celia panted to a stop next to her.

Celia knew her name was Kim, but she liked to keep it impersonal without knowing why. "Yes, Coach." She shrugged and looked down at her feet, feeling uneasy. She wanted to tell her to hurry because she didn't want to keep her mom waiting, but she knew her mom was probably thrilled to see her talking to the coach, hoping she was being buddy-buddy or getting compliments.

"Celia, do you enjoy coming to soccer?"

Celia glanced up at Kim without expression. She wasn't sure whether to be honest. Might this be a trap?

"Truthfully?" Kim added as if she could read her mind, worrying Celia.

"No." Celia shook her head and looked away. She didn't know what else to say.

"I didn't think so." Kim brought her hands together and looked at her sternly. Celia's face felt hot, and she drew her shoulders inward. "You know, that's okay, right? I mean, it doesn't hurt my feelings. I know soccer isn't for everyone." Kim grinned.

Celia felt so relieved, tears filled her eyes. She wiped her face and looked up at her coach.

"But it's kind of a bummer isn't it that you come out all these days and don't have any fun? Is there anything I can do to make it better for you?" Kim reached her hands out in question.

Celia couldn't talk. She thought the coach would get mad or tell her to get her act together or be tough like the team stars. Her mouth dropped open.

Kim smiled again and touched her hand. "So, here's what you do. Maybe try to find something you like at each practice, just one thing. Maybe there's a kid on the team who's fun to be with? Or maybe you want to try to be better at stealing the ball when you're on defense? You're pretty fast and strong." She lifted one foot to kick her cleats together and clods of mud fell to the grass.

She raised her eyebrows. Nobody had ever told her she was fast or strong.

"But then. Think about what you'd rather do with your time so that the next time your mom tells you to sign up for soccer you're ready to pitch something else. Okay?" Kim pulled the end of her auburn-haired ponytail, tightening the skin around her face. "She probably just wants you to be involved or find something you like. But don't think of it like being the best in something—just something you really want to do with your time." She took a deep breath, then clapped her hands together as if to signal the chat was over.

Celia could hear the din of players' voices from the next team preparing to practice on the field. She smiled shyly. She sensed Kim had been nervous and was relieved to be finished.

"See you next week." Kim gently touched the top of Celia's shoulder.

It still surprised Celia for a coach to share such meaningful words to an eight-year-old; also teaching her a better way to handle her mom. She did start thinking about what she liked.

The next time her mom started after her about soccer Celia was prepared. "I plan to walk dogs." She could tell right away her mom wasn't thrilled with that idea, not quite the thing that was equal to a sport. But Celia had already lined up walking a neighbor's dog for one dollar which kind of impressed her. She grumbled a bit, but Celia always thanked Coach Kim for helping her. She understood how relevant this three decade's old lesson was to her now.

Kate cleared her throat, and Celia blinked open her eyes, startled. She straightened out of her slouch.

"Sorry about that." Kate rolled her eyes. "Brian had some emergency come up at work and wanted to vent." She sat again across from Celia, this time keeping her feet on the floor. "You know, when he needs to talk . . ." She hesitated. "And because of all that, he doesn't think he can go to the game tomorrow and needed to chat about making morning plans."

"Oh, I'm sorry." Celia felt bad to be relieved she was heading out on the water and unable to help out. "You okay with it all?" She pulled her arm through her jacket sleeve.

"It's fine. It must be, you know? He does a lot to be a good dad, and the kids would be disappointed if neither of us made it. It just bums me out on my full day without work as he'll probably be tied up all day. Hmm?" She shrugged and looked at Celia. "Any other ideas to keep two active kids busy for the rest of the day that will tire them out so much they need to sleep at seven?" She shook her head and let out a low breathy chuckle.

Celia knew it was a rhetorical question but shook her head anyway. Retreating to her memories of the past in the silence of the café made her feel even sleepier.

Kate drained the coffee and bent to put her shoes on. "At least it's all done here for now." She brushed her hands together. "Hey, what do you think about painting the interior here?" She looked up at Celia after tying her laces. "You okay? You seem quieter than normal?" She was fidgeting, probably eager to get whatever alone time she could with Brian that evening.

Celia looked at the nothing much neutral painted walls of the café and shrugged. "Yeah. I'm tired. But too, I think I've got to be done with this fishing gig." She had more to unpack. About an urgent quest to find the thing to satisfy an emptiness she felt. She appreciated their deepening friendship but wasn't one with energy to talk for hours. She too had a big day ahead, though gratefully not at the soccer field.

# Chapter 4
## Celia
### December 9, 2024

CELIA SHUFFLED THROUGH the grocery store for a quick dinner; sorry she hadn't thought to grab a meal to take with her before the café closed. She selected a to-go container and loaded it up with potatoes and chicken and some overcooked veggie from the hot bar. She knew it was all a bit gross but had neither time nor patience to address epicurean or nutritional ideal, and she hustled through the checkout counter. She was the type to eat most anything, although she tried to eat healthy. Mostly, though, she focused on eating enough to have energy to do the things she did.

During the ten-block drive home, she returned to thoughts about her mom. She'd been triggered by two women and a girl in the store, reminding her of grocery shopping with her mom and grandmother those years ago in Portland's Fred Meyer. She always begged for frozen chicken strips and chocolate chip ice cream. After she parked her car at her apartment, she peered past the darkened parking lot and wished she could afford one of the newer apartments adjacent to the Astoria Riverwalk with water view.

"Hell." She crammed her gear and food between her arms but dropped the cardboard container as she unlocked her door. Bits of brown sauce leaked onto the carpet. "Jesus." She exhaled, pretending she'd clean it later.

She dropped her gear on the floor and set her food on the kitchen table, grateful her roommate was out that night. A hot shower was at the top of her list, and after waiting for the pipes to warm, she stepped in. Nothing felt as good as a shower at the end of a long, damp day. She luxuriated in its heat, unable to prevent the steam from sucking out more memories. She squeezed out a dollop of shampoo on her hand and massaged it into her hair, breathing in its jasmine scent.

Celia knew motherhood was hard for her mom. She had been left alone when Celia was born, and although fortunate her parents offered support, they were also disappointed their daughter, Sheila, was unmarried and pregnant. Yet, with help at first, Celia's mom provided for the two of them to live in a decent neighborhood in Northeast Portland with good schools then and low crime. As a pre-teen, Celia told herself she had it better than a lot of kids abandoned by their fathers. Yet, her mom's attitude got more frustrating as Celia got older—giving her a permanent chip on her shoulder—as if she was owed something. Celia was less bothered about occasional referrals to the deadbeat father, but more about how her mom seemed to act as if she deserved more than others because of it.

After rinsing her hair a final time, Celia stepped out of the shower, grabbed a towel, and stared through the foggy mirror at her reflection. How could she at her age be engulfed in childhood memories? Before wrapping herself tightly in one rough towel and her hair in another, she wrapped her hand around a firm bicep then pressed the hand against her taut stomach. *If she gave up fishing would her body change too?*

"Whatever," she muttered and padded to the kitchen.

Leftover pizza and old vegetable odors escaped as she opened the fridge to grab a can of seltzer. She took a sip and slouched back into the straight-backed chair, its wooden slats pressing into her spine. As she stared out the kitchen window above the sink, she could barely make out newly planted pine trees across the parking lot.

"Celia!" She heard her mom's voice from long ago. "Make sure you tell your Mrs. Clement why I need you to stay after school today."

"Sure, Mom." Celia had tried not to roll her eyes but discounted the request; she knew this favorite teacher liked having her around after school. Mrs. Clement allowed kids who didn't have daycare to occasionally hang around for an hour or so after class.

"Celia!" Her mom repeated loudly as she sat in their kitchen, finishing breakfast and reading the back of a cereal box. Her mom wouldn't buy the sugared stuff advertised on TV. No, she had to have the whole grain topped with fruit, usually a banana, and milk. Not even a sugar bowl in sight. And eggs on the weekend; never frozen waffles or pop-up pastries. Celia had been mystified why her mom was particularly wound up that morning; only years later did she fit the pieces together.

"I need you to pay attention to me. It's important Mrs. Clements understand what I am doing and not think I'm just like other parents who poorly planned their week." Her mom spewed out a bunch of details, something about some important meeting.

"Mom," Celia began to argue. After all, nobody cared what her mom was doing, Mrs. Clement included. Besides, she thought her teacher liked her company because she wasn't a chatterbox and sat quietly in the corner as she drew in her notebook. She loved the peace and quiet of it all and having someone around who didn't bug her to do this or that. Even then, she knew arguing would fire up her mom, and she'd have to listen to the spiel about how hard she worked to create this amazing life for Celia.

Soon after, Celia became vigilant, identifying moments her mom launched into her superiority rants. It might start with a simple comment about how amazing she was to provide more than a peanut butter sandwich in her lunch, going on to recite stupid facts about protein and fat content. She might mention someone who didn't do things that way or as well as she did. Celia could never figure out why her mom had to be the way she was, but this conflict became a gigantic thorn in their relationship. Much later Celia realized the pattern stopped her from chasing dreams bigger than what she sensed others seemed to think she deserved.

She once had a boyfriend who insisted her childhood had messed her up, making her incapable of being in a successful relationship. At the time, she resented it and silently retreated before getting up the nerve to bark back: he had more than enough of his own shit to contend with. Their relationship was largely physical, centering mostly around sex. At least she had that. But before long they drifted apart finding everything except sex to be a dead end.

Celia groaned. She had wasted too much time overthinking this nonsense. How could she ever find energy for tomorrow? She was chilled in her damp towels and headed back to the bathroom. She hung up her towels before hurriedly coating her legs and arms with peppermint scented lotion, slid on her ratty sweats, combed her wet hair, and returned to the kitchen. As she sat down and finally forked cold dinner into her mouth, her mind unwound all that was ahead of her. She needed to try to get some sleep before her 4:15 a.m. wake up but first had to pull gear together. She peered into the last of her dinner. She should have felt hungrier after the day's work and forced herself to swallow the last mouthfuls of stringy chicken and greenish vegetable, mushed up in an unappetizing leftover slop.

Celia set out layers of clothing for the morning. It was freezing when she first untied at the dock, some mornings the damp cold numbing. After a few hours of pulling and hauling, she couldn't remember how cold felt, until a storm broke loose, or surprise waves splashed over, or she sat for a few minutes staring out into a winter day of thick mist. She couldn't imagine the horror of drowning in the icy ocean but pushed the thoughts aside and headed to the bathroom to brush her teeth.

# Chapter 5
## Emma
### January 23, 1913

TWO YEARS EARLIER had Emma learned about the girls who worked in the paper mill's bag factory. Several newly graduated from her high school and another who left school early were among the mill's workforce.

"Emma," Her mother had interjected when she dared bring it up after supper. "Young ladies do not work in dirty, noisy factories. Think about your reputation." She scowled at Emma.

They were sitting in the front room after putting the younger children to bed in one of the home's two bedrooms. Her father put another log on the fire; it crackled loudly as he pushed the glowing embers toward the back of the hearth with an iron poker to keep them going through the night. Mother shook her head and bent back over her mending of a tear in Mary's skirt. The orange-yellow glow of the kerosene lamp created shadows on the wall while rhythmic stitches emphasized the finality of her words.

Emma crossed her arms and frowned at her feet.

"Yes, Emma." Father lowered his voice. "We appreciate your desire to help us but listen to your mother. There are other things you can do to help out or even bring in a few cents." A gentle smile formed on his lips, and he returned to read the *Oregonian* perched on his lap. Father was more educated than many and the unsold newspapers from the store were a luxury he enjoyed. Emma might have been surprised he did not encourage his children to attend college if it weren't for growing financial fears. She wondered if that too weighed on him. The room returned to silence, punctuated by the soft sound of a needle pulled through fabric and rustling of newspaper.

Emma did not contradict her parents back then, but her spirit ached with disappointment. She would graduate later that month and knew without asking that her parents expected her to help even more around the house. At least until she was ready to marry and begin a family of her own like her sister Martha had done.

"Emma." Mother set aside her mending and looked up. "I heard at church that Mrs. Scott was looking for help in her kitchen and with other chores." She looked Emma in the eye. "Just a few hours each week. I recommended you to her." She nodded twice and returned to her handiwork as if it was a finished deal.

Her comments infuriated Emma, outraged by Mother making decisions for her when she was nearly eighteen. Father pressed his lips together and gazed sternly at his wife. He better understood Emma, often acting differently than other fathers she encountered by giving more latitude to her mother's voice. Emma wished now he would overrule Mother's opinion. When she spent time at girlfriends' homes, she was surprised by some parental interactions, especially frightened by one girl's father's rigidness in contrast to the mother's timidity. Emma knew she would never accept that type of relationship in her own future life.

As it turned out, after Emma graduated, her older brother, William, helped win over Father's approval to apply at the mill. William also encouraged a mill manager to consider hiring another girl, in this case his sister. Her brother was well-liked, a hard worker, and natural leader, even though he was only twenty. Most of his friends and the fathers of families they knew worked at the paper mill, making enough money to put food on the table and pay for other things like electricity if their home was fortunate to have it.

"Father," William had said one Sunday after church. "The mill is hard pressed to find enough men to hire as they up production. And you know, all of us in Camas rely on the company."

"Yes," Father said. "But that does not mean your sister must join the ranks."

Mother nodded vigorously in agreement. "William, your boots." He uncrossed his legs and moved his boot off a rung of the wooden kitchen chair, the creak of the wood interrupting the conversation.

William eyed Emma. He shook his head and put a finger to his lip. "Thank you, Father. I understand. However, we must remember our loyalty to the mill. Think of the life it has allowed us to build here. Even your work at the store is dependent on its success to retain workers." He released a breath and glanced at Emma before focusing on Father.

Emma suppressed a smile.

Their parents exchanged glances.

"Yes, William. We will consider it." Father nodded to Emma while Mother frowned and shook her head.

Through some miracle, two days later Father agreed to the hiring and overruled Mother. Once Emma began working at the mill's bag factory, it was also Father who encouraged her mother to relax expectations about Emma's help with the children and chores. Mother even stopped asking Emma when she would secure a beau and marry, although Emma was certain she hoped it would happen soon. She knew Mother expected her to continue to help with the cooking and her siblings, even once married.

Many of Emma's girlfriends were determined to secure a husband once they left school, if they had not already abandoned their education to marry and start families. A few pushed out to learn to be teachers. Emma knew teachers were important, and she loved to learn, but had no interest in pursuing teaching. Besides, it required money to resettle in nearby Vancouver or Portland or to pay for more education. Even more so, she was fascinated by manufacturing processes, like papermaking. The act of harvesting the evergreens growing all around them to produce useful products intrigued her. She never tired of watching boats move milled lumber and finished paper down the river. Her brother first explained how paper was made when she was small. Imagine, she had thought to herself then, reading newspapers and books made with paper from their mill. And even more so now, her, a mere girl to some, being part of that important work.

Now, these two years later, Emma felt part of something bigger than she had first imagined. Larger than family or church. She also understood how paper bags were important both to their economy and to improve the life of people in communities all over. She now understood how this simple invention made life easier for people. Even then, she was embarrassed to tell anyone this, other than her younger siblings. She knew many did not think women deserved high-minded ideas beyond running a household or volunteering at church. She let Father and Mother believe it was about bringing in earnings, even if in her heart she knew the job was important to her because of something grander than that. No, she was not ready to abandon early womanhood only to find a husband and have children. Women must be allowed to hope for more.

Emma knew she romanticized paper making. The real job was dirty, noisy, and dangerous. Some of the mill's floors were hard packed dirt, not even concrete, and part of her job was to remove waste and scraps often tracked about. The men smelled, bragged, and swore, and either ignored her or made flirtatious comments. Even then, she felt important as she joined five hundred other workers strengthening their community with the mill the center of town. She did love the hum of the dozen bag-making machines and presses, even if they were loud and dangerous. Occasionally she had a fleeting thought: if she could succeed at this, what else might she be able to accomplish? Emma wondered if other women might be jealous of her independence in this world of work? No, they were too busy toiling in their own lives to give it a second thought.

Elizabeth was Emma's closest friend, and the only other girl from her class to work at the mill. Although Elizabeth's parents had the money to send their daughter to college, she had not wanted to leave her longtime beau, so instead joined Emma in pursuing mill work, much to her parents' surprise. "It's only because they think I'll marry soon and quit," Elizabeth once confided to her.

From the start, Emma recognized she fell into a different society class than her friend and was nervous to be around Elizabeth's family in the beginning. While Emma's house was one of the original homes built for mill workers, Elizabeth's home exuded elegance: its wide porch supported large columns, and its windows boasted more than a single pane of glass. What Emma most loved, though, were the darkly stained built-in bookcases in the front room stocked with neatly shelved books. Emma's family owned only a handful of books in addition to the bible, and they sat lonely on a side table in her parent's bedroom.

Once, as they talked on Elizabeth's porch, Elizabeth asked Emma about her grandparents.

"Father has told us about his mother. Her name was Nellie, but she died before I could meet her. Everything I have heard about her reminds me a bit of Cassie." Emma bit her lip, embarrassed to divulge her fascination with Cassie at work. Besides, she was silly to imagine she knew enough about either of the two women to liken them to each other.

"That sounds like the opposite of my grandmother." Elizabeth laughed, then clapped her hand over her mouth as her grandmother was visiting from Portland.

She looked toward the house and rolled her eyes. She clasped Emma's hand, as if they shared a secret, and Emma released a breath of worry and grinned.

Elizabeth drew closer to Emma and whispered, "I think my grandmother thinks she was related to a queen." Emma eyed Elizabeth's new dress with its lace collar and decorative buttons down the front bodice. "I think my father likes to rile her up. You should have seen her reaction about me working at the mill." She giggled.

Elizabeth's family was close to relatives and wealthier than anyone Emma knew. Emma was embarrassed to admit how little she knew of her own extended family. "No, I never met them, not even my one aunt. When my grandmother Nellie died, Father took the steamship alone to the funeral in Portland. Mother felt it better to stay here. For all of us to stay here." She had not understood this decision and wished she had stories to share like Elizabeth. "Mother's parents died long ago."

Elizabeth grabbed her hand, just as her mother called them inside.

These days they woke up before light, mill operations relying on natural lighting even though parts of buildings had become electricized. Emma slept on a fold-up cot in the front room of their home and reignited the fire in the morning. She savored her last bits of sleep by quickly layering the necessary chemise, union suit, corset, work dress, and apron. She even learned to put her hair up briskly. A light snack of hot tea and dry toast carried her through the morning. She wished the women were provided better shoes as her feet hurt after the long workday.

Emma suspected their upcoming week would be even harder. Her previous Saturday shift lasted until daylight disappeared through dirty factory windows as they finished up a large bag order, but Cassie had appeared flushed and excited. Now, it was Sunday evening, and Emma's family was at Camas's First Church of Christ's sponsored dinner. Father had insisted to Mother they choose this church when they moved to Camas. While not denigrating the Catholic Church, he carefully explained he had never felt comfortable with their formal rituals after marrying Mother. He had been raised Presbyterian in a small church in northeast Portland and found Catholicism overwhelming. It had been a major disagreement, and Emma wondered if Mother had ever forgiven him.

"Hello, Emma." Elizabeth looked unusually nervous. Although their relationship was more formal on Sundays, something was different.

"Hi, Elizabeth." Emma touched her hand.

Elizabeth wore a large hat trailing ribbons and feathers. Emma self-consciously touched her own, unadorned and made of felt.

"Emma." Elizabeth looked around nervously and she fidgeted her fingers together. She edged back toward the wall, signaling with the smallest movement of her fingers for Emma to follow. The community building had been added adjacent to the original structure which still housed its altar and pews. A handful of families remained in the room, socializing after sharing a potluck meal. Emma had only eaten bread and cheese but was eager to return home.

"What do you think about the talk at work? The discussion about wages," Elizabeth whispered.

Emma pulled her mouth tight to keep her expression stoic as she stared at Elizabeth.

"You know. The protest." Elizabeth sounded exasperated.

Emma knew she was forcing herself not to call it a strike. "We are not supposed to talk about it around others, you know that." She glanced nervously around the room and kept her voice low.

She and Elizabeth were two of thirty-eight women doing nearly the same job as some men. For months some of the women had complained more vehemently about the unfairness of being paid less than their male counterparts along with problems with the workplace conditions. A week earlier Emma had brought the topic up at dinner one night, but Mother shushed her. Later in the evening, when Mother was putting the children to bed and Emma was washing dishes, Father stiffly arose from his chair and stood next to her. He looked toward the closed bedroom door. "Talking about mill problems frightens your mother. You must remember your brother tried to bring the cause of my injury to management's attention?"

The fire crackled across the room and water dripped in the sink. Quiet murmurs escaped from the children's bedroom.

Emma nodded. "Yes, and Mr. Bolton nearly had the same accident not long before." She tried to calm her voice, knowing it best to hold her tongue. She had been told back when her father's accident happened that work issues were for men to discuss, not women. Those first days after his injury had been difficult, both the loss of income and her brother's bold insistence that their family deserved to be compensated. Yet Emma was younger then and had not felt the anger she held now.

"Even your brother knows to be more careful now. To not be seen as disagreeing with management." Father patted her head. "Remember, the company has been very good to us and our livelihoods. They are always there for us in need." He smiled but gently massaged his back as if triggered by the old memory.

"Yes, Father," Emma grumbled, unconvinced.

She shook her wet hands in the sink and tried to push strands of hair that had fallen out of her bun back with the top of her shoulder. Father gently pulled the hair away from her eyes.

"But . . ." Emma could not hold her tongue. "It doesn't seem fair to do the same job for less pay does it? Just because we are women?" Her father lowered his chin, eyeing her. "I mean, women do have the vote now. Things should be changing." She knew she was echoing the same words she heard from Cassie. She was excited now that women had the vote in Washington to be able to vote in the 1915 election.

"Emma, I understand." Father faced her and gently put his hands on her shoulders. "But you need to know there are people, people not from here, who are showing up in cities and perhaps soon, even towns like ours. They are making trouble while insisting companies do more for their workers. And some . . ." He turned to the closed bedroom door. "Some say they are socialists." He took a breath to collect himself. "We are a town that stands behind our mill. The company provides for us. You must remember this."

Emma had seen a headline in a newspaper Father had brought home about a strike at a Portland fruit packing company where people, even women, were arrested. She heard rumors at work that some were beaten by the police. As terrible as it was, she knew a lot of horrible things happened in cities, even like Portland and Spokane. But her town did not have people like that, and she was certain Father was overreacting.

"I understand your feelings, I do." Father wiped her cheek before taking a step back. "I am simply advising you to be careful. You do not want to give people the wrong message. Try to remember how much your mother cares about you." He looked at Emma intently. "She is worried about anything that might cause a commotion."

Emma knew she should respect Father, but she wanted to tell him this was different. She wanted to tell him Cassie had assured her only women from the bag factory were striking; that there would not be outside agitators. She could not contain her frustration. "Mother is only worried about what people think about us. Not about the things that matter most. About improving our lives. And if we do not stand up now, who is to say things will ever improve for women?" Her face felt hot, and she was breathing so hard she was gasping.

"Emma," her father warned in a harsh voice he rarely used.

At that moment the bedroom door opened and softly closed. Father moved to the back door to head outside to finish chores and nodded at her before he stepped out. Emma watched Mother pick up her knitting needles, drape her shawl around her shoulders, and sink into the rocking chair, releasing a tired sigh. Emma rubbed her fingers over her face and turned back to the sink, grateful Mother had not heard their conversation. She knew she could never speak like that to her.

But now things were finally happening. Cassie had quietly advised her during Saturday's shift that it was important not to openly discuss the impending strike, and how no outsiders were influencing it. She reasserted nobody from afar followed what happened in this small town, and that Camas residents would support their protest.

As conversation continued around them in the community room, Emma nodded vaguely to Elizabeth. Father's warnings had unnerved her, even with Cassie's assurances, and it was important to keep Cassie's trust.

"Elizabeth, yes. But that's enough now." She forced a fake smile and clasped Elizabeth's hands. Elizabeth had once told her how most women factory workers in cities were immigrants. And how many Americans were bothered by people from places like Ireland and Russia taking away opportunities for Americans, like the Chinese did with the railroads. Emma could not imagine others willing to do the hard work of railroad building. She wished her parents would talk to her about important topics like this as Elizabeth's parents seemed to do.

Elizabeth shuffled her feet. "Yes . . . I'm just . . . I'm a bit nervous," she whispered, in a voice different than her usual. "I worry what Robert will think."

Emma nodded and tried to feel sympathetic. Robert was Elizabeth's fiancé who also worked at the mill.

"It will be okay, Elizabeth." Emma tried to sound confident, even though she too was nervous about the impending strike. But she did believe in Cassie.

Elizabeth waved goodbye and returned to her family across the room. Emma spied her mother signaling her. Mother extended any opportunity to socialize with her own friends. She carefully walked toward her mother, first looking down at her navy high necked dress to ensure she was presentable. She smoothed her hands over its gathered waist. It was important to her mother that she cared about her appearance.

"Emma," Mother said in her polite, public voice. She smiled at Emma. "You remember Mrs. Miller?"

Emma nodded and smiled weakly. "Yes, Mother. Pleased to see you again Mrs. Miller." She bowed slightly.

"How lovely to see you, Emma. Do you remember my son Patrick? He is visiting from Vancouver, and I was certain you two might remember each other."

Emma looked at the young man in his dark trousers, waist coat, and tie. He had been standing slightly behind Mrs. Miller but now moved into the small circle of women. Emma eyed him and hoped her expression did not reflect the impending dread she felt of Mother's attempt to set her up with another young man, one she remembered as boring even as a boy. She hoped her expression exuded disinterest only Patrick could identify. She forced a stilted smile, but all she could think about in that moment were their morning plans.

# Chapter 6
## Celia
### December 10, 2024

UPON AWAKENING, CELIA felt sick to her stomach as if her gut perceived misery on the horizon. She was normally a morning person, not like the folks who rolled into the café and could barely spit out the word coffee. What was wrong with her? She didn't feel sick, even though a few folks at the café worried they had COVID every time they felt off.

No, she felt a deep-seated impending feeling of doom. She tried to shake it off as she hurriedly readied for the morning. She shoveled down her bowl of generic oat cereal, then jammed two power bars into her jacket pocket, certain the bars were a gimmick. She never felt power or energy after eating them. The other guys relied on cans of Red Bull, but she refused to succumb to that caffeine addiction. Although she preferred working on a day boat, she had enjoyed meals provided by the trip boat she'd worked on before, even though they didn't make up for nights away.

"Hustle up, Celia," Ed shouted gruffly as she neared the dock at five o'clock sharp. He was usually boisterous and enthusiastic when they headed out with pots to drop or haul, no matter what. She wondered if he'd had another disagreement with his wife. Later, she poked herself for not questioning him.

"Coming, coming." She was exactly on time. Under her breath she muttered. *What's your problem?* She glanced toward the eastern sky for any hint of lightness. The parking lot and wharf were beginning to boast signs of life, men hauling totes and gear across the harbor docks. She tossed her bag on board, grabbed the railing, and climbed onto the boat. Across the deck, Trevor was baiting up the first few pots, pulling the frozen bait from large plastic totes. An aroma of rotted fish and salty air seeped into her. The nearly three hundred pots were stacked and organized around the periphery of the deck as usual. Gratefully, the crew always got a last-minute energy surge the day before leaving in these first days of the season. Gear dump or drop day was easier than opening day, when they knew each subsequent visit to the pots over the nine-month season would yield fewer crab. Each empty crab pot weighed more than some women could lift—she prided herself by her ability to handle the work with her lanky buff arms and shoulders. If she gave it all up, what would that say about her perseverance? She knew she could physically handle the job, but the weird queasiness continued in her gut. Maybe she was getting sick. She hoped the rolling waves wouldn't make her puke, or the guys would never let her live it down.

Around them the marina buzzed louder with an energy different than the night before. Not all outfitters tried to cross the bar and drop their pots by the eight o'clock opening, but it felt like it. Some, like Ed, got to the spot to drop before it was time and spent minutes circling the area and cracking lame jokes. The cloudy darkness muted the Meglar Bridge lights.

"Early bird gets the worm. No loafing about to get the pots dropped!" Ed called out, as if to the seagulls hovering around them, their piercing cries begging for bait. While the words were typical, his voice sounded angry. Normally Celia enjoyed watching Ed's excitement on both drop and opening days. She had prided herself working for a captain who so loved what he did.

Trevor and Justin were cutting up the rest of the bait and making last minute adjustments to the pots. Celia knew the bigger boats had equipment to automatically mince bait and trip boats boasted larger wheelhouses with room for a crew to enjoy a meal. The guys nodded at her but continued their private banter. They weren't rude or macho like guys she'd fished with before, yet they didn't always include her as part of their team as if she made them uncomfortable. That was part of what led her to think working on a woman-captained boat and crew would be different.

The cold damp air snuggled under her wrists at the glove line and pricked at her neck. She pulled down her black knitted watch cap and tugged at the straps of her insulated yellow bibs. The smell of today's bait, salmon heads and smashed clams, worsened her stomach churning. If she didn't know better, she'd think she was pregnant. Not that she had ever been but her friends who had been gutted by morning sickness told her enough about it. Yet she hadn't had sex in so long it would be impossible. She wished they were baiting with chicken, although she knew the smellier the better the haul.

She peered at Ed from the corner of her eye; not wanting him to see her stare at him. He seemed oblivious. Suddenly he dropped his hands from the ropes he was holding and grabbed his upper arm, hesitated, and then retrieved the ropes.

Celia couldn't see his face. "Hey Ed! You okay?" She hated to butt in, but he seemed off.

Ed didn't turn toward her. Instead, he grunted, "I'm fine," and climbed up to the wheelhouse. "I'm fine!" he shouted louder.

He didn't sound fine. She kicked the totes by her feet. Normally Ed seemed years younger than his age when they set out early in the season, as if these were the days he lived for. A captain had to be in top form when the waves were big, some days surging to twenty-five or thirty feet even without a significant storm. People didn't realize it wasn't just the size of the waves, but how currents from the powerful Columbia River could branch out in different directions. Visitors seemed surprised to learn big ships were required to use bar pilots to help cross the bar, first Native Americans in canoes in the olden days. Local folks knew the danger of crossing the bar where the mouth of the Columbia River met the Pacific Ocean. Ed had first told her how large breaking waves mixing with the river current and tidal systems could surprise even the most experienced boater. She had to believe that some of the pressures on local commercial boats to bring in decent harvests sometimes triggered bad boating decisions in this complicated water.

"Untie the bow line!" Ed yelled at Celia from the wheelhouse.

*What was his problem?* She was already uncleating and coiling it as she always did. She stepped carefully to finish her work at the bow. They were among the earliest boats to leave the dock that morning, she was sure they'd be too early yet again. Within the next hour boat lights would shimmer across the water, though it would not be as busy as opening day. She could imagine folks not from here thinking it to be some kind of early morning boat parade. Even then, it wasn't until opening day when they could start hauling: day trippers like *High Hopes,* heading back and forth to pull up pots, count and dump their harvests into the holding tanks before dropping rebaited pots. Some days working nearly twenty hours straight. It seemed a weird sport of chance: who knew where a crab might wander? She knew crab was the most sustainable seafood as the male crabs sized big enough to legally keep would die in a few short years anyway. One old fisherman once told her, in an oddly sinister voice, about how the males would start to cannibalize their young if crabbers didn't trap them.

"Hey Celia," Trevor called, barely audible. He pursed his lips together and wrinkled his nose, then shook his head. She walked past him to head back to the stern. "Just ignore his mood."

He lifted his eyebrows toward Ed in the wheelhouse, shrugged, and went back to tightening the winch used to lower and raise pots. Occasionally the guys would say something to insinuate her being of the weaker sex or a worrier, which she ordinarily wasn't. But Celia dropped it and tried to put concerns about Ed out of her mind. She bent over the totes to cut up remaining salmon heads and distribute them into awaiting pots. She could do that in her sleep and looked out toward the ocean as they strategically navigated out of the harbor. A few seagulls hovered above the boat, screeching *cow-cow-cow*, no longer laughing at her but begging for breakfast.

She was glad it was dry, although the winds were picking up and she spied darker clouds laden with rain further east. She hoped soon the golden glow of an awakening dawn would burst through the lower edges of the dark towering clouds. Cape Disappointment, located at the southern tip of the Long Beach Peninsula, was hidden, and it looked as if the river melted into the ocean, though she could just make out the edge of the land mass forming Fort Canby nearby. This was the reason she once said she chose this job; hours to bask in the ocean's briny, ferocious glory.

She disliked the weirdly macho attitude infiltrating some fishermen as the season opened, though, each one jubilant to outdo another. There were hundreds of commercial crabbing permits and only so many crabs, with profits dependent on pricing set by distributors and buyers. Ed complained about state regulations telling them what they could do and how, and especially when the tribes got special advantages. Most knew the Coast Guard would have to rescue some each season; less experienced fishermen taking more risks or just catching plain bad luck. She believed Ed understood the dangers of this part of the bar and ocean, turning back in prior seasons if the weather was nasty even though it impacted earnings. After all, the top rescue folks for the Coast Guard trained on these waters. Yes, she reminded herself of this even as her scalp tickled and stomach churned.

Justin and Trevor were nearly shouting lyrics to some song she didn't recognize, their words muffled between the boat engine and crashing waves. "Get it, got it," something or other. She shook her head and focused on the bait and pots. The weather was cooperating as their boat joined dozens of others heading over the bar to claim their preferred pot spaces, weirdly like a freeway where if you didn't pay attention, you might get sideswiped. Celia looked up toward the wheelhouse but could only see the back of Ed's head.

"Come on Celia! Celia, you're breaking my heart . . ." Justin yelled laughingly at her, but she pretended not to hear.

She shouldn't blame them for her crappy mood. Justin was young, and she knew he could still act like a kid with half a brain. She tried before to imagine him as a younger brother but, without brotherly experience to guide her, she failed. While she'd always been on the quiet side, she had been more talkative in her first crabbing seasons on *High Hopes*. Back then, she had been grateful to be hired by Ed. She wondered if he noticed a change in her, or if he was relieved by her silence. His wife was a talker, and he once said what he most loved about his fishing life was the peace and quiet.

Having finished baiting the pots within easy access, Celia focused on coiling up the remaining ropes. Usually there were last minute tasks to prepare the pots and get the deck in order as they began to make it through the surf, but she felt more hurried than usual. She reminded herself that they'd probably get to the first drop spot too early anyway. She looked up to give her neck a break from its crooked position. Justin was in the back port side bending over to untangle a rope attached to one of their labeled buoys. Each buoy would denote their line of pots, essential for tracking and later harvesting, all of it computerized, with the captain in today's world needing to understand technology too. The waves were big but not as overpowering as they might become later. It wasn't uncommon during the bigger storms for breakers to crash over the bow or the stern, leaving icy water to slosh around on the deck. Without a doubt, the boat might get tossed a bit uncomfortably. She hoped her gut would calm down rather than heave, although it might be good to vomit out whatever nastiness splattered inside her.

The boat jerked suddenly to the left. "Shit!" She looked across the stern to Trevor.

"What the fuck?" Trevor yelled back, but his hands were caught between the winch and the pots.

A sudden knowing fear filled Celia. *Was this it?* Since she was closest to the wheelhouse she yelled, "Ed! What's up?"

She heard only the movement of the boat and crashes of the waves, but *High Hopes* was floundering off course. She glanced back at Trevor as she moved toward the wheelhouse, holding on to its back railing for balance. She peeked up, her heart pounding. Ed was slouched back in his chair, eyes closed, and mouth contorted in pain. He had dropped the helm and his hands were shaking. He opened his eyes, but they looked glazed, and he was unable to grip the wheel. The waves took the boat on a crazy amusement ride, plunging with each new crashing wave and turning sideways. Even in her bibs and cold weather garb, Celia felt an iciness slip through her body. She wiped mist from her face.

Celia looked back toward the stern. "Trevor! Something happened to Ed!" She panicked, knowing Trevor was the next most experienced helmsman. The boat flopped to the left, and she grabbed the helm and attempted to right the boat. Ed slumped further into his captain's chair, his lower body splaying toward the deck, one arm grabbing the other. He was breathing but looked at her in terror. Within minutes, out of nowhere, Trevor appeared and grabbed the helm from her.

"Help him!" he screamed. "I'll radio the Coast Guard!"

Celia moved out of Trevor's way and grabbed hold of Ed, as Trevor yelled, "May Day, May Day," until gusts muffled his voice. Just then another wave crashed over the stern gunwale, splashing water onto the boat. She moved to the back of the wheelhouse and saw water pooling on the deck, puddles waxing and waning as the boat bobbled in the water, some of it seeping back into the ocean through the scuppers.

"Justin!" Her voice disappeared into the howl of the wind. The powerful wave jarred the boat, moving it parallel to the attacking waves. The impact jammed into the starboard side, and Justin launched above the rail with the wave and into the water, momentarily disappearing.

"Justin!" She screamed, panicked.

She was unsure if Trevor knew what was happening as he worked to right the boat. Without thinking she held on tight to the railing and moved as quickly as humanly possible toward the gunwale where Justin last stood. She grabbed a life buoy and threw it toward him.

"Oh my God! Oh dear God!" she yelled.

The buoy hit him, and he pulled it to his chest. She knew she was crying but could only feel the cold spray of the waves on her face. She pulled on the rope tied to the ring.

"Celia!" Trevor screamed. "Grab the helm!"

She heard his command before it too disappeared into the wind, as he strode toward her reaching to grab the line. Celia was unaware of anything outside the boat as her reflexes kicked into order and she hurried back to the wheelhouse, accidentally pushing Ed off the seat as she grabbed the helm again. She knew she had to attend to Ed, but they had to save themselves first, even Ed would agree. Although she was less experienced at the helm, she wasn't an idiot, and appreciated Trevor's getting the boat righted, although she wasn't certain she could get them back to shore. Before, she had reluctantly appreciated Trevor's experience; now she felt indebted. *Why was she such an ass before?* Relief washed over her, knowing he'd grown up fishing and crabbing. Her love of looking out to sea didn't cut it during an emergency like this.

She glanced at Ed. He was still breathing, and his eyes were open, although his skin was pale and his eyes glassy. They did not have the resources to prevent capsizing their boat and save both a man overboard and one with a medical issue. Nobody had thought to don their government required immersion suits as it had all seemed routine. Celia felt angry with Ed, even as he lay there possibly dying. It bothered her to feel angry, and she wanted him to live, but she felt certain he knew he was feeling poorly before the boat departed.

"Thank God!" Celia blurted as she stood up and peeked back toward the stern. Trevor had pulled Justin to the deck. His eyes were open, and he seemed to be breathing as he lay on his back fully soaked. Warm tears mixed with the icy salt of the ocean as Celia clutched the helm in relief. Even with her strength, she did not think she could have pulled Justin up on her own. Once someone goes overboard in tossing ocean waves, it's unlikely even to find the body. It had to have taken extra human strength for Trevor to get him back.

Trevor appeared back at the wheelhouse faster than she thought possible with the boat bounding up and down in the breaking waves.

He gently pushed her off the helm. "Help Justin. Whatever you can to warm him and keep him out of shock."

Celia was about to ask about Ed when she heard the chopper in the distance. *How had they arrived so fast?* She thanked God Trevor knew what to do and when to do it; she knew much less than she thought she did. Although she understood the importance of the Coast Guard and had even visited their station across the river near Ilwaco, she could not have imagined the relief she would feel to be rescued.

As if from a vacuum, Celia heard Ed whimper, "No. Please don't call. Please. No Coast Guard."

Celia raised her eyebrows, and felt her veins might pop out of her head. Every kind feeling she had for him dissipated, even if she wanted to be sympathetic. Now she understood why he made such a stupid decision that morning to go ahead as scheduled, even though he felt unwell. He loved this work and could not imagine his life without it, no admission of consequences.

"Justin," Celia called as she steadfastly headed to him.

The boat felt more stable, and she hoped it wasn't an illusion. She pulled off Justin's wet gloves and tried to pull him close. She knew she had to get him dry and warmed up, but he was bigger and heavier than her. Trevor was too consumed in communicating with the nearing chopper to offer tips.

"Hang on Justin, you're going to be okay." Celia tried to sound calm and soothing. "They are coming. You'll be okay." She let go of him and moved to a tote to grab two wool blankets.

"Justin, Justin, it's all going to be okay," she repeated over and over.

He looked as vulnerable as a baby. All her feelings about him being a stupid-asshole-twenty-something man dissipated. She knew he was close to his parents and a girlfriend; how awful it would be if anything bad happened to him.

She knew it was good he was still shivering. She pulled off his soaked outer parka and wrapped the first wool blanket as fully as she could around his body, and the second around his bottom torso, then pulled him to her core as if a small child.

She was vaguely aware of Trevor talking on the radio with the Coast Guard. The helicopter hovered above the boat and dropped a line with a rescue swimmer on the sling. She had watched practice responses before but living it felt surreal.

"Justin, Justin," she sang as if in a trance, watching the rescuer slowly descend to the boat. "It's okay, it's okay."

She tried to think of other comforting words and all that came to her was an old Beatle's song. "Everything's gonna be alright," she repeated over and over between stifled sobs, holding him as tightly as possible, willing her body heat to enter him.

The rescue diver was in the wheelhouse. It felt like hours, although perhaps only minutes when the rescue basket with Ed, wrapped in its blanket, floated its way to the copter. She vaguely wondered which medical center he would be transferred to and when his wife would get news.

"Hey, nice work." The Coast Guard responder appeared behind her, startling her.

Without saying more to her, he talked to Justin as he pulled medical devices from his bag. Celia backed away as tears of relief broke loose, while he checked Justin's heart and temperature. Celia stepped to the gunwale on the opposite side of the boat and gushed her breakfast and stomach acid into the churning ocean and then wiped her face with her wet slicker.

The whoop whoop of the helicopter softened as it disappeared into the skyline and the rescue swimmer motioned to her. "He's doing okay, and we're just going to head to shore. I'll keep him under observation," he said in a calm but loud voice. "Can you let the captain know the plan and to return us to the harbor?"

Celia's fear trickled away like water gurgling through an unplugged bathtub. She could not find words and nodded.

She walked unsteadily back to the wheelhouse and placed her numb hands on the stacked pots for balance. "Hey, Trevor." She couldn't stop her sobs. "He said that . . ." She shrugged as she tried to stop crying.

"Yeah, I got it. It's okay, Celia."

Celia could barely hear Trevor's words, but they locked eyes, and he tiredly smiled. He took one hand off the helm and quickly patted her shoulder before grabbing the wheel again. Although the wind silenced his next words, she saw him mouth, "It's gonna be alright."

She felt the boat slow as it neared the harbor and broke into salty tears of relief.

# Chapter 7
## Celia
### December 10, 2024

THE BOAT JOLTED as it shifted into reverse, and Celia grabbed the railing to steady herself as she moved toward the bow to secure mooring lines. While cleating a rope, she spotted two Coast Guard officials standing at the top of the dock watching them. One had his arms crossed over his chest, and the other was on his phone. The ambulance was parked next to the dock, its lights flashing as two responders pulled a stretcher out through its back doors.

Celia tried to ignore the officials and walked back to the wheelhouse, focusing on steadying her feet as the boat was secured. The gentler waves of the harbor lapped against the boat's sidewall, and its fenders groaned when they hit the dock. Seagulls darted toward the boat as if sensing their reappearing breakfast.

"Trevor, what do we do? I mean, with all this?" Celia pointed to the stacks of baited pots. Only then had she thought about the load of bait that would rot onboard.

"Yeah." He shook his head and frowned. "A hell of a waste and no way is the boat going to be allowed to go back out."

Although the harbor was quieter than when they had left, Celia spotted several clusters of folks on the dock staring at them.

"Just leave it, Celia. Take care of yourself. Someone will be happy to take it back out on their boat." He nodded toward the officials. "You know, they'll want to talk to us."

Celia groaned. She removed her gloves and stuffed them and her hat into her dry bag. She looked around the boat and was filled with an odd mix of relief and unexpected sadness. They both turned to the sound of the two medics climbing onto the boat. One of them spoke gently to Justin and then the two lifted him onto the stretcher and strapped him in, wool blankets and all.

Celia wanted to call to Justin but couldn't find her voice in time. She exchanged a look with Trevor. "You did good. You did really good." She smiled through the tears clouding her vision.

"You too, Celia. You too," Trevor said, looking as exhausted as she felt. She was certain tears would come later even for him.

Celia nodded then climbed onto the dock, followed by Trevor. She felt relieved to be on steady land.

One of the uniformed Coast Guard officers stepped toward them as they headed up the dock. "I know this may be difficult, but I need to chat with the two of you for a few minutes. Um, separately if you would."

Celia turned to watch the other officer board the boat.

"Yes, sir. If it's okay, could you start with her?" Trevor pointed to Celia. "I'd like to make arrangements for someone to unload the bait, or we'll have a royal stink on our hands."

The officer nodded and signaled Celia to follow him. She shivered uncontrollably as they walked along the dock toward the parking lot. *Why did she feel responsible for the shit happening?* She wanted to escape and wash her hands of the disaster.

The officer eyed her closely. "We can stand out here." He pointed to an area behind the car and away from people. "Or, maybe you need to warm up a bit, here?" He pointed to a Coast Guard vehicle parked behind the ambulance.

The stretcher with Justin poked out and she wanted to check on him, although she knew he was in better hands now than onboard. The officer opened the passenger door of the vehicle. Celia nodded and bent to get inside, willing to do anything to warm up. The officer stopped in front of the car and spoke to the medics before returning to the driver's side. She was relieved when he turned on the ignition and cranked the heater, even though she felt reluctant to speak. The hum of the heater was comforting, and her cheeks quickly felt hot with the rush of warm air. The official handed her a plastic bottle of water, but her numb fingers couldn't grasp the twist off, so she set it on her lap.

"I'm sorry. Sorry for what you've been through." The man introduced himself as Eric from the Marine Safety Division.

He wasn't much older than her, and his neatly trimmed black mustache kept her from being able to fully read his expression. A black USCG watch cap covered his head, and he looked incognito—like any other guy in a similar uniform. She wondered if he was curious about what had happened, or if it was just another routine incident to document.

Celia nodded but could not maintain eye contact. Her brain felt as numb as her fingers, and she wished she could plead something to be able to go home. He grabbed a notebook from the console.

"So, tell me what you remember from start to finish." Eric hesitated. "Can you do that?"

Celia's mind flashed to the dark night in downtown Astoria those years ago when she hurriedly left the police scene when the man was arrested for killing the old guy. Back then she insisted to herself she hadn't witnessed anything, unnerved to stick around in case she was questioned by the police. Oddly, she did not feel any more at ease with this Coast Guard guy, Eric. She was beginning to feel her fingertips but could not keep her hands from shaking and jammed them under her thighs. She fingered her soggy bibs and wet car seat.

"Oh no." She nodded down at her bibs. "I'm getting your car wet. I should have taken these off."

Eric's laugh punched through the somber ambience. "That's the least of my concerns, but thanks." He looked back at her, again, expectantly. "Hang on." He grabbed a rough white towel from the back seat and handed it to her. The marine radio crackled, and he turned the volume down.

She took the towel and inhaled the oddly calming smell of institutional laundry detergent as she pressed it to her face. No, she would find no Zen moment here. She knew she only had to share what she remembered, but saying anything felt final. Her head pounded, and she turned it slowly side to side, knowing she was dehydrated but wishing she could claim amnesia. With her fingers warmed a bit, she opened the bottle and sipped, even though it felt like a delay tactic.

Celia took another sip and eyed Eric. He looked bored now, and she wondered if he'd rather be out at sea. She tried to revive the feeling of relief she felt as the copter showed up with its arrival of heroes and when they had arrived back on shore. She knew the Coast Guard was cracking down on drug use among crew, and she was grateful that wasn't something she'd have to admit to or worry about. She wondered if they would drug test Ed. She heard some captains were frustrated trying to find folks who could fish without being stupid or lazy, and drugs like marijuana sometimes worried them less.

"Well, maybe, let's begin with some basics," Eric said encouragingly. "Can you tell me if everyone was wearing PFDs, and anything else about the other required safety provisions? And maybe about the weather and waves as you were heading out."

Yes, she reported out about how they always wore flotation devices, telling herself at least when they crossed the bar. Yes, they had the required first aid kit and several of them had CPR training. When she hesitated or stopped speaking, Eric waited, allowing long silences to be just that without tapping his finger or his feet.

Celia took another sip. She set the bottle down and rubbed her temples with her cold fingers.

"You're doing fine." Eric looked at her and checked his phone, then looked up again. "Nothing to be nervous about you know. You did the right thing to help your crew mate." He shrugged. "But just try to relax."

Celia sat upright and rubbed the pins and needles from her fingers. "Thanks." She hesitated. "But that's about all I remember. I mean, you know, until you all arrived. I mean the Coast Guard. Uh, the rescue swimmer. And then the ambulance."

She had told him about Ed dropping his hands from the helm, and how she knew she had to do something. "I was surprised, and I didn't think through my actions." And she went on to tell him about Justin having been tossed overboard, her throwing the life ring, and Trevor finally pulling him in. About taking over the helm and then Trevor bringing them back across the bar and to shore. She was surprised to be able to speak matter-of-factly, finding it easier to share than expected. She was feeling better to have shared the story. As if now, she could be done. They could move on. Well, some of them.

"Um, about Ed? Is he okay? I mean, the captain?" Why hadn't she asked earlier?

Eric's lips narrowed, and he tapped his foot. "The captain has been transported to the medical center for evaluation. I don't have the details, but as you know, he was breathing and conscious during transport." He looked down to his notebook and then his phone, before jumping back in to confirm information about her prior work and age. He asked her a few things about the condition of the boat, most she didn't know.

"I think Trevor will be more helpful with those details." Yes, she was trying to feel better about what she also felt she was omitting.

"Can you tell me if you had immersion suits onboard?" Eric kept his tone even and informal.

"Well, I thought we had them. I had training on them once." Celia quickly inhaled. *But maybe they weren't on the boat?* She felt caught, even though she knew that too was ultimately the responsibility of a captain. She pushed her hair back from her face.

"Okay," he said simply. She knew the inspection would confirm it or not. "We do appreciate your time. I'm sure your crewmate's family is appreciative for your quick thinking. Is there anything else you'd like to share before we finish up?"

Celia bit her lip. "No. I'm good."

She wanted to add that Ed was a nice guy. That he had been good to her and was a good captain. That his crew respected him. That he had given her a chance. But now she only wanted to be done. Besides she answered all the question she had been asked. She could not handle the intensity any longer and was grateful to see Trevor returning to the dock.

"Thanks. But if we're finished?" She shuffled her feet and looked for her dry bag, but remembered she'd dropped it outside the car.

Eric nodded and opened his door. Rather than wait for him, Celia found the door handle and welcomed the rush of fresh salty air, even if she still felt chilled. She climbed out of the car, ignoring the protests of her thighs and lower back.

"Just give me a call if you think of anything more." He handed Celia his card.

Celia as if by habit walked back to the dock and grasped the railing as she peered out from the harbor. The day had mostly cleared, and the dark clouds of the morning had pushed further west. She looked at the card and jammed it in her pocket. Her stomach felt empty, but no longer queasy. She felt surreal, as if she could stand there and watch the world go by. Her days ahead were unplanned, as if she had reached the end of a long assignment. Yet rather than the relief of completion, an emptiness threatened to engulf her. Expectations for payment at the end of the season were in the toilet. She had no idea what would happen to the pots or Ed's boat, or what would be next for Trevor or Ed. For any of them. Part of her wanted to walk away as if from a chapter in a book and never reread it before moving on to a new story. She looked back toward the parking lot and spied Trevor drinking a Coke, talking to the officer as they stood next to his car. Celia didn't know what she was supposed to do and inertia rooted her on the dock. She looked out at the ocean. She could barely make out the specks that she knew to be fishing boats circling, dropping pots and lines, setting buoys.

"Hey, Celia!" Trevor was walking to her as the two officers were leaning over the hood of a car, trading notes. "You okay?"

"Yeah." She brought her hands to her face and then touched Trevor's sleeve. "And you?"

Trevor nodded. "Pretty wiped out, I guess. I got the guys." He nodded at two men wearing bibs in the distance. "They'll remove the bait and stuff. I'll come back tomorrow and figure out what else, depending on what Ed says. I guess." He shrugged. "Fucking day."

Celia nodded. She didn't have space for more talk nor energy to care if she was shirking crew responsibilities.

"You should go," Trevor added.

Celia nodded. "Yeah, you too?"

Trevor nodded.

"Okay, take care." She touched his arm again before heading to her car.

# Chapter 8
## Emma
### January 24, 1913

"THERE IS A bright new dawn ahead of us." These words, once shared by Cassie, circled within Emma's brain like a golden testament. Yet, that day felt long ago. Before the strike after especially draining shifts, Emma questioned why she demanded to keep working at the mill, especially with Mother's desire for her to leave. Today she was a different person since first being intimidated by Cassie's commanding personality. She knew she wanted to be part of making change happen. She believed it would take small acts like this to create a better world for future generations of women. It simply had to.

Emma had to admit it made sense for her to be treated as someone who knew little during her first days working at the factory. After all, working around machines and producing paper bags had been new to her, then. Each day she would show up for work and be instructed what to do and how to do it by every man on the site. "Hey there, girlie, run and get me more glue from the storeroom," one machine operator might command her if she was nearby. It was bad enough not to ask her kindly, but to refer to her as girlie. Emma clenched her fists. Not all men were like this, but it only took a few to enrage her. Her sister Martha told her she was naïve to imagine such attitudes to ever change.

As the days became months, and then years, Emma grew adept at her job but observed how men were promoted to better positions and higher pay. Other than Cassie and one other female machine operator. Was Mother right? She wondered if she should leave her girlhood dreams behind; that was, until the strike loomed ahead. Although nervous, she felt more excited and determined than she ever had before.

"Emma," her father said.

She sat hunched over her dry toast, as if the same as any morning and not the first morning of the strike. She wondered if he could hear the thumping of her heart and hoped he recognized the significance of the day. He was up earlier than normal; rarely did she see him before leaving for her shift.

"Yes, Father?" She tried to hide the shakiness in her voice.

Father rested his hands on the kitchen table stiffly. "Your mother and I will be out this evening when you return from your shift." He was freshly shaven and dressed for work. "And Nina will be here. Martha asked that you watch her along with your siblings."

"Yes, Father," Emma grumbled, unsure if she was relieved or disappointed he didn't mention the strike. She was frustrated by Martha's expectation to watch Nina after a long day at the mill, strike or not. Was it not enough that Emma took care of her siblings, cooked and earned wages to help the family? She wondered what Martha had to do that evening.

She nodded to Father, understanding his role as peacekeeper. She had more important things ahead of her.

Emma drained her tea and shoved the last crumbles of toast into her mouth. Her hands shook as she rinsed the cup in the sink.

"Bye, sweetheart." Father shyly pecked her cheek. "Keep making me proud."

Emma stared at him. Father rarely said anything like this to her, the subtle smile his way of showing support without openly advocating the strike.

"Have a nice day, Father." She returned his smile before putting on her coat, gloves, and hat. As an afterthought, she took her brown knitted scarf from the hook and wound it loosely around her neck. "And yes, of course I will watch Nina." A sliver of grumpiness siphoned away.

Father nodded and turned to stir the fire. The logs popped heartily, and he carefully opened his bedroom door and softly closed it behind him.

Emma looked out the smeared kitchen window as the first soft rays of early daylight creeped in. She pulled her scarf closer to her neck and snuggled herself further into mother's old wool coat before grabbing her bag to set out into the drizzle of the new day.


"IT'S HAPPENING, EMMA. It's truly happening," Elizabeth cried out in her high-pitched voice as they neared each other on the street. Elizabeth's eyes were shining, and she was bundled from head to toe in her heavy wool coat, knitted mittens, and laced leather boots. She had a sign tucked under one arm and a bulging cotton bag under the other. Her home was perched further up the hill on Garfield Street, and Emma was relieved to have intersected before arriving at the mill so they could join the group together.

"Umm . . . Yes." Even though Father's smile had boosted Emma's courage, she did not feel as bold as Elizabeth seemed, a change from the night before. Emma wished her parents were as openly supportive as Elizabeth's, imagining them to have helped with her sign and perhaps even packing food for the day. It surprised her that Elizabeth's family seemed to be more open to changes in the world.

They hurried down the final two blocks to join the small group of women gathering outside the entrance to the mill. The Columbia Slough was barely visible at the bottom of the hill beyond the mill, and she knew a large bag order was heading out by boat even as they protested. Cassie expected all the nearly forty women and girls from the bag factory to strike. Early requests for change had been ignored, and mill management was notified at the end of the prior day's shift about the possible strike. Three women held up signs already, though the streets were empty other than a few workers heading to the mill. "A dollar and a half a day!" read one, "Equal pay!" shouted another.

That first day on the picket line was exciting and nerve-racking. The women believed management would miss them in the factory and quickly accept their terms.

The woman named Mildred next to Emma turned to her. "This is the start of real change." She took a drink out of a jar, releasing steam into the cold, damp air.

Emma wished she had been wise enough to bring along hot tea. As the minutes crept by, Mildred told stories about her earliest days in the bag factory. Elizabeth had once told her Mildred was the oldest of the women in the bag factory, though she didn't look older than thirty. "Yes, I told them they did not have to treat me as if I did not know anything."

Several women nodded. One of them made a remark Emma could not hear, and a few erupted into cackling laughter while a younger girl reddened in embarrassment.

Soon after, a woman named Ruth sang a line and urged the others to repeat it. Cassie had told Emma about how protest songs were important to keep their energy together and remain unified.

"There is power in a band of workin' women," Ruth sang, motioning for the women to repeat it.

Later, Emma learned how Cassie instructed Ruth to create a new song to sing each day, although Emma was certain they weren't all original.

Men continued to trickle into the mill past them, outfitted in boots, suspendered pants, and a few wearing caps. Some pointed at the striking women. A few looked surprised; several laughed. Others looked embarrassed.

"Ha! As if anyone will notice," one howled.

"Or care!" another yelled as he elbowed the man next to him.

Two men nearby snickered.

Emma worried they wouldn't be taken seriously. She overheard some predicting the "girls" would give up after a few hours and go inside to get out of the cold or get back to work to claim partial wages for the day.

Word must have spread by lunchtime on the first day, as town folks discreetly crept nearby to stare. Emma felt emboldened rather than embarrassed, as she might have two years prior. During the past months she had become more committed with each passing day to be part of the change.

"I bet they are getting nervous inside. After all, they need us to get the orders out." Elizabeth beamed at Emma as she removed her heavy scarf and unbuttoned the top of her coat. "They may not have realized it before, but they will learn quickly how much we do." She was nearly shaking with excitement; her nervousness from the evening before vanquished.

The morning mist had abated, and a small ray of sun penetrated the clouds.

"Robert told me he understands why I am striking." Elizabeth smiled broadly. "Emma, look." She pointed up the street.

Emma looked up the street, and her mouth dropped open. She brought her hands to her heart. "Father," she whispered.

Father strode the final half block and as he neared her, he tipped the brim of his wool black hat. Sharing this demonstrative act in public was not like him.

"Here. I figured you might be hungry. Elizabeth too." He nodded toward Elizabeth and tipped his hat again. He handed her a handkerchief-wrapped bundle. She need not open it to know she would find bread, cheese, and a bit of meat inside.

"Thank you, Father." She brushed away the tears in her eyes. "This means a lot to me." Her voice cracked.

Father nodded and stepped closer. "The community is behind you girls. Keep that in mind." He nodded again and tipped his hat. "I'll see you this evening."

Emma wanted to ask him what he meant, but she knew he needed to man the store. She wondered what conversations he might have had in the store already that morning. She smiled as he retreated up the block and then looked at Elizabeth, who grinned before pushing her sign high into the air.

As they continued to stand through that first day, waving signs and crying out, "What is Fair is Fair," and, "Same Pay for Equal Work," Emma thought of her father's mother. Although she knew she risked romanticizing the few details she had heard, she believed this grandmother would support the women in this strike. She too would have wanted better conditions for her granddaughters. Emma knew they were doing the right thing, even if they were sacrificing pay and some men taunted them. That first day emanated energy, excitement, and the thrill of fostering change.

During their final minutes before heading home, Cassie approached Emma. "I'd like you to join us in any negotiations to settle the strike. Can you do that?" Her hands were on her hips, and she nodded at a quieter woman named Hattie.

Emma stared at her with surprise. "Me?" She caught her breath. "Why me?"

Cassie smiled sternly and dropped her arms to her sides. "Yes, you. Please join me. Come early tomorrow and we will talk more."

As if already decided, all Emma could do was nod in agreement.


AS THE DAYS wore on, Hattie and Cassie reported to the gathered women that mill management asserted they would not budge. Cassie informed Emma privately how she and Hattie would be the main negotiators, but they wanted Emma and Cassie's younger sister to come along to learn, pay attention, and watch for specific things.

"They will come around to understanding," Emma advised Elizabeth as the days dragged on, trying to reignite the passion from the strike's earliest days. Elizabeth's fiancée worried troublemakers might show up and even rough up the women like they had in other places, but so far it hadn't happened.

"They are insisting, since the mill is an open shop they refuse to meet with any groups of workers," Cassie reported late in the first week. "Then they went and hired two women and an operator to make up for all of us." She laughed. "Mark my words. It will not take them long to understand they cannot maintain production without us. Don't forget how those women in Spokane kept at it and they won."

After feeling like forever, but actually only two weeks, management agreed to meet with the women. Emma followed Cassie and Hattie into the top management office for that first negotiation meeting and was surprised to see the men dressed formally in ties, vests, coats, and bowler hats with not a cap in view.

She touched the top of her buttoned blouse nervously and adjusted her hat; grateful Cassie and Hattie planned to do the talking. She tried not to cough in the smoke-filled room. Cassie had told her ahead of time what to expect—that both the bag factory superintendent and their town mayor would lead the negotiations, with several other men on hand, some simply to intimidate the women.

Cassie and Hattie explained their demands, starting with fans and other things to improve the quality of the factory and only later discussing the pay increase. Neither side backed down and no progress was made during that first meeting. Although she never mentioned it, Emma knew Cassie hoped for the mill and bag factory to be unionized in the future.

Finally, after two more unsuccessful negotiations, the owner of a local store appointed himself as mediator and threatened the women if they continued to take up public space. The women spent a few scary days and were lucky none of them were physically roughed up.

One early morning, two of the louder women raised their signs and yelled, "Fair is fair!" Other women echoed in refrain. Elizabeth shared a tired smile. Ruth broke into yet another song.

Emma had no idea how she kept thinking of new words and lyrics to lead. She did not want to admit protesting was becoming more difficult than she had imagined. At least Father continued to be supportive, arriving with food nearly each day. Emma knew it reflected what he heard from others in the store. At dinner, Father would shush Mother if she criticized the strike or complained about the missing paycheck. Emma wanted to remind her mother that some in the community were sharing food and money with the strikers, even creating a small fund to help. Even though the mayor had insisted that shop owners not issue credit, many in the community felt closer to the girls than to those high in mill ownership who didn't even live in Camas. A few of the striking women relied fully on their mill wages. Yet Emma did not want to belabor the dinner time talk. She knew Father cared more than she had understood before about public sentiment.

Cassie warned them to be patient. "Change takes time."

Emma repeated the motto to others, and quietly to herself. She refused to admit how she was tiring of the daily protesting. She was used to staying warm and even overheating at work, running errands and working near hot machines. Now, standing outside in the late January drizzle, her fingers ached with cold. She worried they all might have a change of heart if the strike continued for weeks on end.

As the unsuccessful negotiations continued, Emma sensed lethargy among a few of the women, especially the younger girls. Some found places to sit for increasingly longer parts of the day, others spent more time chatting than crying out or holding signs. Emma wondered if the community tired of it as well. Most workers ignored them, passing between shifts and home, with only a few men giving them a nod or smile.

Emma pulled her knitted scarf tighter to her neck and sipped tepid tea from her mason jar. She wished her scarf had a tighter weave. The gray days with early morning drizzle continued nonstop, although at least it had not sleeted or snowed. Fewer community members stopped to bolster their energy, although some still provided evening food or money, and Father stopped by nearly every day if only for a moment.

"Stay strong, my young friend," Cassie said as she walked by, checking in with the two dozen protesters still on the line. A few of the younger girls had left, talked into a more womanlike existence by their mothers.

"Cassie," Emma began. She didn't know how to share her thoughts without sounding like a quitter.

"You are fine," Cassie interjected brusquely. "We never said it would be easy. But I'm sure they are getting close to giving in. I heard they are considering negotiating again, but this time with real changes." She brushed her hands together and nodded at Emma before moving on to check in with others.

One woman caught Emma's eye and neared her. "I agree with you," she said softly with a German accent. "They are all getting tired of us. I mean, all of them." The woman's braids were coiled on top of her head, and she waved out to the street and town, and then finally toward the mill. "My husband tells me it is all bad effort. If it is not better by next week, he demands I stay at home. Or go back to work, which he prefers of course." She looked down at her feet.

Emma nodded, unable to find energy or motivation to disagree.

"He says the big business people. The ones in fine dress and hats. The ones in the big houses on the hill." The woman motioned behind them. "They do not care about us and know we will give up soon. He thinks they are laughing at women thinking they can change something." As if what she was saying was dangerous, she stepped back to where she had been standing and gripped her sign but kept it at her feet.

Emma picked up the sign Elizabeth had given her. "We cannot give up," she reminded herself. She repeated it aloud to the women around her. If not this, then what? It was this final question that haunted her and helped her understand the only alternative.

"Equal pay, same job!" she shouted.

# Chapter 9
## Celia
### December 11, 2024

CELIA AWOKE TO the annoying sound of her Celtic harp phone alarm and a pounding headache. It took her a moment to figure out why she felt crappy, and she wished she had remembered to turn off her alarm the night before. Kate encouraged her to use the soothing ringtone, but she found its tinkling new age strumming irritating. Her head spun, and she felt confused. She heard footsteps in the kitchen and grabbed a sweatshirt before stumbling to the bathroom to pee. Her toenails needed trimming, and she wondered if she should consider a pedicure for the first time in her life. Maybe it would prevent arthritic toes someday like her roommate Sophia insisted.

"Jesus," she muttered. *What a stupid thing to think about now.* She looked in the mirror and wondered if ice would relieve the pain she felt in her puffy, red eye sockets. She could barely tell she had been born with green eyes.

Sophia looked at her in surprise as she dragged herself to the kitchen. Her eyes widened. "What? What happened to you?" Celia had forgotten Sophia would be home. "You look like crap." She hesitated and forced a smile. "Um, sorry."

Celia was in agony. She turned on the tea kettle and grabbed her ground coffee and pour-over filter. Now she understood how those folks who weren't morning larks felt. She stood in front of the sink and peered out the window into a soft mist blanketing her view of buildings beyond the parking lot. She had exhausted her supply of tears and wanted to climb back in bed.

"There was an accident," she sputtered, staring blankly at the mist.

Sophia gasped.

Celia had no memory of driving home the previous day and felt emotionally dead. Even though they weren't particularly close, Sophia worried about her when she was on the ocean. Once she had read an article aloud about a boating fatality, and Celia had yelled to leave her alone. Adding, "At least I'm out doing something challenging." Sophia worked in a day care center, and Celia knew what she said was both a lie and mean-spirited.

She poured hot water over the ground beans. Normally the earthy smell of coffee gave her a feeling of pleasure. Not now. All was wrecked. Her world felt ruined and empty, her future blank.

Sophia went to Celia as she poured more water through the filter as if it stopped time. "Do you want to talk?"

Celia knew Sophia's keen sensitivity had been a problem for them. Sophia wanted to talk more; Celia preferred silence.

Celia stiffened at her touch, and Sophia backed off to sit at the table. Sophia knew her well enough to let her make the next move. They had met over a year before at the café, both picking up extra shifts during the busiest tourist months before Sophia began working full-time at the center. They spontaneously decided to share housing. They tended to often work opposite shifts, and Sophia spent a lot of time at her girlfriend's place, leaving Celia alone in the apartment. It would have never worked otherwise.

Celia placed the dripping filter in the sink and sat at the table opposite Sophia. She didn't think she could communicate without screaming or crying, and she didn't want to do either.

"We had an accident." Celia tried to steady her cracking voice, before sipping her coffee. The bitter liquid felt right as it scalded the roof of her mouth and trickled down to her gut. She cleared her throat. Ordinarily she liked the first sip of hot coffee as if a testament to being awake and alive.

She put the cup down, rested her elbows on the table, and ran her hands through her hair. It was stringy and she felt dirty and exhausted. She could not remember if she had showered after she got home the day before. She hovered over her coffee, her hands on either side of her face, as if its aroma would offer resurrection. She rubbed the bump of the large mole on her cheek and closed her eyes. Her eye sockets still ached as if she had bawled all night. Her body had never felt so weak. Not strong enough to pull pots or stand upright on a boat. She stared at the floor before settling her eyes on the fir tree tattooed just above her left ankle. Her celebratory act after graduating college when she had great hopes for her future.

The kitchen was quiet with only the muffled sound of a car door slamming outside. Celia knew Sophia had never seen her like this. While talkative, Sophia had recently become more sensitive to Celia's disinterest in chatter.

"Do you want to talk? At all?" Sophia reached for Celia's hand, but Celia pulled back. "It might be good for you." She stood up and poured hot water from the tea kettle over the used tea bag in her cup. She returned to her seat and stared at Celia.

Celia sipped her coffee and straightened. She stared into Sophia's dark eyes. "It was horrible," she whispered. "Nobody died at least." She caught her breath, as if the allotment of words wiped her out. She returned her hands to her face and pushed her hair back. Finally, she shared her story in broken sentences, a bareboned account of Ed's sudden medical issue, how they now knew it was a heart attack, and about Justin falling overboard. She glossed over details about what she did next, other than the rescue by the Coast Guard and the boat's return to shore.

Sophia's expression changed from concern to horror. Her long, black, glossy hair shined under the weak overhead light. Celia stopped talking, and Sophia's face softened, as if she were looking at a scared child.

"But it sounds like you were a champion. I mean, it may not feel like it, but you helped save him. You saved the situation."

Celia nodded, smiling as she recognized how the old Sophia would have kept chattering.

"Yeah. I guess." Celia stared into Sophia's dark eyes, nodded, and smiled. "But I felt so helpless, really. And if Trevor hadn't been there, I don't know what would have happened? I would never have gotten us back to shore after all that." She wrapped her hands around her coffee cup, feeling panicked.

"But stop." Sophia gently touched Celia's hand over the cup. "He was there. And that wasn't your job. Make sure you return to remembering everything you did do." She waited a few breaths to let it sink in. "How is Ed?"

"You know," Celia said, eyeing the rim of her cup. "Maybe that's what gets me. I'm still damned mad at him, and I don't want to be. I feel guilty. I mean, he's been good to me. He's a good man." She looked at Sophia. "Oh, he's okay, they say. I know they took Justin for observation to Columbia Memorial, but I'm not sure where the copter took Ed." She sucked in a breath. "Like I said, Ed was conscious and breathing when they transported him. But I know he knew things weren't right and he just didn't want to admit it. He risked our lives. That's what pisses me off so much." She raised her arms and shook them. "And I know I should check in with his wife, which I will. Later. I do feel bad, and of course I want him to be fine. I just need to give myself some time." She stood and returned to the sink to look out the window, as if the mist would numb her anxiety. She rubbed her lower back. How could she be in pain when they hadn't even dropped pots?

Sophia rose and placed two slices of whole wheat bread in the toaster. "You need something in your stomach."

Celia shook her head at Sophia's attempt to adapt tricks she might use for a child in crisis to a grown woman. She sat back down, pushed her cup away, and lay her head on her folded arms. Maybe she should go back to sleep. But what if she was haunted by new nightmares? She groaned. She had been exhausted the night before and had no memory of dreaming. But now? After all, she knew people deep in the throes of PTSD, and not all of them were veterans. Kate told her about a friend with long COVID who had regular nightmares about the virus eating away at her organs.

"What about Justin?" Sophia asked. She knew Justin's girlfriend; it was a small community after all.

Celia raised her head and watched her grab the toast, butter both pieces, and return to the table.

She pushed a slice toward Celia. "Eat this."

Celia sat up. "Thanks." She felt bad for being pissy. For the first time, she was grateful for her roommate beyond her paying her share of the rent. "Yeah, Justin is okay, I think. I heard them say it's good he's young and hardy. They actually used the word hardy." She didn't know why this seemed funny to her now. Maybe she was on the brink of hysteria. "I doubt he had to stay overnight, though who knows. The whole day is a blur. It happened early in the day, and here it is the next morning." She shook her head and closed her eyes. "My timing is messed up. I don't know how the hours passed or even when I went to bed." She took another small bite of toast, but it tasted like cardboard and her stomach felt queasy again.

"I'm off work today," Sophia said. "I mean, if you need anything. I've got time."

Celia nodded. She knew Sophia was trying not to be overbearing, and she suddenly felt awful. She had underappreciated this roommate; a kind friend during a horrible time.

"Thanks. I mean, really. I know I can be bitchy. I appreciate this." She finished her coffee and ate a bit more of the bland toast while peeking out through the bit of window. Dark clouds were billowing in the distance, typical of a coastal winter storm. "You know, I felt like something bad was going to happen. I know that sounds woo-woo, but . . . I had a premonition or something." She looked at Sophia, deliberating how much to share. "Now I worry that . . . that, maybe I caused it?" She felt childish, knowing she only wanted someone to invalidate her crazy thought.

"Come on. I mean, get ahold of yourself. I get it, but you know you don't have that much power." Sophia smiled and twisted one of her ear studs.

Celia reluctantly laughed. Their laughs broke the somberness, as if to invite sounds from outside to return. She heard a car door slam in the parking lot and footsteps in the apartment above them.

"Yeah, I know." This time, Celia guffawed a hysterical sounding laugh, as if swirling pent up energy only then could escape. She threw back her head and pulled her shoulder-length hair into a fat ponytail before letting the curly strands fall free again. "Okay, so maybe I didn't cause it, but I did feel something bad was going to happen. Maybe I could have prevented it." She slurped the coffee dregs and stretched. Her shoulders ached as much as if she had hauled full pots for days. "I think I should tell the Coast Guard guy that. You know?" She took a deep breath and made eye contact. Sophia's parents had been born in India, but Celia was embarrassed she didn't know more about her life.

"But you were already interviewed. Remind yourself instead, about the good you did. I'm sure Justin, well, all of them, understand that." Sophia stood and touched Celia's shoulder. This time Celia didn't shrug it off.

"Yeah, okay, But it's more about being honest about Ed." Celia stopped as if this part was too hard to say aloud.

"What? What?" Sophia looked at Celia expectantly.

Celia sighed. "That he was covering up how he was feeling that morning so he could keep fishing. You know, it's been his whole life. I think I finally understand why he was so grumpy. And worried. Oh,

I don't know." She put her hands to her face and peeked through her fingers. "But I should have stopped him."

Sophia grabbed a napkin and wrapped the toast crumbs from the table inside it. She eyed Celia's empty cup. "Do you want more? I can make you a cup?"

Celia shook her head.

Well, again, that's Ed's issue," Sophia replied. "I'm sure his wife knows if that's the case. Anyway, it's not your problem, remember? Besides, when can we ever tell a stubborn man what to do?" She rolled her eyes.

"Yeah." Celia stood. "I'm going to get cleaned up. I might take a walk, even though I feel like shit. Maybe the air will snap me out of my funk."

Sophia took her cup and washed it in the sink. Then she turned and gently hugged Celia, catching her off guard. Celia was a full head taller and began to resist, but Sophia held strong, standing on tip toes. Celia felt herself softening before gently melting into Sophia's arms but being careful not to allow her weight to pull them both over. She sniffled, and the more she tried to hold back tears, the louder she sobbed as Sophia held her without saying a word.


LATER IN THE afternoon, after waking up from a fitful nap, Celia knew she had to address what was bothering her. As feared, she dreamt she'd been out on a desert, and someone was warning about a huge storm coming. She had two children with her, but they had no shelter. It was all weird and disturbing and she woke with damp tears on her cheek, although her face felt less puffy. She sat up and grabbed her phone from her night table.

Eric picked up on the third ring.

"Hi. Um, sir. Eric. This is Celia. We met uh, yesterday."

"Hi, Celia," Eric said. "Thanks for calling. How can I help you?"

"Well, there was one more thing." Celia hesitated as she tried to slow her breathing and speak quieter. "I could tell something was wrong. I mean wrong with Ed before we headed out. He wasn't himself. I mean he was grouchy. And I think, maybe . . . well. Maybe he didn't feel well." She clamped her hand over her mouth before blurting out she should have stopped him. She took another breath. "So that's all. In case it matters." She was shaking and her sweaty hands could barely hold the phone.

"Thanks," Eric replied. "Yes, we know he had a medical incident. Unfortunately, cardiac events can happen like that."

She had wistfully hoped he might reassure her it wasn't her fault. Instead, he thanked her and told her to feel free to contact him again if she thought of anything else to share.

Celia went to the kitchen in her stocking feet to make a second cup of coffee for the day. Sophia had stayed true to her offer and hung around the house, keeping out of her hair but nearby if needed. Celia repeated her ritual of peering outside as the water heated and tried to decide if she felt better or worse. Eric had made her admission sound inconsequential. Yes, after all, Ed had a heart attack. Heart episodes surprised people all the time, and maybe this was no different. She knew it was time to check in with her crew mates and captain, and to give herself a break.

# Chapter 10
## Celia
### December 16, 2024

CELIA WAS NOT certain how Ruth fit into her life, although she had spent at least two holiday meals with her in previous years. She did know what the call was about when it came in weeks before. "Oh thanks, Ruth. That's kind of you. I'm so sorry but I have already accepted another dinner invitation," she had lied. "Yes, another time." She rolled her eyes. When Ruth suggested meeting for coffee soon, she agreed mostly to be able to get off the phone. She felt bad, suspecting her mother had somehow urged Ruth's persistence in checking up on her. *Ruth had to be her mom's spy.* Finally, as promised, Ruth called to "get a date on her calendar" and Celia felt obligated to say yes. A short coffee alone with Ruth would be okay, she tried to convince herself. Soon after setting the date, she realized she'd likely be out hauling crab and intended to cancel.

Celia had grown up without a network of relatives, unlike friends who socialized with cousins and aunts and uncles. She did get the sense that whatever stories existed within her family, over time were fractured and lost. The idea made her sad when she let it get to her, especially when Kate went on and on about the fun she had hanging out with huge pods of relatives. "They know me best, Celia," Kate had once told her after returning from a family reunion. "It can be embarrassing but also oddly freeing."

So instead, Celia reminded herself about the other stories she heard over the years. Sisters and brothers and fathers and mothers infighting and becoming estranged. She didn't need any of that, for sure. Although she knew her one set of grandparents, she had been embarrassed in school when other kids charted out extensive family trees, exclaiming this or that one came over on the Oregon Trail or some other hype. Those with longtime Oregon roots annoyed her. Her family also went back several generations in the west, even if she didn't know details. But she found it tiresome how longtime locals got off on the privilege they held to the land because of the people in their past. And the ones she heard talk about it didn't have Native American blood, so it seemed a joke. Yet deep down she felt an emptiness not knowing her family's past.

Ruth was older than her mom and married to Bob, a successful and well-liked retired charter fisherman. At one Thanksgiving dinner, Bob had gone on about his earliest Alaska fishing days, explaining how he and his family had since then lived in Astoria. When Celia first moved to the coast, she received an out-of-the-blue, what she thought to be half-hearted, invitation to work on a boat Bob owned but no longer captained. His boats were popular with tourist adventurers and consisted of all male crews. Celia didn't blame him for operating a lucrative operation, knowing it also carried hidden worries and stressors. Her disinterest back then wasn't about the life Bob chose, more that she knew she would not fit in. But now she had even less of an idea than she had back when receiving his invitation as to what was next for her.

Ruth invited Celia to the prior three Thanksgiving dinners. She had joined twice before, feeling obligated to accept Ruth's welcoming efforts. Yet Celia felt uncomfortable around Bob and the crowd he gathered. Their guests had been polite, although not one had gone out of their way to say much more than hello to her, and Celia felt inhibited to initiate a conversation or share her true, albeit introverted, self.

She had been grateful to dodge the recent Thanksgiving dinner invitation. The thought of sitting around the table again with people she barely knew sounded unappealing, yet she felt an odd sadness after turning it down. As if she was missing an opportunity for a romantic meal with people who cared about her; a mix of *Little House on the Prairie* meets Martha Stewart. She had tried to laugh at herself as she headed to Kate's house for dessert later that night. She remembered some of the holiday dinners with her mom and grandparents as a kid, until they started butting heads when she hit her teens and tried to refuse to go.

Celia attempted to be empathetic to her mom's worries about her only daughter living miles from her or asking Ruth to spy, although they did talk regularly on the phone. She had once told her mother to stop pressuring her to find a boyfriend or husband. Gratefully, it had been a long time since her mom whined about how Celia was her only chance for a grandchild.

But now, with the demise of *High Hopes*, it felt oddly comforting to have a date on her calendar, even if she had originally planned to cancel. She felt too exhausted to make up another excuse and admitted she was curious about how Ruth fit into her life. The two had never had a lengthy conversation alone. During shared holiday dinners, Ruth was quiet while Bob filled the room with his loud personality. Unlike Ed and his wife, Bob was the big talker and Ruth the supporting player. Celia knew enough to give credit to fisherman wives. Businesses would never make it without someone to organize it all—accounting, billing, paychecks, licensing, food, and supplies. Yes, from what Celia could tell, Ruth seemed to exist to make everything around Bob okay. It drove her crazy to observe this relationship structure. If that's what marriage meant, she was fine without it.

Celia entered the Coffee Girl and saw Ruth standing next to a table, waiting for her. She had pulled out a sweater and fresh jeans to up her game, although she knew she needed a haircut. Sophia offered to tweeze her eyebrows during their extra time together, but Celia laughed, hoping she didn't hurt her carefully preened friend's feelings.

She had to give Ruth credit in finding this local spot sitting prominently at the end of a pier just upriver from downtown. Most people she knew worried for the locally owned spots—coffee shops, restaurants, grocery stores. It was kind of like the local tuna fishers up against Star Kiss or Bumblebee. She was glad to support local, rather than the chains growing their empires. She had strolled the Riverwalk to their meet up, eyeing the pilot boat stationed near the maritime museum. She imagined how terrifying it would be to climb from a pilot boat to a large ship in the middle of the breakers or river bar. No, one could not get away from the lure of the ocean and its history in this town: shipwrecks, old ferries, barges, and steamboats.

"Celia, how wonderful to see you. Let me treat you," Ruth said.

"Oh, you don't have to. But sure. Thanks." Celia looked around the shop. "What a nice spot." Only two other customers sat at a table in the corner, but the windows opened out to the powerful river highway.

Celia laid her raincoat on the chair and followed Ruth to the counter. The barista looked at her expectantly. Celia wasn't an espresso fanatic; certain she would never order anything fancier than a simple plain cup of black coffee. "A medium drip coffee would be great. Black. Thank you." The woman rang up the order. "For here, please."

"Would you like a treat?" Ruth asked, pointing to a platter of scones and muffins covered with clear plastic wrap.

Normally Celia loved morning glory muffins, chocked full of apples, coconut, and nuts. "No, I'm good. Thanks." She forced a smile. Her stomach hadn't regained its appetite in the days since the accident and none of the treats looked enticing.

She took her drink from the counter and headed back to the table while Ruth waited for the barista to steam hers. Celia eyed Ruth in her jeans, probably one of those brands with a hidden elastic waist. Ruth wore a bright flannel shirt under her unzipped raincoat, and a pair of rubber-soled oxford shoes popular with the elderly boat crowd. She liked that nobody seemed to care what people wore here at the coast. It would be fine with her if all fashion-conscious times were gone for good, leaving elastic waists, droopy sweats, and all else that was comfortable, except for the sagging pants leaving half of an adult man's ass for show.

"It's been a long time." Ruth set her latte something or other on the table.

She pulled two napkins from her pocket, placed one under her drink, and set the other near Celia's coffee. The latte wore a creamy heart on top, making it more appetizing than Celia might have thought.

Ruth took her coat off and carefully arranged it over the back of her chair before sitting down. "How is it going with you? I mean fishing and, well, everything?" She looked at Celia sideways and smiled indulgently.

Celia felt like a deer in headlights. Ruth asked the question innocently, yet it seemed impossible for her not to know about the accident in their small community. Nearly a week had passed, and although she had brief phone conversations with both Ed's wife Janet, and Trevor, she had evaded lengthier conversations about the incident other than with Sophia.

Celia dodged. "I think I'm done fishing." She was surprised by her calm, confident sounding voice. "I'm taking on more shifts at the café and, well, just thinking about things. Sorting it out. Next steps, you know." *How could she sound so measured and confident?* She focused on steadying her voice but raised her eyebrows. She wondered if Ruth knew but didn't want to be the first to bring it up. Sophia had encouraged her to process her experience, but Celia found it difficult to verbalize the details. She didn't want any of it to get back to her mom who would say "told you so" or try to pressure her to move back in with her. Ruth's sidelong glance confirmed she knew.

While Celia rarely chatted to fill space, she wanted their talk to be frivolous. She knew Ruth was trying to be kind and wished she had more energy to accept it. "So"—she tried to channel Kate—"you didn't grow up around here, did you?" She knew she hadn't, but it was the first thing she thought to ask.

"Oh no, not me. My parents would never have chosen Astoria back in those days. I grew up in Portland." Ruth gestured expansively backward to point upriver. "Of course, back then was nothing like now." Her eyes crinkled, and she smiled indulgently.

Celia eyed her perfectly coifed silver hair and wondered how often she visited her hairdresser. Her hairdo contrasted with her rugged plaid shirt and jeans.

"I can't imagine living in all that now," Ruth continued. "Although I think your mother is fine. I mean in Portland."

Ruth became animated, and she gestured often with her hands. She talked on about how she could not imagine driving around in so much traffic in Oregon's largest city. "Just to get to the grocery store." She stretched her hands out as if in question. She added how horrible it was with all the homeless people living on the street. "And then all those people on drugs and picketing this or that. I feel bad for anyone trying to run a business in that city." Her voice rose. Celia imagined Bob ranting on this at home. "But you know . . ." She stopped as if out of fuel and put her hands in her lap. Her face reddened, and Celia wondered if Bob cut her off if she started rambling.

It seemed everyone was complaining about the homeless problems. And more recent cuts to social services and government grants made it feel even more hopeless. She was as guilty as anyone, just trying to move herself forward without drowning in worries about the future. Just half an hour earlier she neared a guy "down and out"—his body and belongings outspread on the sidewalk near the corner. He had two overstuffed plastic garbage bags near him and a small dog tied up with rope. Although Celia caught his eye and tried to give a sympathetic smile, she walked on.

"But my Bob came from a fishing family." Ruth amiably changed gears. "Skipped a generation, though, his grandparents fished. We met at Oregon State where I thought I'd be a teacher. But. Well, I didn't make it past the first year." She looked at Celia cautiously, as if expecting criticism, before smiling. Yes, Ruth was a smiler. "I hated it when people thought I was merely looking for my M.R.S. degree." She shook her head and frowned into her coffee.

"M.R.S?" Celia tilted back her head and pursed her lips as she tried to figure out the acronym.

Ruth rolled her eyes and released a glorious peal of laughter. "You know, marriage. That's what everyone called it back then and it always made me mad because . . . Well, that's not why I started college. And I did love Bob. I mean, I do love Bob." She laughed again.

Celia smiled. This Ruth had more spunk than the Ruth she had seen during those boring dinners. She had to admit she was enjoying their time together.

"Really, though, it is hard to be honest about it all now. That is what a lot of women did then, although we hoped more for our daughters. Yes, I did love Bob and still do." Then, Ruth put her hand to her mouth as if telling a secret and stage whispered, "Even if he talks too much. He means well."

Celia smiled. She heard a buzz. Ruth pulled her phone from her purse. It seemed funny to see old people use cell phones like everyone else.

"Speak of the devil. It's just Bob." Ruth returned the phone to her purse as if to prevent him from intruding on their visit. "Anyway, enough about me." She brushed her hands together as if dusting off invisible crumbs. "All those times long ago. I watch my kids now, especially my daughter. I know things are hard. But I'm still glad you girls don't have to put up with what we did." She wiped her mouth with her napkin and shrugged. "Even though old folks like me go on and on about the good old days." She laughed. "But I'm not complaining. I've had a good life. I just like to see women get more choices. That's all." She tapped her hands on the table but stopped, winded. She dabbed the napkin at a drop of spittle at the corner of her mouth. Celia wondered what she felt about recent stabs at women's rights, but didn't have the energy to bring it up.

Ruth's cup was more than half full and it was too soon for Celia to politely excuse herself. The visit had been enjoyable, but she did not want to be stuck answering difficult questions about her own life. Ruth sipped her coffee luxuriously, as if tasting the most delightful drink in an elegant restaurant and glanced at her watch.

"How do you know my mom?" Celia asked, startled by her own bluntness.

"Your mother? Oh, honestly, I don't know your mom very well. It was your grandmother who was my friend. First, I mean. I met your mother through her. Your grandmother and I were close back in those days." Ruth put her coffee down and drew in a breath. "Oh my. Look at that barge." They turned to look at the barge moving downriver, passing close to the pier. "Probably wheat?"

Celia wasn't sure how she could tell the steel vessel contained wheat over any other export.

"Anyway, I still remember a visit one day at your grandmother's house, if you can believe it." Ruth laughed and looked off into the distance, as if retrieving long ago memories. She looked at Celia. "Yes, it was your grandmother who reached out to me when you first moved to town. She occasionally calls to check in on me but always asks if I had seen you or knew how you were doing."

Celia felt embarrassed and blushed. *Not her mom?*

Ruth dropped her chin and looked at Celia as if about to lecture. "Yes, now, now. She just loves you, you know?" She looked back at the barge now further downriver. "Goodness gracious, she was so worried about me back when I moved here, afraid I'd become some rough, unruly fisherman's wife or something." She smiled gently and fingered a hand through her hair. "Maybe I have."

Celia felt bad it had taken her this long to learn about their connection. "What about that day you first met my mom?" She pushed her empty cup to the side and rested her face on her hands and elbows on the table.

"Oh, it was long ago. Your grandmother and I were volunteering for some such thing. Your mother had just arrived home from high school, and I think your grandmother was serving tea." Ruth took a sip of her coffee. "Back then, many of us housewives searched for worthwhile things to do, service projects here and there. You know, besides raising our kids. And there was a lot of community need for us," she added as if a justification was needed. She nodded at Celia, her lips forming a gentle smile. "I did meet Sheila that day, but most anything I knew about her, or you once you came along, was through your grandmother. Just like she heard about the lives of my two kids and their kids. You may not realize it yet, but we women need each other throughout our lives. Not just when we are girls."

The espresso machine squealed, and Ruth looked toward the counter and giggled. Celia looked at the barista to see what had set Ruth off, but nothing seemed amiss. Ruth tried to stifle her giggles, but it seemed to make her chortles louder.

"Ruth?" Celia leaned forward.

"'Oh, I'm sorry." Ruth picked up her napkin and wiped at her tearing eyes. She took a long breath, clawed into her purse for a tissue, and shook her head. "It's just I haven't thought about that day in so long. I know I've forgotten so much, but then, once in a while, a memory comes to me crystal clear." She laughed softly. "And it's always some insignificant thing. Not something I've tried to remember, mind you." She shook her head. "They say doing crossword puzzles help, but sometimes I think it just makes me concentrate on meaningless details."

Celia didn't care about crossword puzzles and waited for more. "What did you remember? That was so funny?"

"Oh, I'm making it out to be grander than it was. Please excuse me." She shook her head again and peered off across the river. "There were a group of us there for tea to discuss some volunteer project. Mostly your grandmother and I helped plan events so the YMCA could raise money for kids and the elderly." She looked down at herself, and then back at Celia. "People my age now, I guess." She smirked. "Anyway, I knew most of the other women, but one of them only your grandmother knew. Oh my, this lady was like something I'd never seen before, not even in college. Loud and funny, as if she wanted to have her own variety show. A regular ham. I could tell your grandmother was embarrassed and kept trying to quiet her."

Celia felt disappointed but politely feigned interest and nodded, hoping to hurry her along.

"Oh, she was this cute thing, a bit older than us. Alice. Yes, her name is Alice. I still get Christmas cards from her, if you can believe it, even though I never thought we were close. Oh my, I should reply sometime." Ruth hesitated, and Celia hoped she wasn't getting lost thinking about writing cards. "Oh yes. This Alice. She was determined to tell everyone this story of a woman she claimed was related to your grandmother. Your grandmother's grandmother or some crazy thing. A woman who had lived long ago." Her cheeks were rosy, and she was animated again. "She kept raving on about all the important things this woman had done. Oh, I wish I could remember her name. But this woman lived up the river in one of those mill towns." She pointed out the window at the river and motioned toward the east. "Anyway, she apparently shut down the whole mill all by herself because of something, speaking up for a whole bunch of women. I can't remember what. Alice was fired up and began telling your grandmother she owed it to her to make a tribute. To me it was as if Alice was an entertainer who had finally found her stage. But, oh, I felt badly for your grandmother. She kept shushing her, embarrassed, and I think she wondered if Alice had been drinking in the middle of the day. Honestly, I loved listening, but your grandmother was oddly upset by it all. I was never sure how true any of it was, and your grandmother would never talk about it afterward."

Ruth sputtered to a close and looked up, her cheeks rosy with excitement. She leaned back in her chair.

Celia raised her eyebrows and forced a smile.

"That was so long ago. You must forgive me. I don't know what got into me and I'm sure you have places to be. Although it sure was fun to laugh like that." Ruth looked at her watch and then pulled out her phone and held it in her hand.

Celia sensed she was eager to return Bob's call. "I know it's time to go, but, well, do you think my mom knows about this Alice? Or about this story?" At least she finally knew how Ruth was connected to her family.

"No, I wouldn't think so. I would doubt if she remembered much of any of it. She probably thought we were a bunch of old bitties, ranting on and being silly. I don't even know if she stayed with all of us in the room during the so-called show." Ruth smiled tiredly.

Celia nodded and stood. Their time together had been much longer than she had expected. Being surrounded by laughter had been a welcomed respite from her solitude of heaviness. Her head felt clearer and her heart a bit lighter. She returned the cups to the plastic tub on the counter. Back at the table she grabbed her jacket. "Thank you again for this."

Ruth pulled her into a gentle hug. "You've had a lot. Don't forget you've got people who care about you."

*Yes, Ruth had known all along.* "Thanks." Celia's voice cracked, and she fidgeted. "Are you still in contact with Alice? I mean, I'm kind of curious." She was afraid to look Ruth in the eyes after asking an off the wall request about a long, ago crazy story. "I don't know much about any relatives beyond my grandparents."

"You could ask your grandmother," Ruth said. "After all, she was the connector then although I have no idea if they are still in contact."

Celia sighed and forced a nod. She didn't want to whine that Ruth had just told her how her grandmother hadn't wanted to talk about it even back then.

"Okay, I'll tell you what," Ruth said. "Yes, as I said, I do still get cards from Alice. I'm sure I have her address. I'll send it to you, and you can decide."

Celia smiled and looked Ruth in the eye. She knew it was silly, but learning about a preposterous decades' old story was a nice diversion. And what if there was truth to her relative having been important and pushing back, even way back then? Learning more might take the stress off figuring out that next thing. She gave Ruth another quick hug.

"Thank you," she added and stood as she watched Ruth's hunched form slowly walk toward her car.

# Chapter 11
## Emma
### July 20, 1913

"COME, CHILDREN. IT is time to wash up and ready for our guests." Emma had not looked forward to supper that night. Referring to them as guests felt false and lofty.

"Emma, can we take Nina to the river with us after dinner?" Helen asked quietly.

Helen adored her niece Nina who seemed more like a cousin. It was not enough that Emma had to corral the children, but had also spent all afternoon assisting Mother to make an especially fancy supper. All to only host Martha and her family. While Emma loved little Nina and tried to never treat her otherwise, her sister was increasingly difficult to be around. Emma knew Mother shared her frustration about Emma privately with Martha but wished she would speak her mind with her directly.

Emma smiled at Helen, their quiet sibling. As frustrated as she was at the number of times Martha dropped Nina off, she had to admit it made the days that much better for Helen. "I am not certain. Although it will be a beautiful evening I do not know if there will be time."

Camas was enjoying gorgeous summer weather, cottonwood leaves shimmering in the gentle breeze, especially along the shoreline. Early evenings were capturing bits of waning daylight before the sun set over the mountains west of town. Emma knew the Pacific Ocean was well beyond that and prayed she might one day see it.

"Come now." Emma nodded, observing her three siblings as they washed their hands. She grabbed a rag, moistened it in the pitcher, and scrubbed at two dirt stains on John's jumper. She should have insisted he take it off before he went outside that afternoon. She ran a brush through Mary's hair and inspected Helen's braids, not worrying about herself.

Emma heard the front door open, followed by excited commotion. She inspected the children, nodded to them, and put her hand on the doorknob. "Remember, best behavior. Even if it is family." All three nodded, looking seriously at her. John and Mary tried to be polite, but together they were often rambunctious, and Mother seemed to expect Emma to keep them in line. She often wondered why Mother nearly always lacked energy. She opened the bedroom door. "Go ahead."

Emma knew she should feel badly not to look forward to their monthly meal with Martha's family. Yet, the house always seemed too small and shabby, and she wished instead they could travel to her sister's home in Vancouver. It would be nice to have less responsibility, especially on her only day off work. Some weeks, she even had to work a seventh day if there were extra shipments backlogged. She knew it was wrong to complain but did not force a smile.

"Hello, Martha." She gave her an unenthusiastic hug.

Martha smiled and nodded, but her arms barely touched Emma.

Emma wondered what bad thing she had done to have to work so hard to gain her love. After all, she tried not to complain when Nina was added to her workload. She knew better than to bring any of it up to either Mother or Martha and instead reminded herself what a delightful girl Nina was. No, she knew it was less about her niece and more about the principle. Was the time Martha spent in her social and women's group activities as she tried to elevate her society status more important than Emma's own demands?

"Emma," her mother called sternly, nodding to the prepared dishes on the sideboard. "The biscuits." She motioned to Emma.

Emma grabbed the quilted potholder and opened the wood burning oven to grab the biscuits, grateful they were evenly browned. She slammed the oven shut and Mother gave her a warning look. Emma knew she would be blamed if the biscuits weren't perfect. They required more butter than the family often used in a week, and Emma knew Mother tried to impress Martha and Peter, even if she might not admit it even to herself. Martha's women's group had received a copy of a new cookbook from some women in Portland, and for weeks it was nearly all they talked about, this recipe or that. Her mother first insisted that Martha share the biscuit recipe, and then for Emma to ensure they had the ingredients on hand when they made them that afternoon.

Without reminder, Emma scowled as she stirred the bean soup, perhaps too vigorously. The dish did not seem particularly fancy, although now as she stirred it, she was reminded how much more bacon it contained than what might be typical. Her stomach growled. She would be lying if she did not admit to being happy to get more bacon in her stomach, and she was eager to try the blackberry pie she had baked that morning. The children loved to pick blackberries with her in the sticker patches nearest the river. There seemed more blackberry briars invading each summer. She and Helen did most of the picking, and John and Mary ate more than they added to their pail, all of them returning home blackberry stained and scratched.

"Come." Father eyed his children and waited to sit until only Emma and Mother remained standing. They squeezed together around the wooden table. Father had added their two extra wooden chairs, leaving little elbow room, but at least everyone had a seat and none were left-handed.

Mother placed the platter of golden biscuits on the table, and small clouds of steam hovered over the tops. John's eyes opened wide, and Emma knew she would need to monitor him trying to sneak extra jam from the jar. She was grateful they had set the table earlier. She stood over the stove, ladling soup into bowls, before handing them to Mother who placed them on top of the awaiting place settings. John put his finger in the soup to grab a piece of bacon, but Father's stern frown and head shake made him return his hand to his lap.

Finally, Emma joined the rest of them at the table.

"Let us say Grace," Father began. "Lord God, Heavenly Father, bless us and Thy gifts which we receive from Thy bountiful goodness, through Jesus Christ, our Lord. Amen."

"Amen," the children and adults repeated.

"May I have a biscuit please," John exclaimed.

Mother put her finger to her lips but nodded, spread a small bit of jam on two halves, and gave one half to Mary.

"So, Peter," Father began. "How are things going at the mill?"

Peter worked at the sawmill in Vancouver. Emma knew he was a top manager and Mother often boasted to her friends about the possibility of him being elevated to superintendent.

The children kept busy eating, knowing that talking at the table was reserved for adults. Emma often felt more relaxed after food was served, as if it was the luxurious time of day when she neither had to work or mind children. She inhaled the smell of the bean and bacon broth but gripped her hands tightly in her lap as she took a break from eating. Yes, it seemed a perfect meal, and she was grateful everything seemed to turn out as Mother had hoped. She lost track of the conversation and took another bite of her biscuit. Although she may complain about using too much butter, even she admitted no other bread tasted as good.

"Well, Emma. Was it?" Peter asked.

Emma looked up surprised, only then understanding her private savoring of her meal had caused her to ignore the conversation. She looked at Peter.

"Worth it. The strike? Of course, we all heard about it, even in Vancouver. Probably even Seattle I suspect." Peter chuckled. "I'm wondering if it was worth it? Losing wages all those days. Standing outside in front of everyone."

Emma felt put on the spot and knew she had to be careful in her response. The strike was months ago, and she didn't understand why only now he brought it up. As management, Peter had little tolerance for workers rebelling and insisted that operations already treated workers just and fair. Unions were absent within Washington's lumber mills.

"Thank you for asking, Peter," Emma replied evenly, hoping her cheeks would not flush. She gripped her hands tightly in her lap. "Yes. I suppose you could say it was." Her heart raced, and she hoped she could leave it at that. While she did have much to say about all of it, the honest answer was far too complicated. And not what Mother would like to hear.

"Well, I guess for your sake, I am glad to hear that. It is not what I learned. Perhaps you can share more?" Peter asked.

Martha shook her head and covered Peter's hand, but Peter moved his hand away and stifled a laugh.

"Excuse me, Peter, but would anyone like another biscuit?" Mother glanced around the table before raising her eyebrows at Emma.

Emma knew she would anger Mother and Martha and felt warmth rise in her cheeks. If she were William, Mother, and Father for that matter, would be fine with him talking openly about mill business.

"Yes, Peter, I'd be happy to." Emma ignored Martha and Mother's staring daggers. "Although we did not get the full wage we asked for, we did get an increase that began just a month later. Yes, we made a difference!" She forced herself to sound more pleased than the women had felt with the outcome. After all, in the end they raised their pay from $1.10 per day to $1.25, but not the demanded $1.50. Emma hesitated and glanced at Father. "And you may not have known I was requested to represent the bag factory workers at the negotiations. Yes, I was there with the mill manager. And the mayor."

Mother gasped, and Martha covered her mouth with her hand. Emma could not contain a nervous smile. Peter's smirk told Emma he thought of her as a simple child. Nearly as if he did not believe her. A small hand grabbed hers under the table. She turned to Helen who stared at her and gave her an ever so slight nod.

She knew Cassie and others were disappointed in how they had not been taken seriously by management, but being put on the spot made her stretch the truth. Cassie had insisted that even though they didn't achieve full success, it made a difference for future organizing efforts in Camas. "And we also received new fans to improve the air. To make ventilation better. In fact, the health inspector came because of us. The company has promised to provide even more fans." She felt bold, better understanding the significance of ventilation within the factory. "You do understand that the odors some days make our workers ill." She tried to ignore the increasing heat she felt in her face and straightened. She pushed her fingers gently on the table in front of her and tried to keep them from shaking, proud of herself, even if it shamed Mother. She looked at Father, and he nodded slightly, although he did not smile. Martha stared at Father as if to get his attention, but he kept his eyes on Emma, nodding again.

Peter smiled at Father, as if as men they shared an inside joke. Although Emma did not want to give him the benefit of the doubt, she knew the rumors that had gone around. How some people teased the men in the factory about how these women had more courage than they had. About how the community supported them, giving them food and supplies to help make up for lost wages, only because they were young or innocent or not capable of standing up for themselves. Some of the townspeople felt it all a trivial exercise and reassured each other that the mill, in the end, had graciously taken care of everyone. Some even blamed the striking women for leading to their mayor stepping down after the difficult negotiations.

"And." Emma knew she could not fully contain her fury but tried to keep her tone and voice even. "You should know that the management understood they could not continue without us. Even after hiring three people while we were striking." She felt a kick under the table and looked at Martha who was glowering at her. "So, thank you, again, for asking." She stoically eyed Martha.

"We have pie," Mother said, louder than normal. "Emma, would you please get the knife?"

Emma's momentary enthusiasm for sharing a bit of their work win cascaded into frustration. As she rose, Helen patted her hand and smiled at her. Emma smiled gently back. Helen understood more than she ever verbalized. She pushed back her chair, not intending to scrape the floor as loudly as it did.

Emma avoided looking Mother in the eyes as she handed her the knife. Mother cut small pieces of pie and placed them on saucers and then nodded to Emma who served each of the guests first, followed by the others.

She had lost her appetite for the special pie. Instead, she gathered the soup bowls and spoons and washed them in the tub of hot soapy water she had heated on the stove just before dinner. She wanted to clatter them in a torrent of anger but forced herself to slow her washing. Although they had hot running water, it was not scalding enough to properly clean bacon grease from dishes. She thought Mother would ask her to join them, but she seemed content to have Emma initiate the cleanup. She felt no need to participate in small talk about how business was at the store or the sawmill. She looked out the window between scrubbing bowls and spoons, wondering how a similar conversation might go at Elizabeth's house. She knew Elizabeth's parents openly shared their pride in Elizabeth participating in the strike, along with general support for unions.

"Yes, we simply adore our church and community," Martha was saying. "Although, it appears as though Peter may down the road have opportunities in Portland."

Emma caught a glimpse of Martha as she added more boiling water to break down the soup bowls' greasy residue. Martha was beaming and had placed her hand on Peter's as if in honor. Emma knew Martha had always wanted, as much as a husband and family, to someday live in one of those big houses in a tree-lined neighborhood of Portland.

Emma dried her hands. She knew she could finish the remaining dishes later. She returned to the table and tried to get a sense of evening expectations.

"How about I take the children to the river?" she asked quietly. She knew she had to regain Mother and Martha's good will. Mother seemed less nervous with Mary near the shore now that she had gotten a bit older.

Martha and Mother exchange a look. Martha nodded.

"That would be delightful," Mother said. "I'm sure it would make the children happy."

Mary clapped her hands, and Emma, even in her sour mood, could not help but smile at her. Nina and Helen arose from the table and held hands.

"Then, children." Emma eyed the four of them. "Please wash your hands at the sink and get your jackets, it's still a bit chillier in the evenings."

Although she longed to be respected as an adult, she knew Mother and Martha only wanted their own time together to share stories and gossip. "Woman talk," Father would say. Emma did not know if they would ever see her as one of the women, rather than a child or the children's caregiver. But tonight, being outdoors away from indoor conversation and stagnant smells of onion and bacon in full view of the river was what her heart desired. Even with children tagging along.

# Chapter 12
## Celia
### December 18, 2024

"HI," CELIA SAID as Ed's wife opened the door. She had knocked several times and half hoped they might be out. Janet had left a message for Celia two days prior, asking her to stop by their house, adding she had something for her. Celia felt unnerved not knowing more.

"Oh, yes. Thank you for coming." Janet looked exhausted. "It's nice to see you."

Other times Celia had seen Janet, she had been well put together with makeup and styled hair even if dressed for the out-of-doors. Today, her mostly gray hair was disheveled like someone who had just woken up, dressed in a plain gray sweatshirt, jeans, and fuzzy slippers.

"Come in. Sorry, the house is a bit of a mess." She ushered Celia into the front living room.

Celia bent to take her boots off just inside the door, but Janet brushed her off.

"It would take a lot to make all this worse." Janet released a heavy sigh and moved a magazine and folder of papers from a chair.

"Thank you." Celia wished she had gotten this over with earlier.

"You should sit. Just for a few minutes." Janet ushered her to the chair.

"Thanks." Celia anxiously tapped her fingers on her thighs. "Um, how is Ed?"

The last she had heard he was home and doing fine. They'd done some procedure at the hospital right after the incident and put him on a drug or two. This she had learned from Trevor with their relationship strengthening over a few phone calls as if they were co-conspirators. Or perhaps, co-survivors.

"He's doing okay," Janet said. "Yes, he's good. I guess better than I might have expected." Tears welled in the corner of her eyes, and she balled her hands into tight fists and shuffled her weight uncomfortably, too agitated it seemed to sit. She looked at Celia and sighed as she dropped her shoulders. "You know, the thing is, I've wanted him to be done with this." She waved a hand toward the accordion files piled on the coffee table. "All this. This business. I'm sure he complained about me to you, my nagging about this or that. But I just knew." She rubbed her eyes with her fists. "But it's still hard." She sighed. "Anyway, we'll get there. We're getting there."

Celia teared up. She cared about Ed, even as angry as she had been. He didn't deserve to have it go the way it had. But she didn't know how to articulate any of this to Janet and felt unsure what to say next. She looked toward the kitchen and wondered if Ed could hear them.

"Janet, I'm very sorry," Celia said "And, well, I feel responsible."

Janet's eyes widened, and she stared at Celia. Then she smiled sadly. "Oh, don't do that. None of us could have gotten this stubborn guy to do anything differently. If anything, it was my pushing him that upped his frustration. And his insistence." She hesitated. "And, Celia, I'm sorry." She shook her head and pursed her lips. "I don't suspect Ed is up for seeing you. He's not met with Trevor yet either. He won't really talk about it much, but I think it's only now he understands the danger he put you all in. He's embarrassed but he's also flat out angry." She took a breath and floated her arms toward the ceiling. "Oh, not at anyone. Just life. Maybe just disappointed." She sank down on the couch, leftover agitation morphed into exhaustion. "I think deep down he's trying to find somebody to blame." She forced a smile. "I guess you could say he's not dealing with this aging stuff very well. Neither of us are, really." She looked up at Celia. "Realizing how those years have flown by."

Celia looked at the wall leading into the kitchen, covered with pictures of their three kids at various ages. All older than her now. She couldn't see them clearly but knew a few photos boasted grandkids. She was glad he had a family and wondered if his kids felt the same way Janet had, or if Ed harbored disappointment none of them fished. She shifted uncomfortably on the couch and brought her hands together in her lap. She felt growing empathy and sadness for Janet. She must have been a trooper to support him in this world of fishing, chasing the harvests, long days alone and worries about when he was out on the ocean or if they'd bring in enough to pay bills. Just like Ruth. Celia wondered how much choice either of the two women had in some of their life decisions.

"Of course." Celia nodded and tried to sound cheerful. "I understand. I mean about him not wanting to see me." And she did. She was curious about what happened with the boat and the Coast Guard investigation, but did not want to raise the question or further upset Janet. Trevor hadn't known any more than she the last they had talked on the phone. She had finally tried to reach Justin on the phone, after Trevor told her he was doing fine, but only got his voicemail and decided not to leave a message. She wondered if he too felt embarrassed.

Janet looked uncomfortable and tired, and Celia knew not to ask more questions. She shuffled her feet, wondering why Janet had asked for her to stop by. She wanted to leave but didn't want to be rude.

"Um, well, I'll be getting off. I'm glad he's home and doing okay. Maybe tell him I stopped by and said hi?" Celia knew she should have brought a gift, flowers, or a card. She was terrible at remembering things like that, unlike her mom who seemed to have the perfect card or gift for every occasion, sometimes giving a gift if only for show, it seemed. She had a flash of her mom walking to deliver flowers to a neighbor who had lost their spouse while under her breath she talked trash about the very neighbor before the widow opened the door.

"Oh wait, I'm sorry. You'd think I lost my head. Well, I kind of have." And for the first time, Janet offered a full smile and laugh.

Celia knew she had to say more. "You know. I mean, I know how much you've done to support the boat. All of us, really. I'm sure, if it wasn't for you, it may not have been so successful. I mean, you know. Before all this. Really."

Janet's smile broadened. "Thank you. I appreciate that." Then she slowly boosted herself up off the couch, walked over to a desk in the corner, and grabbed an envelope.

Celia stood up, sensing this errand was nearing its end. She could see there was one other envelope remaining on the table.

"Of course, there's the issue of the end of season pay. I know it isn't what you expected, but we do hope it can get you through the next bit of time. I mean, you know, until you find something else. Let us know if you need any kind of recommendation. Of course, Ed would be happy to put in a good word for you." She handed Celia the sealed envelope.

"Hang on," Ed called from the kitchen.

Celia looked at Janet, who looked surprised as she smiled.

"Give me a minute. Hell, I'm soon to be a cardiac rehab patient, I guess." Ed lumbered in, looking frailer and skinnier than before, even though it had only been a week since the accident." Hey, Celia." He dropped into a chair she understood was one he regularly claimed, reading glasses and an issue of *Fishing News* on the nearby table. "Sit for sec, would you?" He straightened out his legs and groaned.

"Hi, Ed." Celia lowered herself back to the couch. She had not understood how much she needed to see him in person. "You . . . you look good."

"Oh, kind one you are. Yeah, I'm preparing myself for what all they'll do to me at that clinic. They gave me a reprieve till after Christmas." He frowned but let out a skeptical laugh. "Get me in better shape than I was, who knows. Unless she gets to me first." He jutted his chin at Janet.

Janet screwed up her face and waved him off, but Celia could tell she was pleased.

"Hey." Ed looked at Celia and then down at his shoes. "I'm sorry. You know, if I was a bit of a jack ass. You know, that last day." He looked at Celia, raised his eyebrows, then back at Janet.

Celia drew in air. He looked as if he might say more but thought better of it. She nodded, wiped her eyes, and looked away. A long breath escaped, one filled with worries and dried up anger. "Yes, yes. Um, thanks." She looked back at him and hesitated, not sure if she should ask. "What's the plan for the boat?"

"Oh that. Yes, I might have a buyer. Good old *High Hopes*. You know, a younger guy willing to get it back to its beauteous days." He shrugged. "Unless you have an interest?" He smiled at her and chuckled.

Celia quietly laughed and shook her head. "No, I'm good. But, um, thanks." She knew he wasn't serious. A dishwasher swished in the kitchen. "I guess I should be going." She stood, clutching the envelope. "Thank you. Thank you both. And, Ed . . ." She smiled at him, blinking back tears. "You look good. I'm glad." Ed and Janet walked her to the door.

Celia stepped onto the front porch, still stunned. "Thank you." She had given up imagining any of this: seeing Ed or acquiring pay for any part of the season, and she hoped the lost harvest would not impact their future. She felt embarrassed to take the money but equally ready to leave.

Janet gently grabbed her arm. "Thank you, Celia. Check back. Any time. Let us know what you stay busy with. And Merry Christmas."

"Of course. Merry Christmas." Celia had forgotten the holiday was near.

She walked to her car and, although she was dying to know what was in the envelope, drove several blocks before pulling over. She didn't want Ed to see this to be the first thing she did. As if all she cared about was money. Celia stared at the check for twelve thousand dollars. *Oh, my God!*

# Chapter 13
## Celia
### December 18, 2024

CELIA STOPPED BY the grocery store. Her half of the refrigerator was nearly empty since the accident. In the past week she had eaten little, bits she had either at the café or thanks to Sophia sharing meals. Her jeans felt loose which seemed impossible; it was easier to lose sight of needing sustenance when she wasn't fishing.

She parked in the far corner of the lot and walked toward the store. Most prior winters she had appreciated the coastal gray days, punctuated with frequent pounding rainstorms. The cloudiness of the last few weeks, though, made her feel stagnant and nearly nonexistent. As she neared the store, a glimmer of brightness broke through the clouds. She stopped and stared at the sun. She felt a small bolt of energy and picked up her pace. Although she might attribute it to the sun's weak greeting, she knew it was more. She hated to admit the guarantee of cash improved her mood, and yet it would pay for months of rent and food. Or enable her to make a change, if she could only identify what this transformation might be. She felt bad to think of Ed's loss in that way, though seeing him made it feel like a gift generously bestowed. She knew it would still be a struggle for him to accept his changed life, and she hoped they received a decent price for the boat.

The break of sun steered her away from the store aisles, and she wandered instead toward 12th Street and the Farmer's Market. Being December, she knew vendors would be targeting holiday shoppers—maybe its cheer would rub off on her. The market, at least in summer, brought in tourists and folks eager to be social. Celia preferred to walk through and look without vendors being present to avoid meeting questions about what she was looking for or an expectation for her to exclaim at the beauty or coolness of this or that. Maybe it'd be easier to move out of this funk if she had an interest in making new friends or take on a new hobby. Although the market wasn't the best place to do either, walking aimlessly outside helped her brain. Nearly as much as looking out to sea.

"You look like someone in need of freshly roasted coffee beans," a young energetic woman called.

Some of the stalls next to her were still setting up. The coffee vendor sported the Pacific Northwest uniform of jeans and down jacket, and her broad smile overwhelmed Celia. Coxcomb Hill rose just beyond them, touting historical homes and the Astoria Column. Steep streets shouting history with a spectacular view of the Columbia River, Youngs Bay, and the distant Pacific Ocean.

"No, thanks. I'm good." Celia forced herself to sound polite but disinterested.

She eyed paper bags of coffee carrying a label she didn't recognize adjacent to paper cups boasting a variety of beans. She bought the cheapest ground beans she could find, certain she didn't have the pallet to taste any difference, freshly roasted or not. She walked past the coffee vendor and stepped back toward the street, out of reach of tables. More than a dozen others stretched onward marketing their holiday greens, fresh pastries, and even local books. Although she felt better than she had in weeks, it wasn't enough to drum up genuine interest in what was on display or pretend small talk. The smell of fish and coffee, spiked with a yeasty sweetness from the nearby bakery was enticing. She was surprised by the growling of her stomach and looked at her phone. She had visited Ed's house first thing, and it was only just after ten o'clock. She wasn't ready to head back to the grocery store, but the market wasn't doing it for her. As she turned to return to the store, she spotted the local library across the street.

Unlike her roommate, Celia wasn't one to spend a lot of time with books or on the internet, rarely jumping on to social media to follow others' lives. The laptop her mom had bought her in high school died as she was finishing her program at Clatsop Community College, leaving her reliant on her phone for connectivity. She was sure her mom believed her associate degree in outdoor recreation was a waste of time and money.

As she approached the library, she had a glimmer of inspiration—what about that paper mill? Researching at the library felt simpler and safer, for now, than asking her mom or grandma. Even she knew the basics of researching online, and maybe she could glean something. Maybe she could figure out, somehow, if this Alice had fabricated a big lie, or if some woman long ago had done something important at a mill. She had used the library computers back when her own was dying to finish a research project. And time, yes, she had nothing but time, even if she should use it to figure out what the hell she would do with her life. Although Kate had been happy to have her take more shifts, Ed's check gave her a cushion. It relieved the panic she felt late at night doomsaying her need to move back in with her mom. But now breaks of sun, and the knowledge of the check safely zipped in her pocket, instilled bits of relief.

"Good morning." A librarian welcomed Celia as she entered the building. She hadn't seen him as she turned to prevent the glass door from banging while he straightened books on a display shelf near the front of the room.

"Hi." She jammed her hands in her pockets, ineffectively shrinking herself as she glanced toward the carrels housing computers.

"Can I help you with anything?" he asked.

"Um, no, I'm okay." Celia hesitated and wished she better knew what she was trying to find. "Actually, I hoped to use a computer. Um, to do a little research?" The library was warm after being in the cool air, and she slipped off her jacket and tucked it under her arm. She pulled up the waist of her jeans.

"Oh sure, right over there." The librarian, about her age in jeans and a collared shirt, pointed to computer stations in the corner. He looked at her again, as if sizing her up, and scratched his neck. "Just let me know if you need any help." He hesitated. "With using the computer or finding what you're looking for." He turned and headed toward an information desk.

Celia strode to the computers. An older man and woman were sitting on soft armchairs near the window, reading newspapers, but the computer area was empty. She placed her jacket on the floor, sat down, and logged in as visitor, grateful not to need to remember her old library account password.

"Paper mills," she whispered. With that, she began to learn about paper making. Before long, she was overwhelmed by all that popped up in answer to her general search terms. What she was looking for felt elusive among too much information. She combed her hands through her hair and stretched her arms above her head. *What was she thinking?* She closed her eyes. Other than reading about how mills worked and their importance to the Pacific Northwest, she didn't know how to dig deeper. She glanced at the librarian as he spoke to another patron.

She sighed, looked at her phone, and stifled a yawn. She felt an odd mix of feeling overwhelmed yet inspired by this new spark of interest. She pulled up digital maps near Portland, and with her finger on the screen, traced the Columbia and Willamette Rivers, and nearby towns like Vancouver, Washougal and Oregon City. Finally, she closed the computer search window.

She sighed with disappointment, wishing she could steer herself toward an answer, yet feeling awash in this sea of information. Paper making, logging, steamship travel, and early settlements; all of it interesting yet too detailed. She gathered her coat and bag as she stood up. She nodded in thanks to the librarian at the information desk. She hesitated, took a deep breath, exhaled and walked to him.

He looked up from the books he was checking in. Celia tried to up her courage, telling herself librarians probably liked questions; maybe it helped relieve boredom during long days. But she didn't want to bother him.

"Um. I'm trying to find some information about a certain papermill? Well, like from a long time ago." She cleared her throat. "To be honest, I'm a little overwhelmed, and I don't quite know what I'm looking for. I mean, yet." She ran out of steam and felt foolish, slumping as she looked down to her feet.

"Well, that's what we're here for," the librarian said.

Celia looked up at his cheery voice and felt relieved by his patient smile.

"Actually," he said, looking around. "It's what I like best, even though most of the time I'm busy with other things."

Celia wondered how long he had worked there and if he really did like his work.

"There is a lot of interesting history in this town and many folks who call themselves experts, if you know what I mean." He smiled again. What was it with all this smiling? Between this guy and Ruth, you'd think there was a lovefest going on in her community. "Usually, it's people asking about John Jacob Astor or the Astoria fire. But between you and me? I'd love to help you with something a bit different." She wondered if he was always this chatty, or simply compensating for her awkwardness.

"Thanks. That's good to know. I'm out of time now." She needed to think all this through. "But, maybe, you know for a start. Is there a paper mill up the river from Portland? Like Vancouver or St. Helens or Hood

River? Or I guess, was there one a long time ago?" She felt even sillier once the words escaped her mouth. Of course there were paper mills all over. She had just read about there once being nearly two dozen in the Pacific Northwest. She looked back at her feet.

"That's a good question."

Celia looked at him in surprise.

"While there were many mills, a few were larger and better known. I'm no expert on paper mills, but of course St. Helens and Vancouver aren't upriver from Portland if that is what you are looking for."

Celia nodded, feeling stupid. She of all people should recognize which direction Oregon's Columbia and Willamette Rivers flowed.

"However," he continued. "One of the best-known early mills—and it's still partially active—is the one at Camas. I think it was once called LaCamas."

Celia frowned.

"Camas, Washington," he clarified. "Just up the Columbia River from Vancouver, and not far from Portland."

Celia nodded. Finally, she had one nugget of information to go on. "Oh yes, maybe." Overwhelmed with the information from her search, she hadn't had any idea where to start. But now, a single town name was helpful, even if it was wrong. "Maybe another time you could help me again? Before too long?"

"Of course." He handed her his card. "Anytime. I'm here every day except Sunday and Monday. We're closed Sundays. And I can always help pull some books for you, even if they aren't at this library." He gestured at books on the shelves. "Just keep that in mind." He smiled again at her.

"Thank you." She looked at the card. "Thank you, Matthew," she added before heading to the door.


CELIA WAS TOO amped up to concentrate, but her stomach whined for sustenance. She headed into the Blue Scorcher a block away and opened the door to the exquisite smell of just-out-of-the-oven bread. She loved this old building, which also hosted the storefront to her favorite brewery, even if she didn't go out often. Kate once told her this Fort George Building was built on the exact location of the original Fort Astoria. See, she teased herself. Even she knew some local history. There were apartments built above the bakery, and she wondered what it would be like to awaken to the smell of pastries and bread each morning. She didn't think she would tire of it. There was a line at the till, and she peered into the pastry case. If she were on the other side of town she'd stop at Kate's place and eat a real breakfast, but the croissants and muffins were better here.

"May I help you?" the barista asked when she got to the head of the line.

"Yes, a drip coffee. Black. And, how about a morning glory muffin. Please. To go. Thanks." Celia inserted her card into the card reader and picked up the steaming coffee and bagged muffin. She eyed an open spot at the counter and sat on a stool facing the street.

She cautiously sipped her coffee and then broke off a piece of the perfectly baked muffin. Her favorite. If she were ever to bake, she would make these first. She closed her eyes and chewed, delighting in food tasting good for a change. Her phone vibrated, and she pulled it from her pocket. She had missed three texts from Kate. She wasn't one to check her phone every two minutes like Kate but typed out a reply. *Yes, I'm fine. Thanks for asking. More soon.* She knew Kate thought she wasn't sharing enough about what was going on with her. She still had two scheduled shifts later in the week and knew it was time to talk.

She ate another bite of her muffin and opened her phone browser: Camas Mill. "Bingo."

The guy next to her looked over, and Celia shook her head to let him know she wasn't talking to him. She finished her muffin as she read about the start of this mill town, and the various changes in ownership of the papermill. She wondered what it would be like to work in such an operation. She knew a few fishermen who had left both paper and lumber mills that had shut down over the past years. One of them was outspoken about the granolas trying to save owls instead of good paying jobs. She crumbled up the paper bag and stuck her phone in her coat pocket. She watched a couple on the street. They stopped and faced each other, then the man pulled the woman's coat collar up, as if to bundle her against the elements. They kissed, and Celia looked away. She grabbed her coffee, tossed the balled bag in the trashcan near the door, and pushed out to the sidewalk.

Astoria was bursting with vendors and shoppers. Downtown boasted holiday decorations, green and red streamers garlanded over lamp posts and storefronts lit up with twinkling lights. Her return to this holiday exuberance began to wear down her renewed energy. She wandered down the final block of vendors, looking longingly toward the Astoria Riverwalk Trail.

As she passed a final vendor, its green tablecloth shining with silver jewelry beckoned her. Celia wore little jewelry, rarely changing her earrings, other than to occasionally remove them at night. She knew she didn't have an eye for style, nor could she tell much difference in quality. Yet, she was drawn to a pair of silver earrings that reminded her of something Sophia would wear. Maybe it was holiday spirit infiltrating her tough shell. Her roommate had been good to her, and Celia knew she had done little to thank her. Maybe she could learn to bestow gifts yet. She fingered each of the angular silver pieces. "I'll take these." She grinned at her impulsivity and shook her head. She couldn't remember the last time she bought a gift to surprise anyone.

With the earrings paid for and tucked into her coat pocket, she left the market. Ahead of her were a handful of people holding signs on the block between her and the Riverwalk. Oh no, a protest. That was the last thing she wanted to encounter, having surpassed her social burnout index, even if she felt a different person than the day before. As if a balloon filled with bits of hope had released into her spirit.

She turned toward the whistle of a barge upriver and walked quickly to the Riverwalk. Other than her coffee with Ruth, she had avoided the river since the accident. Now, she felt finally ready to revisit a favorite spot where she could stand on land but look downriver toward Cape Disappointment. Somewhere miles past the upriver bend lay Camas to her east. "I'm glad I'm not fishing." She nodded as if in conversation with herself, willing to finally put it in the past. In that moment she knew with absolute certainty she was done. And that she would not miss it.

"How you doing?" asked a gruff, unkempt looking man, sitting on a bench. He had a dirty backpack at his feet, a small empty cardboard box, and Celia knew he hoped for money.

"Good." Celia walked past him, hesitated, and fished out a five-dollar bill from her pocket and placed it in the box.

She crossed the last street before the Riverwalk and took final steps to the spot. She rested both her arms on the railing and stared at the barge slowly moving upriver. She wondered where it might be headed. She thought about this mysterious woman rumored to have lived upriver all those years ago. What if, in fact, her great great something was a woman who did something significant in her life? Who was relevant because of something. She knew it didn't really matter who she was related to. Yet something about this story fed into her own hope for herself. Maybe there was something still out there for her to do. If not to make a mark on something, to at least find the satisfaction she sought.

Celia wondered how long it would take to drive to Camas. She closed her eyes and rested more of her body weight on the railing. Its damp coldness soaked through her clothing. *What would it have taken for any woman to have felt relevant back then?* The bits of protruding winter sun softened her eyelids and warmed her cheeks. Opening her eyes, she took a single deep breath and exhaled. She had no idea what she'd do next, besides put her check in her bank account and work the café shifts. Yet, she felt different than she had when she had awakened that morning.

She walked back to her parked car, deciding once again to delay grocery shopping. She pulled out her phone and speed dialed the café. "Hi. Yes, this is Celia. How are you? Can I just order my usual to go? Yes, dressing on the side. Thanks, I'll be there in ten." She pulled up "Wide Open Spaces" on her phone, cranked up the volume, and drove out of the lot.

# Chapter 14
## Celia
### December 20, 2024

CELIA SHOPPED MOSTLY at her nearby supermarket, certain she couldn't afford the prices at the local food co-op. She worried whatever cushion her recent windfall provided would slim down if unprotected, evaporating like summer's final sunshine. She did prefer how she blended into the woodwork at this grocer, blurring into non-descript aisles laden with dozens of brands of chips and cereal that people could not live without. And populated by folks in a rush to pick up this and that, hustling out the door to whatever was next.

She hadn't thought life would be this way on the Oregon Coast, and yet it seemed ever since COVID hit, the newly claimed aura of impersonality hadn't reverted to life before. Kate claimed it was all the newer blood infiltrating town. With housing costs rising and no end in sight in Seattle and Portland, and more folks working remotely, life in once small towns like hers had changed. Of course, more people with money benefited Kate's business. At least folks weren't running around with masks on, although even when they might have, others refused to believe COVID was a real thing. At first Celia had enjoyed the anonymity of masking, it made it simpler for her to keep to herself. And she did worry about the virus like most folks she knew. But now, these few years later when many seemed to forget the weirdness of the pandemic, Celia was relieved not to be surrounded by a sea of masked people.

"Good afternoon," the cashier welcomed, as Celia placed her items on the conveyor.

Sometimes she felt all she did was go to the grocery store, walk the Riverwalk, work a shift in the café, and sleep. The store was otherwise quiet, and she was glad holiday music wasn't playing on the public address system. The cashier was friendlier than any harried Saturday morning clerk.

"Hi." Celia entered her phone number before sticking her credit card in the reader and deliberately took her time putting it back in her wallet.

"Did you find everything you need?" the woman asked chattily, as she took her own time bagging her selections, even rotating the tomato sauce jar to read its label. "Is this one good?"

Celia nodded to both questions, tapping her toe impatiently as the cashier bagged the pasta, carrots, apples, and the usual.

The checker finished by carefully placing the package of Oreos into the bag. "The most important item." She smirked and Celia forced a smile.

As she carried her single forty-dollar bag of groceries to the car, she wished she had adopted her mother's meal planning skills. Though even then, her mom's militant insistence on the power of the list, and her refusal to buy anything not written down, even as an afterthought, annoyed her. Celia had to admit how often she returned home from the store without getting the thing she needed most. She stashed her groceries on the back seat, then spied the sticker on her windshield reminding her she was past due for getting her car serviced. The brakes had been making a weird noise, and she knew better than drive around with them sounding like that.

"Shit," she muttered, frustrated at this mood buster, and wondered if she had enough mechanical know-how to fix them herself.

Craving her optimistic mood from the previous day, she pulled on her stocking cap and headed to the Riverwalk. Her spirit needed another feeding. It was the middle of the afternoon and the sky solid gray. She wasn't one who always hoped for sun, even when it was a full out storm spiked with thunder, lightning, and rain. Although she'd prefer not to be on the water, she liked a good crash of thunder and pelting rain as much as the next storm watcher.

Loud voices and car honks shocked her back to the present, and she regretted not having taken a different route. She looked down to avoid the sidewalk cracks, and when she looked across the street, she saw a handful of people with signs. Even when asked to sign a petition, she often said no thanks and moved on. Not to be rude but signaling to be left alone. Today she was in no mood for confrontation or explanations. She did not like conflict, which was a trait she hoped to someday become mature enough to outgrow.

Covertly she looked across the street to read the signs: "Save Democracy from Fascism," "Save the Earth and its Creatures too!" "Hate isn't Great." She slowed her steps and stared at the group of six. The streets were slow with afternoon traffic and several cars honked, in support she guessed. One guy stuck his hand out the car window and flipped off the protestors. She tripped on her laces, bent down to retie one, and then the other. She slowed her pace and looked across the street again. The man holding the earth and creatures sign looked at her. She glanced down at her daily uniform of sweatshirt and jeans, her rain parka still smelling like fish, picked up her pace as if she had an appointment to get to, and forced herself not to look back.

Celia considered not answering her phone when it rang. She had walked farther along the trail than she often did, beyond the Megler Bridge, and near the docked ferry and cruise ship that brought folks in to enjoy the port town. The pilings from docks long gone jutted up from below the water. She had tried reaching Justin several times. It had been nearly two weeks since the accident, and she imagined they both needed time to sort their thoughts out before talking.

"Hey," she said on the fifth ring, gripping a railing next to her tightly. She peered at the few seagulls standing on a sandbar visible with the tide out. She waited for Justin to speak, but silence echoed back at her. After weeks of avoiding her crewmates, it felt odd to connect with Justin as she stood near the marina. "I was just wanting to know how you're doing. I mean, you know, since I haven't seen you." She tapped her fingers on the railing. "But, well, Trevor told me you were doing okay."

"Yeah, all is fine." Justin's voice sounded boyish, and she would not have been able to tell if something was amiss. "I'm doing fine. Thanks. I mean, thanks to you. You know, saving me and all."

"Oh, it's just what we do, right?" Celia felt stupid. It wasn't like any of them had ever thrown a lifeline to a person from a boat heading off course. "I mean, you know. What we know we are supposed to do, right?" She twisted her body side to side.

"Yeah, I guess. I mean, I feel like an idiot. But, of course, I'm happy not to have drowned." Justin laughed as if it was funny now.

"Yes, of course." Celia rolled her eyes. They sounded inane, as if they couldn't or wouldn't say what really was on their minds. Or how harrowing it all had been. It had been horrible. It was not funny, that she knew.

"Well, Ed put a good word in for me, and it looks like I might start on with another crew. Not crabbing. But maybe that's okay." Justin sounded upbeat.

Celia had no intention of breaking his mood, and she knew he was different than her. He was young, and it was a way to make money, get experience, and gain more responsibility. She wondered how his girlfriend felt about it, but didn't want to prolong the call. She focused on the bit of land across the water. She wished she had been alive when folks ferried across the mouth of the river and was distracted as she tried to remember if the original ferry docking was visible on the other side.

"Okay, well, thanks again. I'll see you around."

Celia wondered if he was embarrassed. Then again, maybe she was reading too much into it all.

"Sure. You take care." As Celia put her phone in her pocket, she caught a glimpse of threatening clouds developing far out at sea and headed back toward her car.

After walking a few minutes, she neared someone sitting on a bench ahead. This was the first person she'd seen on the trail, and the poster "Save the Earth, Save the Creatures" rested at his side. Her pulse quickened, and she wondered if she should cut off the trail to a main street. The man was looking upriver, a classic bearded beach hippie wearing Birkenstock sandals and Levi's. Dark gray socks peeked up under the sandal straps. She drew in a courageous breath as she neared him, just as he turned toward her. A smile broke out between his dark black beard and mustache.

"Hi," she said. Still nothing from the Beard, although he kept his brown eyes focused on her. Her palms felt sweaty, and she shoved her hands into her coat pockets. Yet, curiosity grounded her to the spot. "Did you draw those?" She pointed at the pictures on the sign. "The crab and salmon? I like them." Silence. *What an idiot she was.* If the Beard didn't say anything soon, she would move along, rude or not.

His smile faded as he looked back out toward the middle of the river.

"Hey. Are you alright?" Celia softened her voice. She knew there were a lot of folks around who really weren't alright. Traffic had slowed in town, making the river sounds seem louder, water lapping at the shore and a few distant barge engines and horn blasts. She looked toward the water and then back at him. She touched the crab on the posterboard.

The man looked at her fingers and then briefly back at her face. "Yeah. Thanks. Just sad." He brought his fingertips together. He looked back at her. "I just come to this spot sometimes and think about a guy I knew. Didn't really know him, but he died near here. That's all."

"Oh. I'm sorry." Celia knew whatever she thought to say would sound inadequate. An image of Justin thrown overboard flooded her. She caught her breath. "Did . . . did he drown?" She wiped her eyes.

"Oh, no. not that." He brought his hands to his lap and looked at her thoughtfully.

"It's a pretty spot. My favorite is back there a bit." She pointed behind her along the trail.

The man nodded. "I guess you could say I'm memorializing a bit of something too." He gazed at her with what felt to be patient understanding. The seagulls hovered, seeking tourists with handouts of bread and dinner scraps.

"Hey, can I ask? I mean about you out there, on the street. With the others." Celia pointed back toward town. "What was that about?" She felt like sitting next to him but worried how it might be taken, all of this out of character for her.

The man picked up his sign and traced the letters. "Oh, we're all worried, you know now with who won the election." He looked at her and back out to the river. "Protesting, I guess you'd call it. That this guy isn't fit to be in office. Worried about change that will be bad for everyone and everything."

"Like crab and salmon?" Celia tried not to smile. "And dogs?" She could not suppress a laugh as she touched the smaller picture of what looked to be a shaggy puppy.

"Like everything." He let go of the sign. His eyes darted back and forth, and then he inhaled deeply. He looked at the dog and shrugged. "I work at the clinic down the street. Columbia Veterinarian."

Oh, so he did have a day job and wasn't just parading the streets restlessly with unfilled hours of time. But still an activist? Celia stepped back. She too held worries about the current political woes but mostly was trying not to think about it. Yet might he be one of those radical activists blowing up things and building towers in the trees? He didn't seem like a monkey wrencher.

"You probably need to get on your way." The man seemed to sense Celia's discomfort or maybe felt his own.

Celia dropped her shoulders and frowned. She felt surprised not to want to be dismissed. *Not yet.* "No, really. I am interested." It was more than just him being cute.

He gazed at her as if he was trying to tell if she was pulling his leg. "You can always join us. I figure if things get bad enough more people might. Oh, and if not that, I'll be making a request at the next City Council Meeting about climate change. I mean not just for me. It's in three weeks at City Hall." He pointed toward the street. His words flowed between long moments of silence. What a contrast between this careful parceling of words with the last guy she had dated, albeit months ago, who talked about nothing incessantly. Although awkward, the meagerness of words was refreshing.

"Um, okay. I'll look into it." Celia doubted she would but was unusually attracted to what she sensed as his gentle spirit. "I'm Celia." She straightened and pushed her bag higher on her shoulder.

"Hi, Celia. I'm Paul." He rose, and they stood shoulder to shoulder. "I'd shake your hand, but I've been out here on the street all day." She had never met a man like this, and hoped her coat still emanated its fishy smell. He shrugged and looked away, and Celia saw a hint of a blush beneath his beard.

"Um, how would I learn more?" *Good God, Celia, now you're being forward.*

"There's some info on the City's website." Paul looked down at his feet, but he smiled.

"Oh, thanks." She shook her head a bit and slumped with disappointment.

Paul looked at her. "You know, okay, just to be clear. I never do this." His brown eyes sparkled with quiet laughter, but the blush creeped over more of his face. "Seriously, I don't think I've ever made a pass at a woman in my entire life." He glanced at a passing bicycle. "But you could always leave a message for me at the animal clinic if you wanted to learn more." He glanced at her and then looked down. "Or wanted to talk."

Celia laughed, shaking her head at her own feet. She had to admire how, although shy, he didn't seem bothered in the least to sound foolish. Maybe cute foolish. *Who is this guy?* She laughed again. "Sure." She took a deep breath and hesitated to scratch an itch under her hat. "But, I mean, don't you have a cell phone?" She knew she would never call a business to ask anything about a guy. She raised her eyebrows.

"Oh, God." Paul covered his face with his hands. "You know, I'm kind of a dork. At least that's what others tell me." He removed his hands and shook his head. "I have a hard time reading people sometimes. I mean.

Well, I read them but . . . Oh never mind." He waved a hand and sighed. "I just didn't want you to think I was one of those guys, you know. You probably get it all the time, and it just seemed like if you were honestly interested it could be on your own terms. Like, you wouldn't have to worry about having some creep's phone number or something."

"Sure. Sure. Hang on." Celia grabbed a scrap of paper and pen from her bag and scribbled on it "Why don't you call me?" She shook her head. "But no pressure."

Paul took the bit of paper and looked at her as if trying to figure her out.

"No, really, you should. And, honestly, it's not like me to hand out my number to guys on the street. Even when they draw very good pictures of crabs." She laughed in a way she hadn't since having coffee with Ruth. "And puppies."

"Oh, sure." Paul looked at the paper again, then back at her. "Celia." He smiled at her, and his right eye twinkled like a distant star. "Have a nice day." He smiled down at his feet and then caught her eye.

Celia continued toward her car. She turned back one final time and saw Paul watching her from the bench. She knew she had a stupid smile pasted to her face, but she didn't care.

# Chapter 15
## Emma
### June 10, 1915

EMMA KNEW THIS fib was bigger than any she had ever told her parents. Yet, she was now twenty-one years old. In fact, she was eligible to vote. Many women her age led households, and did not always abide by their parents' wishes, although she knew they might need to contend with their husband's approval. No, she was not doing anything wrong. And it was time for her to break away. To take the next step on the journey to making her own mark.

Her friend Elizabeth shared stories about the fancy parade that happened each summer in Portland. Although one year Emma's family attended the Independence Day Celebration in Vancouver, this Rose Parade was more elaborate. It amazed Emma that such a flamboyant sounding city in another state could be reached by a short steamboat ride. And now, she might finally get to see it. Even then, none of her immediate family members except Martha had made the trip to Portland since her parents had stepped off the steamboat landing to move to Camas. Emma knew it made a difference that her grandparents had all passed on. Father and Mother seldom even traveled the twelve miles to Vancouver.

"Please, Martha," Emma had begged as she began to plan for the trip.

Martha's sour expression dampened her hopes. They had spent part of a Sunday together, Martha agreeing to attend their church service even though she hated to miss time with her own friends. Emma knew she would need to create a different fib to have her sister agree to the plan.

"Please don't tell Mother," Emma began, knowing full well Martha kept few secrets from their mother. "Elizabeth has a cousin I met once. Well, he's quite handsome. He will be at the parade." She looked at Martha hopefully.

Martha raised her eyebrows. "Truly, Emma?" They exchanged looks. "Must you make it so difficult?" She smirked. "There are many available men closer to home." She shook her head and returned to her task of gathering her family's things to return to Vancouver.

"Please, Martha?" Emma tried not to drop their wrapped mid-day meal leftovers with a thump next to Martha's pile of coats. She was tired of the childish way she felt she had to deal with her and promised herself this would be the final time.

"Yes. Alright." Martha released a heavy sigh. "This once." She also agreed to doing any childcare responsibilities during the two days Emma was away.

With that detail handled, Emma asked Father later after supper to release two dollars of her wages toward her trip to cover the trolly and ferry fares and any other essential charges. Although he held part of her wages for her future, she planned to tell him soon that she would handle her own money with her next paycheck.

On the morning of her departure, Father gave her a hug and told her she deserved time away to enjoy young womanly things in exchange for the work she did. He handed her an extra dollar. "And, Emma, be careful. You stay close to Elizabeth's family. It would be easy to get yourself lost." He stepped back and lightly touched her shoulder.

Emma did not tell her parents that they would be met at the ferry terminal by Elizabeth's cousin—a girl younger than Elizabeth and Emma. Mother would never have allowed this if she did not believe they were to be chaperoned by Elizabeth's aunt and uncle their entire time away, or a man who knew the city. If she were William, these strings would be looser or nonexistent. After all, women in their state had gained the right to vote five years prior, ahead of much of the country. Now that she was twenty-one, she would demand changes for herself. She would make sure her own daughters, should she be blessed with them someday, understood how important all of this was.

The bigger secret that Emma and Elizabeth held was Cassie's encouragement to be on the lookout for orators in downtown Portland promoting the radical Wobbly agenda. She said because anti-suffrage activists were expected at the parade, counter protesters may take advantage of the expected crowds. Cassie also warned them if they did encounter such events to be careful as even some union supporters distanced themselves from radical Wobblies. Emma could not imagine how Cassie heard about controversy happening in other cities. While Emma knew the Wobblies were believed to be socialists and were frequently arrested, she only recently learned the nickname stood for the Industrial Workers of the World.

Emma was terrified at first as she imagined the possibility of being arrested, but Elizabeth shushed her worries. "Besides, my aunt will be thrilled to know we want to shop after the parade. Nobody will think otherwise if we happen to wander by the Park Blocks."

Emma stared at Elizabeth in awe. She sounded sophisticated to be familiar with Portland.

"You will be able to identify my aunt, by the way, when you meet her. Auntie is the epitome of high society and very fashion conscious." Elizabeth laughed.

Emma nodded, willing Elizabeth's enthusiasm to mute her own worries.

The next morning, Emma woke up before sunrise. She stretched luxuriously in her cot, imagining what it might be like to have everyday feel like she did then along with two days off work. She nestled in the warmth of the bed, pulling the two quilts up to her chin. Finally, she got up and reignited the fire before packing breakfast to take with them. She removed cheese and ham from the icebox, cut herself two small pieces of each, and wrapped them in a cloth along with a leftover slab of cornbread. She tucked the food into her lightly packed satchel. After eyeing the clock on the mantle, she hurried into her Sunday best, a pale blue tailored dress with cap sleeves. She pulled on her stockings, shoes, and coat and quietly slipped out the door.

By the time she walked across the bridge and the three blocks, she shook with excitement as she approached Elizabeth. She could not remember looking so forward to a day.

"Good morning, Elizabeth."

Elizabeth pursed her lips as she scrutinized Emma from head to toe.

Emma gripped her satchel and straightened the brim of her hat. "What is it?"

"You look as severe as if you were going to church." Elizabeth laughed.

Emma peered down at her newest dress as it peeked out from her lighter winter wool coat. She had updated her brimmed hat with two new yellow and blue ribbons, but she didn't have much more wardrobe to choose from. Too, she felt Mother might be calmed to see her dressed as she might for a day of service to God, although she left before Mother arose. If she had a closer relationship with Martha, she might have borrowed something more celebratory for a day in the city.

"You look nice," Emma muttered. She would not let it destroy her excitement for the day.

The first trolley of the morning pulled into the stop, and they hurried to climb on. Emma was grateful Elizabeth had not insisted they take the steamboat, even though she badly wanted to travel by one. The trolley fare, however, was five cents, and combined with the ferry and Portland streetcars, she felt certain she could save money. She might feel differently if she had full control over her entire paycheck.

"Wait, where's your brother?" Emma asked.

"Oh that." Elizabeth laughed, her eyes twinkling as she motioned to a seat toward the front. "I never wanted him to come in the first place. When he told our parents he had no interest in spending his Saturday with us they agreed it was fine."

Emma settled her petticoat and skirt on the trolley seat, now feeling dowdy compared to Elizabeth's rose-colored laced dress and higher heeled shoes. She bent down to dust off her Sunday shoes, which were a bit scuffed. She wished she had thought to polish them for the special trip. Now, this news about Elizabeth's brother not joining them reignited her nervousness. She gave Elizabeth a questioning look.

"It is fine, Emma." Elizabeth sounded exacerbated. "You worry too much. Besides, it's really a silly thing to imagine his being with us would somehow protect us or make our trip safer." She laughed and grabbed Emma's hand.

Emma nodded. Of course, she knew that. Why did she let herself get trapped into Mother's old-fashioned thinking? She willed herself to relax and recapture her early morning excitement. After all, she was on a trip alone with her dear, bold, and experienced friend. She felt more independent than she ever had, even more than at work where it did feel as if someone was often telling her what to do.

For the next hour, Emma's worries subsided as she mimicked Elizabeth's actions as they debarked from the trolley, walked to the Vancouver terminal, and climbed onto the ferry. On the island in the middle of the Columbia River, they departed the ferry and waited to board another trolley.

Emma looked around at Hayden Island, a town built on this island in the middle of the powerful river. They boarded the next trolley, and nearly as quickly pulled into what Elizabeth told her was the northeast part of Portland. She had heard it was common for people to go between Vancouver and Portland for a day trip, and now she understood how.

"The crossing is so short," Emma said with disappointment.

"Yes. And that's good for us. Just imagine, before long people will drive carriages and cars across this huge river." Elizabeth prattled on about construction of the new bridge that would improve life and working opportunities for many. "Can you imagine a day when going into Portland would seem not much more significant than walking down the street to the market?"

Emma shrugged. She adored Elizabeth but sometimes felt dense and unsophisticated around her. Elizabeth's father was an attorney in Camas, although he seemed to travel to Vancouver often. Emma wondered if their family might soon buy an automobile.

"I cannot believe you have not been to Portland before," Elizabeth exclaimed as she confidently ushered her along the street.

Emma had been relieved how simple it was to transfer to the streetcar after riding in the ferry for the shorter trestle crossing into Portland. But now, after stepping off the trolley into the loud and busy streets of Portland, she didn't know what to think. Around her were crowds of people, women with gloves, jackets, and fancy hats and men in smart three-piece suits. She had not imagined the variety of decorated hats she might see women wearing, feathers, ribbons, and veils and matched with puffy collars and scarves. It was miles away from her daily mill uniform of simple blouse, skirt, and apron. And the buildings were taller than any she could have imagined, with many more than four levels of windows. Nothing like Camas's rough roads and smelly mill. And wide-open views of forested hillsides. She grabbed Elizabeth's hand and held her satchel tight in the other. She felt nearly bereft and alone in the commotion.

Elizabeth smiled at her and pulled her close.

# Chapter 16
## Emma
### June 10, 1915

"WE ARE MEETING Frances down the street. In front of the new Lipman Wolf Building." Elizabeth picked up her pace, and Emma hurried to keep up but was forced to drop her hand. She wanted to slow down to digest the busy car and carriage filled streets and stately concrete buildings. She tried not to think about how much she had already done that differed from what she had told her parents. But no, she was no longer a child. Even if she felt like one in this grand city.

"Frances." Elizabeth ran a few steps ahead and put her valise on the concrete sidewalk. She hugged this cousin who looked older and more sophisticated than both Emma and Elizabeth.

Emma nodded hello when introduced and stared at Frances's tailored dark burgundy suit with matching jacket and skirt. Her wide brimmed hat was much larger than theirs, shadowing her face. Emma shrank into herself, feeling out of place. Although younger than them both, Frances had finished at a private high school that spring and planned to travel by train to visit and enroll at a college in Salem.

Frances reached her gloved hand out to Emma. "Delightful to meet you, Emma. We are pleased you can be with our family during this celebration." She winked at Elizabeth. "We are very proud of our city, just to warn you." She laughed. "Sometimes people find us snobby and overstrung about anything that threatens to change it."

Emma smiled shyly. At least Frances seemed welcoming and not snobby. Emma peered into the nearby window display. Behind the glass were beautifully arranged hats, colorful scarves, and smart purses. Her mouth fell open, and she dropped her bag to the sidewalk.

"Now, come. We will have plenty of time to catch up later." Frances smiled at Emma. "And shop. But the parade has started, and we have two more blocks to our spot with Mother and Father." Her burst of enthusiasm made her suddenly seem younger.

Emma and Elizabeth trotted along behind her, grasping their bags close to their bodies. Although Emma had heard rumors about men committing crimes openly in this city, it felt the farthest thing from her imagination with the elegantly styled men and women crowding the streets, some with children in tow.

As they neared Frances's family, Emma spotted the approaching parade.

"Oh, Elizabeth. So much I had no idea about." Emma breathed in the smells of popcorn, fried food, manure, and even the spicy sweet aroma of roses. "Elizabeth, look." She could barely find her voice. She pointed to a banner hoisted above the approaching parade: "All They Wanted Was BREAD AND ROSES."

Elizabeth gave her a questioning look.

"Yes, it's an unofficial slogan for this year's parade," Frances's father said. "You see, to remind us that we all have a desire to supply basic needs to people but also to live a more fulfilling life." He nodded as if pleased with himself and his town.

Emma tried to keep her face from showing her true feelings. After all, she knew that Bread and Roses was a theme for both labor activists and suffragettes.

"Look at this one, girls." Frances's father pointed to a float with the words "Portland Land of the Roses."

Emma gasped at the dozens and dozens of red, white, pink, and purple roses covering the surfaces of the float. A string of electric lights shined out at them.

"Oh my!" they exclaimed together, their eyes shining.

"Yes, that one is presented by Portland General Electric," Frances's father said. "Think about how this company is changing our lives. Bravo." He gave a casual salute toward the float, his fingers trailing into the air.

"Oh, Emma," Elizabeth whispered. "Here comes Queen Muriel. Oh my, look at her beautiful gown. And the princesses too."

Emma was embarrassed not to have known there would be a queen and princess court in the parade. She had never imagined gowns like this, flowing ivory and white cotton, satin, and lace.

"Those girls are younger than you," Frances's mother added. "The first queen, daughter of Governor Chamberlain, was coronated in 1908." She eyed the court, nodding. "You know, Frances. The princess on the far left is our friend Ethyl and James's daughter."

Frances looked longingly at the women on the float. Emma fingered her own cotton skirt. Everything on the Queen's Float appeared as if a page out of a fancy magazine. None of it seemed real, the flowing gowns, the crown, and armfuls of flower bouquets. It felt inconsistent with the uneasiness some Americans had about the new war abroad and her own family's worries about money. But she shrugged off that concern, feeling fortunate to be able to spectate such frivolousness. Emma had never seen so many roses in her life; shades of red, yellow, pink, rose, and purple. She closed her eyes to try to seal in the sights to retrieve and savor later.

Elizabeth elbowed Emma. "Look."

They watched three women walk past them handing out red roses. They shook their heads and looked back toward the float, having been forewarned that anti-suffrage activists were distributing roses to protest women's suffrage.

"That's it." Frances spread out her hands as she nodded toward the last horses moving past them, followed only by men pushing brooms and shovels. Her father collapsed their one folding chair and tucked it under his arm. The sidewalks swarmed with people, and a fancy car pulled into the street.

"Mother, I plan to take our guests to the nearby department stores. May we meet you at home a bit later?" Frances asked.

Emma stared at Frances and her mother. Her own mother would never think any of this acceptable; young women meandering through a busy city on their own with her fears about droves of hobos and good-for-nothings invading downtown. Yet, she felt relaxed and even safe, the music and noises no longer jarring. She became less frightened about being run over by the trolley or a carriage, understanding the importance of sidewalks. What a perfect way to celebrate being twenty-one years old she thought as she straightened her hat.

"Yes, my darling," Frances's mother replied. "Father and I will see you home by six o'clock. We have a nice supper planned for your guests, so do not be late."

"Thank you, Auntie." Elizabeth gave her aunt a short, formal hug.

Emma shyly smiled. Frances's mother was beautiful, nearly untouchable. Her hair was perfectly coifed beneath a showy hat adorned by several feathers, and she wore a high heeled pair of satin shoes with a buckle.

"Of course, my darling. We are pleased to share our city with you." She stopped for a moment, as if carefully selecting her words. "We know not everyone is as happy with Portland as we are."

Emma glanced at Elizabeth, embarrassed she had shared her parents' beliefs.

She strained herself to take everything in as they continued their way up Morrison Street. The trolleys creaked along their tracks, bells sounding at each block. The sidewalks were still filled with people carrying bags and bundles.

"Here," Frances exclaimed. "This is my favorite store."

Emma stopped and looked up. One, two, three . . . ten. Ten floors.

"Emma." Frances beckoned as a store employee wearing white gloves held open the door, welcoming them as they stepped inside. "And the best thing is the clerks are very kind," she whispered.

Emma followed behind, watching Elizabeth and Frances as they touched scarves and hats placed along a glass display table. The wares looked too luxurious to touch. She stopped to scan the room filled with table after table and racks of various finery.

"Oh wait," she called as the two were halfway across the white shiny floor. She trotted to catch up, losing her courage at the thought of becoming lost.

"If you get lost, just wait for us under the new clock." Frances pointed at the grand pendulum clock positioned impressively in the middle of the room. "Let us go upstairs. Come." She nodded toward an elevator in the corner.

The door opened, and Frances instructed the uniformed operator to take them to the fourth floor. Emma grabbed the bar along the wall and her stomach tumbled with the car's jerk upward. She had not yet had cause to ride the cargo elevator at the mill.

Spellbound, she followed Frances and Elizabeth again as they touched fine garments and accessories.

"Perhaps Mother would let me wear a dress like this one day soon." Frances fingered the gauzy puff sleeves and sheer, lacy fabric of a soft blue patterned dress.

"Oh yes," Elizabeth replied.

Emma gasped. Imagine having the money or need to buy a dress like this. Her family usually purchased fabric each year to replace or update their everyday outfit, occasionally ordering from Sears Robuck. But such luxury she could not imagine.

As they stepped off the elevator back at street level, Emma felt less claustrophobic in the fancy store, but was relieved when they walked outside into fresh air.

"Wait. I need to go to the stationary store. And then, perhaps it is time to go to the Park Blocks?" Elizabeth said. "I almost forgot it is nearly Father's birthday. I know he would love something from there. He says it is one of his favorite shops."

"It is a favorite of many." Frances sounded bored and picked at a fingernail while they hesitated on the sidewalk outside the nearby store. "Father said the owner even lives on our street and his wife carries my name." She laughed. "Although of course I was not named after her."

Emma thought the J.K. Gill Bookstore was the most striking shop she had ever seen, stocked with books and stationery supplies. Walls and tables were piled with volumes of books. As they exited the store, she pointed to the name stenciled on the paper bag holding Elizabeth's new fountain pen.

"I've seen that name at the mill."

"Oh yes, Mr. Gill helped start the mill you both work at," Frances said. "And your town. You must know, with Mr. Pittock." She sounded bored to provide this history lesson. "Now we need to hurry if you want to see the speakers." They trundled on, and Emma was grateful Frances's parents had taken their luggage with them.

A loud voice echoed ahead of them. Elizabeth firmly pulled Emma and Frances to her with her gloved hands. "Now. Father says it is important we do not bring attention to ourselves. Act like we are shopping, stopping only because of the commotion."

Frances shrugged.

This was the part of the trip Emma had been most excited about, although she had no idea how thrilling the parade would be. The mill was still an open shop, with any talk about unionizing whispered privately and only some workers in certain crafts asserted to be individual American Federation of Labor card-holding members. Discussions at the mill about organizing unions had become heated. While the community had backed the women during the bag factory strike those two years prior, it seemed relieved it was in the past. Out of town news tied Wobblies to socialism, and many did not like their radical outspokenness. Her community was, above all, loyal to the mill for all it provided to its residents.

They reached a large park, lined with wooden benches and gardens. Cassie had told them how speakers often appeared unscheduled, orating extemporaneously. A woman, standing on a crate, was speaking loudly to the crowd. She reached her hands to the heavens. "Brothers and Sisters of Portland! While the pageantry of Portland's elite marches by, let us not forget the real roses. The working men and women of this city; those who make this city work, who clean your clothes and make your meal. But where are their rights? Where is her vote? Her wage?"

Emma nodded and Elizabeth jabbed her side. She knew many felt these words to be blasphemy. Yet, Emma felt there was truth to it all. She knew things could be made better at work.

Then, she could not believe her eyes. Across the block, but in her line of vision was Andrew from the mill. She focused on him so much, she stopped listening to the orator. He saw her, nodded slightly, and smiled. Emma did not know whether to be happy or nervous he had seen her. She wondered what brought him to this spot. He was one of the few men who continued to be friendly with her at work, even occasionally offering a tip or encouragement. She forced herself to look away.

"Organize! Educate! Agitate!" the woman droned on in a hoarse voice.

A few people near her nodded and murmured in agreement, while many others quickly walked by without looking at the speaker or gathered crowd.

"Mostly they don't tell people when they are speaking," Elizabeth whispered to Emma.

The woman continued talking about a strike up north. Emma made sure not to nod along, but her personal knowledge made her feel courageous.

Elizabeth suddenly smiled and moved slightly away from her.

"Hi, Emma."

Emma turned and gasped, putting her hand over her mouth. "Andrew. What are you doing here?" She straightened the collar of her dress and glanced back at the speaker.

"I suppose I should say the same to you?" Andrew whispered, smiling. He wore his usual dungarees and button-down shirt but had on a bowler hat rather than his usual cap and brown oxfords replaced his work boots. His freckled face seemed more relaxed than when she saw him at the mill.

"Emma." Elizabeth cleared her throat. "I am so sorry to interrupt you two, but perhaps you could continue back in Camas?" She giggled and looked at Frances. "It's time we head back home." Emma nodded. "Besides, I suspect the police will be here soon." She moved closer to Frances.

"It is nice to see you. You seem to be in agreement." He raised his blondish-ginger eyebrows in question. "Just so you know, me too. It is all important. I will see you back in Camas." His eyes had a mischievous glint, and he touched her arm lightly. "You look nice, Emma."

Emma drew a quick breath and returned his smile before trotting to join her friends back to the shopping district. As they walked, she could only think about her few minutes with Andrew. More than a decade before, he accompanied her brother William around town, along with a third friend George. The three of them were well-liked, unlike some of the brattier hoodlums then. Later at the mill, it was always Andrew, and less often, George, who looked upon her, taking on what her own brother would have done had he not headed off to fight for his country.

The remainder of the afternoon and evening sped by, and Emma began to feel comfortable in its foreignness. The family employed a live-in housekeeper who helped prepare the evening meal. Emma offered to help set the table or clean the dishes but was told politely to enjoy herself. She was grateful to be leaving in the morning. As wonderful as it had been, she had no energy to take in more that was both new and exciting.

That night she curled her body to fit the contours of a velvet loveseat in a spare room and nestled into the soft quilt and feather pillow. The day's events spun in her mind. For many reasons the day felt to be a turning point in her life: from girl to woman. She no longer felt nervous to accompany Elizabeth on the trek home. Too, she wondered where Andrew was spending the evening, or if he had already returned to Camas. She nestled deeper into the soft quilt and finally nodded off.

# Chapter 17
## Celia
### December 23, 2024

FINALLY, TWO DAYS later Celia took action to move her life ahead rather than keep treading water, after giving up on getting a call from Paul. She had time to burn so why not get out of town, even if it was nearly Christmas? She changed the oil in her car and planned her drive to Portland and Salem. Her neighbor Adam calmed the squeal in her brake pads in exchange for a meal from the café. Now, her stomach rumbled as she parked her car. She wondered when she would regain a consistent appetite. Since Ruth brought up the long-ago story about Alice, she felt compelled to track the tale to completion. She didn't believe in God, or predestination, but mysterious prompts gave her pause. It's why she harbored guilt over the boat accident—she should have listened, no matter what anyone said.

Celia drove to her mom's house in Portland and was proud of herself for popping in on her unannounced, especially since the stopover was out of her way.

"Celia," Her mom exclaimed, opening the door.

Holiday lights twinkled on a few neighborhood homes and her mom's door boasted an evergreen wreath with sprigs of holly and a red ribbon bow. She hadn't wanted to freak her out by entering the house unexpectedly, nor was she ready to sit through a meal accompanied by lengthy chit chat. The surprise visit allowed them to see each other near Christmas without added stress or fanfare.

Celia knew her mom would be home as they were scheduled to have their weekly phone call that evening. Yes, her mother was predictable, scheduling quiet Sunday nights at home to prepare for the work week ahead. Celia only recently recognized how that kind of predictability could bring a kid comfort. After all, she always knew where her mom would be.

"Hi, Mom." Celia bestowed a quick hug at the doorstep.

Her mom's neat brown short hair did not show a bit of gray, and she was fully made up as if she was about to go to work. Celia hoped she had done something earlier in the afternoon and didn't put the face on just to lie around at home. "I had an errand in town, and I thought I'd stop by before taking off early in the morning, if that's okay? I'll be out early." Her mom never liked anyone to interrupt already scheduled plans, and yet she expected pushback in not being prepared to see her with the visit so close to Christmas.

"Of course." Her mom shifted in her sneakers. If Celia didn't know her better, she might think her mom was hiding something. But no, her mom did not like surprises.

"Yeah, opening fishing plans changed a bit." Celia had no interest in going down the "told you so" path. She dropped her bag and sat down in the kitchen as her mom finished cleaning up her dinner dishes. Celia removed her sneakers and set them next to the back door.

"Let's go to the living room. Would you like a glass of wine?" her mom asked as she refilled her glass from the half empty bottle of red. "We can toast to Christmas?"

Celia shook her head, took a glass from the clean drying rack, and filled it with cold water from the tap. They went into the living room and sat stiffly opposite each other on the couch. Her mom took a sip of wine and then asked her nearly rapid fire about her friend Kate, the café, and the weather. Celia asked her mom about work and how the house bathroom repair was going. All civil, nothing controversial or exciting.

Celia was grateful her mom had a Zoom meeting scheduled, some women's group. It allowed Celia to keep her part of the conversation no more newsworthy than their weekly call. At one point her mom asked what she was going to do after crabbing season, and Celia expertly delivered a short, vague answer but steered it back to a question about her mom who loved to talk about herself. Over the years, this trait encouraged Celia to talk less about herself. These days they kept a careful but distant relationship, although recently Celia felt her mom sounded wistful, as if she wanted more.

With only a few minutes remaining before the Zoom call, Celia decided to pop the question that rumbled in her head, ever since meeting Ruth.

"Hey, Mom?" Celia tried to sound nonchalant. "Do you remember once when you were in high school, meeting a woman named Alice?"

She forced her hands together on her lap. "Maybe at Grandma's house once? Grandma's friend Ruth was there too." She kept her voice quiet and unanimated. "The woman might have seemed a bit wacky. And she claimed to know something about a relative of ours?" She knew this was an outrageous test of memory and dropped her shoulders as she exhaled pent up hopes.

"Alice? I can assure you I remember nothing of the sort." Her mom shook her head and rolled her eyes. "But, oh, who knows. Your grandmother invited all kinds of people back in those days. And some of them were a bit wacky, I'd say. Although, of course, Ruth is very kind. That is, what I remember of her." She looked down at her watch.

That was her mom. If it wasn't something that directly impacted her, she had no interest. Instead, she stood up and buttoned her cardigan sweater. "I'll be taking my call now, but I'll be done in an hour or so if you need anything." She smiled at Celia, hesitated, and looked at the floor. Celia wondered if she was troubled not to have a Christmas gift for her. Then her mom picked up her wine glass and padded slowly back into the kitchen. She looked older, and Celia felt more sad than disappointed. As if, somehow, they missed an opportunity to connect.

The rest of the evening and next morning were uneventful. After her mom joined her call, Celia put on her jacket and took a short walk, breathing in the smoke from woodstoves and enjoying the crisp but dry evening air. Although she hadn't grown up in this house, she enjoyed walking the neighborhoods of Portland, her mom now living near Laurelhurst Park. Celia walked the sidewalk edging one side of the park, tempted to follow it past the duckpond underneath the fir and cedar canopy. But winter's darkness deterred her. Years ago, she wouldn't have thought twice, but now the neighborhood felt foreign. The next morning, she arose shortly after her mom left for work, leaving a note thanking her for the visit before getting on the road.

Pleased with her easy drive to Salem, Celia took a drink of seltzer before getting out of the car. It had turned out Ruth only had Alice's address, but thanks to the power of creepy internet searching, Celia was able to track a phone number. One evening Celia called, introducing herself as a good family friend of Ruth's. Her daughter Barbara recognized Ruth's name, accepting it as a perfectly natural request when Celia asked if she might visit Alice. Celia presumed Barbara was exhausted taking care of her mom and eager for nearly anyone to sit with her.

She locked her car and walked up the cracked sidewalk to the simple one-story house. Its gray siding was newly painted, but garden beds were full of overgrown shrubs and weeds. A woman a decade older than her opened the door to her knock and welcomed her in.

"Mom made cookies, even though it's nine o'clock in the morning." The woman rolled her eyes. "Don't ask." She shook her head. "She's in her room, this way."

Celia followed her past the kitchen, down a small hall into a bedroom. Weirdly, the aroma of sugar and spice was enticing, and mixed with cold weather, upped the holiday feel. She felt bad this old woman, Alice, went to such an effort to visit with someone she didn't know.

"Mom, your friend is here," Barbara said loudly. She directed Celia to a soft armchair opposite her mother, turned her back to her, and pointed to her ears.

"It's lovely to see you." Alice smiled.

Celia gently shook her hand and sat down.

Alice pushed her glasses further up the bridge of her nose and looked at Barbara. "We're fine, sweetie. You go do what you need. Lord knows you've got enough going on." Her voice was sharp yet appreciative. She wore pink matching sweatshirt and pants, with navy soled slippers. A pair of white tennis shoes with Velcro fasteners were by the bed and a standard silver walker was to the right of her chair. The blinds of the room were opened, showing off a view of a backyard of shrubs and a bird feeder.

"Okay, Mom," Barbara said. "How about I bring in some tea and cookies in a bit?"

Alice nodded and smiled but waited until the door was partially closed before saying anything. "That poor girl." She sighed and brushed a hand in the air across her body. "Stuck with me. I told her I didn't want her to have to do this. Just like I did with my mother. Such a crazy thing we force on our daughters." She shook her head and caught her breath.

Celia and her mom had never talked about such a thing. Now it panicked her to imagine the possibility.

"Oh, I'm sure she enjoys it," Celia said, knowing nothing of the sort. "She gets to have cookies around, anyway?" She laughed nervously.

Alice cackled. She hesitated and adjusted a hearing aid. She moved her head back and forth. "Damn things." She fiddled again with her ear. "So, to be clear, I did not tell my daughter I haven't the foggiest idea who you are. If I had, she would have lectured me again about people trying to take my money." She shook her head and frowned. "Oh, don't worry. I've got a few marbles left. I just get bored, and I trust Ruth, so I figured maybe you'd be interesting? Better than watching a rerun of *Jeopardy* or *Price is Right*. I always liked that host whatever his name was. And now I guess he died too. Goodness gracious. Sometimes I have no idea why I'm still around." She ran out of steam and examined Celia, all the way down to her black Converse. "I bought my daughter shoes like that once." She looked at her own fingernails, as if examining a manicure. "How do you know Ruth?"

Celia felt hot. She was having a hard time following the eclectic mix of conversation topics and regretted jumping into the situation. She shrugged off her jacket anyway, set it on her lap, and told Alice how Ruth was a friend of her grandmother's. "The thing is, Ruth told me something." She hesitated. "We both live in Astoria." *Oh, don't let this be a crazy rabbit hole.*

"Well, get on with it, dearie. Don't be afraid of me. Nobody else seems to be. Besides, I like stories that are exciting or maybe even a bit naughty." Alice cackled loudly. "Something to give me hope I'm not just rotting here." Her laugh sounded like a blender on low speed. "My daughter is wonderful. I don't deserve her." She stared out the window.

For a full minute, Celia wondered if she had forgotten she was there. She looked out at birds hovering at the feeder and cleared her throat. "Ruth mentioned something. Um, she said, once many years ago you had talked about a woman. You were at my grandmother's house." Alice looked at her blankly, and Celia knew she was being obtuse. "Oh, I'm sorry, you knew my grandmother. In Portland long ago? Her name is Dorothy Roberts. Her daughter Sheila is my mom." Now, she was certain this was a silly pursuit she wasted good gas money on. *How could this woman remember anything this insignificant from all those years ago?* She took a deep breath and shook her head, consoling herself by remembering she was still getting out of town for a couple days.

Alice's eyes moved back and forth as she stared straight ahead, as if watching moving pictures. "Hmm." She looked down at her fingernails and examined each one. She sighed and looked outside before returning her attention to Celia. She pushed up her glasses. "Yes, I think so. I can see it in your eyes. Your grandmother, Dorothy." Then a worried look passed over her face. "Your grandmother? Is she well?"

"Oh yes." Celia forced herself to stop tapping her fingers on the chair's armrests. "My question is about a story Ruth remembered you once told about a relative of hers. An old story. A woman who lived over a hundred years ago now. She lived somewhere around Vancouver like maybe in Camas. Camas, Washington?"

Alice stared back at her. "Tell me more?"

"Oh." Celia hesitated. "I'm wondering if she did something noteworthy or that brought attention to her while working at the paper mill? Or something like that?" She pushed her fingers through her hair.

"Something noteworthy," Alice repeated, as if testing the words. "Oh, my chickadee." She clapped her hands.

Celia laughed at the sudden outburst, even though she also felt like crying.

Barbara tapped at the door and entered, carrying a tray with two cups of tea, a plate of cookies, and paper napkins decorated with sprigs of holly. "I'm so sorry but I got caught on a work call. Is peppermint tea okay?"

Celia nodded. She felt like a character in a holiday movie.

"Having a nice visit?" she asked hurriedly, a set of headphones resting on her shoulders.

"Yes, thank you," Celia offered as Barbara touched Alice's shoulder and left the room, again partially closing the door.

"I made these first thing this morning," Alice said, picking up a molasses cookie and taking a bite. "It's one of the few things I can still do. I'll probably make my daughter sick or fat." She laughed.

Celia took one and nibbled a bite, followed by a second, forcing herself to relax. Even if she learned nothing, she was getting out of town for a break, and the old woman was enjoying herself. Those hours she spent with the old maritime guy in Astoria years ago, talking about boats and docks, and even about his daughter, had given her practice in talking to someone with memory issues. She had figured out how he liked being able to tell her stories without needing to worry if they were true or not. Now, as she sipped her tea, she wondered what clear memories of the past Alice had.

"So, you want to know about Emma?" Alice asked.

Celia nearly choked. She put the rest of the cookie on the tray and took a sip of tea. "Is that her name?"

Alice nodded. "You should know about Emma. I'm certain she was related to you and your grandmother." Her eyes looked clearer than before and carried a new twinkle as she began to tell her a story about Celia's illusive ancestor.

# Chapter 18
## Emma
### September 21, 1916

"EMMA. DEAR EMMA, what is it?" Father cried, slowly approaching Emma as she lay crumbled on her parents' bed.

"Oh, Father," Emma blubbered. Her face was pressed against the pillow

"Emma. What is it?"

Emma knew her parents had not seen her this upset in years, and she had not lay on their bed since she had been ill as a child.

"It's George." Emma turned to her father as he crouched on the floor next to the bed. "It's George Smith, you know. From just up the street. He went to school with William. Oh, he and William were close."

She tried to slow her crying to spit words out. She was still in her work clothes, only having removed her apron, not even unlacing her boots. Mother stood in the doorway, her face trembling in fear.

"Father, he's gone. It was horrible." Emma sniffed as more tears spilled from her eyes.

Father touched her arm, but Emma curled herself further into a fetal position and lay in a motionless crumbled heap, her face toward him but eyes closed.

Emma could hear the door quietly close and the clatter of dishes and murmurs from the children. How could life go on? Why should it?

After several minutes, Emma uncoiled her body and opened her eyes. "He was killed, Father. Just like that. There was . . . there was blood everywhere. He was always so kind." She sniffled and wiped her nose with her hand. "I don't normally go into that part of the mill where he worked, but I needed to get more printing ink." Her voice cracked. "Oh, Father, it was awful. I heard men talking that another operator turned on the paper machine while he was repairing it. They said nobody knew."

Father patted her shoulder.

Emma looked at him. "He was so young. Do you remember him? He was quiet but he was always kind." She struggled to pull her body to the side of the bed and pushed her feet to the floor.

"There, there, Emma. It will be okay," Father soothed.

"How can you say that?" Emma shied away from his touch. "It will never be okay. Don't you understand? He is dead. He will never be able to do anything. And what about his family? And the woman he was about to marry. Oh, Father." Emma knew she was speaking rudely but did not care. This was all wrong. She raised her chin and stared past Father at the wall.

He nodded and sat quietly.

She knew he understood there was a time to be quiet and listen, even if she was behaving impudently—a skill her mother rarely seemed to employ.

"He had only worked at the mill for a few months. I think he was trying to earn more money than what he had been making in his father's business, so he could marry and start a family. And I was there as it happened. It was horrible. They said he was trying to straighten the paper in between the rollers, and, oh." Emma covered her face. "He was crushed. I think his head was crushed. And then something must have gotten stuck in the machine and there was blood. Blood all over."

Father pulled Emma into a hug. "There, there. There, there." He petted the back of her head like he would Mary's.

Emma pulled away from him and wiped her eyes.

"It is a dangerous job. A dangerous line of work. We all know this, but it is part of the business." Father hesitated. "Yes, it is part of the business," he said, as if trying to convince himself.

Emma looked up at him. "It should not be. Things happen sometimes that should never happen. It should not be allowed. All these men are making money, yes, but nothing like what the big owners earn. Remember when they gave us two fans? Some of us still feel sick during the day, on bad smelly days. But it is nothing like this. This should never be okay."

"Yes. I understand. I'm sorry." Father hesitated. Emma knew he was choosing his words carefully. "Perhaps. Might it be time to listen to Mother? To finally leave this work? Perhaps it is no longer a good choice for you."

Emma looked away from his penetrating gaze. She crossed her arms and stared across the room.

She knew she would be wise to choose her words carefully, yet now everything felt different. Martha had told her how her outspokenness was increasingly concerning her parents. Ever since the strike, Mother had stopped talking with her about anything other than things relevant to their daily lives. Until now, Father had remained agreeable and less restrained. But now, she couldn't believe his words.

"I do not want to talk about it any longer." Emma shook her head. "And besides, I'm late for something."

Father raised his eyebrows. "It is dark out. You have not even eaten supper. Where on earth could you possibly be going?"

Emma pulled back her hair and stood. "I'm not a child anymore. For several years now I have brought in wages each week to help this family. And, in fact, I've been meaning to ask that I reduce my amount to this household now that I am an adult and need to save for my own future. I must be allowed some independence." She wiped her face with the hem of her blouse and looked away.

Father slumped lower on the stool. Mother would have reprimanded her for speaking rudely, but Emma no longer cared. Father used the bed frame to pull himself up and walked out of the room.

Emma knew she should change clothes, but did not care. How could such triviality matter now? She wiped her face with her sleeve, straightened her mussed hair, tucked her blouse into her skirt, and rearranged her stockings.

Her family was sitting at the table and turned to look at her as she came out of the bedroom. She avoided eye contact but touched Helen's head as she passed by. She hated to see her younger sister worry.

"Emma, we are sorry about your friend," Mother said. "We will put a meal together for the Smith Family tomorrow."

Emma was exhausted after her encounter with Father. "Thank you, Mother." She walked into the hallway to gather her coat from the hook. "There is a vigil in front of the mill and I'm going."

She was surprised by her calm and steady voice but did not need to see her parents' reactions to know they would be frightened by this plan. Earlier in the week, Father had shared news about a growing divisiveness in town between support for the mill, and the small but vocal minority who felt workers deserved better work and wages. Outside labor activists had caught sight of the Camas Mill and were planning to bring their big city organizing to town. Emma knew that was the main reason Father wanted her to leave her job, even though they still needed her wages with the continued threat of war. While there was no vigil she knew about, she wished there was and wanted to prove to her parents she was old enough to make her own decisions.

The cool misty air calmed Emma's hot damp cheeks as she stepped outside. She was glad to feel drizzle wash down upon face, not caring to wash up before she left. Why bother? What was the point after seeing George's lifeless body on the cold cement mill floor? The stories she had heard before were nothing compared to the horror she had witnessed.

Emma headed across the bridge, soon after passing several mill workers hurrying home after their shifts. Production was booming but the mill was low on labor, and many worked longer hours than they had anticipated when they began. Without labor representation, like what Cassie had told her was forming in some factories, contracts mostly served the employer. She too reminded Emma how longer hours often meant more accidents. Emma pulled her scarf out of her pocket and tucked it over her head. She crossed the street, away from the activity of the mill.

"Emma!"

She looked up to see Andrew across the street. She slowed her steps as he signaled a good-bye to two men who walked up toward town, before crossing over to her.

"Oh, Andrew." Emma's voice was still calm and steady, exhausted from her earlier outburst. She could not imagine being more relieved to see anyone else besides George himself. "Oh, Andrew." She could not contain her sorrow any longer.

"Emma, Emma." He looked toward the mill and then up the street, then he pulled her gently to him. "Dear Emma," he whispered, as if to himself.

He hugged her first as an uncle might hug a distant cousin, her head meeting him at his chest. Emma could not help herself, burrowing her face in his rough jacket, as he tightened his hold. His smell of wet pulp and machine oil was comforting. She wanted to hold onto him forever, as if that would allow her mind to forget the tragedy.

Finally, she knew she needed to be respectable and pulled back. She wiped her eyes with her coat sleeve, wishing she had a handkerchief. Andrew nodded. His face was sullen, his eyes tired and red, and he was not wearing his cap.

"Oh, Andrew. I know how close you were. I'm so sorry." Tears seeped from her eyes and she pulled away from him.

He nodded and sniffed. "Yes, horrible. Never should have happened. And to George, of all people. No, it should not be this way." He narrowed his eyes and clenched his fists.

Emma nodded, remembering that day long ago when they exchanged glances in Portland. They had spoken about the Portland orator twice since, quietly in passing at the mill.

"You must know something about me." Andrew sounded angrier with each word. "I have been learning about how we can make work better for a long time now. But this is it." He shook a finger at the mill. Then he took hold of her hands and pulled her closer to him. "There's talk about organizing. You know, really organizing, like they are at the mill down on the Willamette. I've been joining those meetings." He shook his head. "You could too?" He dropped his chin and raised his eyebrows.

Emma knew he was trusting her with secrets. In that moment, she felt she trusted Andrew more than anyone else in the world, perhaps even Father. "Yes." She inhaled and nodded. "Yes."

"Let me walk you home." Andrew hesitated. "It is better for you not to be out alone . . ." He smiled, embarrassed.

"No, I am fine. Thank you."

They walked silently, however, down to where the bridge crossed the Washougal River. After a few steps, Andrew held her arm, as if to steady her. Emma breathed in the damp, sulfur smell of the air, and moved closer to him. She felt relieved to share this sadness with him but felt something else pull at her. She stopped at the side of the bridge, and Andrew tightened his grip on her arm before letting go of it.

"Good night, dear Emma." He looked deeply into her eyes, his smile gentle but tired.

Emma got the sense he wanted to say something more, but he stayed silent.

"Good night, Andrew." Then she turned and headed home, certain he stood watching her until she disappeared from his view.

# Chapter 19
## Celia
### January 7, 2025

AS THE EVENING approached, Celia found herself pacing the small circle of the kitchen, snapping her fingers as if listening to music. Which she wasn't.

"What's gotten into you?" Sophia laughed.

Celia glanced at her, embarrassed. This was not how she acted, and she felt idiotic even if it was mixed with excitement and nervousness. She could not remember the last time she felt like this before meeting up with someone, though it wasn't like it had never happened.

"Oh, blow off." Celia smiled. "Are you leaving soon?" She was not in the mood to do the "meeting the roommate" thing.

"Calm yourself, girlfriend." Sophia laughed. "Let me enjoy this." She giggled. "You are so cute. And funny. Who knew quiet, serious Celia could be like this?"

"Seriously. Can you please not be here when Paul arrives?" She felt like a teenager about to go on a first date. "But hey. I mean, I appreciate your being here for me and all. You know. Since the accident." She smiled and shrugged.

"Yeah, yeah. Don't worry. I'm heading out." Sophia grabbed her purse and coat. "But if he's here in the morning you'll have to introduce me." She smiled wickedly.

"Oh go." Celia smiled but walked toward her with her arms out as if to push her. She had no intention for sex to be on the night's agenda. No way was she jumping into that. Too often before she did that as a way to hurry herself through a relationship. Unknowingly sabotaging them all to demonstrate her independence, Sophia would interpret.

Yes, tonight was a date, a real date. Not just another time to hang together to talk about interesting but impersonal things. She could tell Paul was feeling something for her during the two walks they had taken recently. Simple, nothing but a couple of friends, acquaintances really, enjoying being outside together. That's what she told herself but often circled back to how different he was from other guys she knew. At first it concerned her. His openness and compassion made her want to spill her whole story; but it was safer to lock it in to keep herself together. She was no doubt physically attracted to him. He had once shown her a picture of himself without his beard, and she told him she liked it on him. She didn't tell him, though, how she would take him either way.

Celia jumped when her phone vibrated. She read the text.

*Hi. I'm so sorry but one of our procedures went longer than we thought. I'll be another ten minutes. So sorry but see you then?*

*Of course. See you then.*

She set her phone on the counter and headed to the dryer to grab her clothes. Then she dashed back to her phone.

*Remember, buzz me and I'll come out.*

She hauled the clean, wrinkled laundry to her room and tossed it on the bed, as if to spite this silly feeling that everything should be perfect. As if she would be inviting him to her bed. Then, she thought better of it and quickly folded her clothes, shoved them into her dresser, and slammed the laundry bin into her closet. "Jesus. I'm a dork."

The doorbell buzzed, and she grabbed her coat and bag and hurried down the hallway and stairs to the front door. She pushed the door open and was relieved by the cool breeze carrying a tangy taste of salt. She was always surprised how much the saltiness in the air varied by day and season, like temperature. Maybe it was her imagination.

"Hey." Paul stood at the door in his faded Levis and fleece jacket. Celia was glad it was dry that evening. She smiled as she glanced down at his Birkenstocks and wondered if he owned any other shoes.

"Hi." Celia smiled and led him to the sidewalk.

"You know. Just to be upfront," he began, stopping as she turned to look at him. "I don't do the dating thing. In case you wondered. Or noticed." He looked at his feet and frowned.

"Oh, it's fine," Celia said. "I mean, I don't either. I think dating is for a lost generation. Or I guess the last one." She shrugged, then dropped her hands to her sides.

Paul smiled in relief.

"Shall we walk?"

"Um, yeah. Is that okay? I mean, I don't own a car." Paul shrugged and raised his brows.

Celia suppressed her surprise although she knew car ownership was expensive. After all, she couldn't seem to afford to properly maintain hers.

"Uh, of course. I have one and I'm happy to drive," she offered. "But walking is fine."

"I don't believe in them. I mean it's okay that you have one. I saw you in it once, so I get it. Oh, never mind."

He shook his head, and the hint of blush Celia had come to recognize peeked out from under his beard. This guy was different. And perhaps younger than she thought too. She drew in a deep breath before slowly letting it out.

They walked toward the restaurant. Their conversation lagged, which hadn't happened during their other walks. They talked about the recent coastal storm and the depressing national news. Celia knew Paul was much more up to speed than she was on politics and government affairs, and she recently began to follow several news sources to be less ignorant.

They reached the restaurant within a few minutes and headed toward the counter.

"What will it be?" the server asked.

Celia looked around at the room of mostly open tables. "I'll have the Fort George IPA." She looked at Paul.

"Just water for me," he said.

They grabbed two menus and waited for their drinks.

"Just come back to the counter when you're ready to order," the server instructed.

"How about there?" Celia pointed to a four-seater next to the window.

Paul nodded, and they set their drinks on the table and removed their jackets before sitting down. They both opened their menus to look at the offerings. Celia took a sip of her beer but felt weird drinking alone and glanced at Paul. She wished she had ordered a coke and looked outside at the quiet rainy weeknight, with few people out and about, maybe exhausted from the holidays.

"You know, it's okay you got a beer, if that's bugging you. It's no problem for me to see you drinking," Paul said.

Celia drew in a breath, thinking she had hidden her discomfort.

"There's a long story there, but mostly I don't drink. I'm not an alcoholic. Not that there'd be anything wrong with me if I was." He dropped the menu and shrugged. "Oh God. I'm bad at all this." He clasped his hands behind his neck and looked out the window, as if he couldn't meet her eyes.

She felt sympathetic toward his awkwardness and reached her hand out but placed it on the table instead of touching him. He looked at the menu again and rubbed his hands along the thighs of his jeans.

Just as she began to wonder how they would make it through the evening, Paul began talking about his life. She took a sip of beer and watched his face, his eyes occasionally meeting hers, but more often staring out the window. Celia drew in her breath as she learned his dad had also left his mom shortly after his birth. His mom had been much older than hers and had been criticized for having Paul because of her age. She had been hypervigilant in her mothering.

"She was an amazing mother." Paul looked at her with tears in his eyes. "I was, well, I was a different kind of kid. And she did what she had to. A lot of that I didn't understand until I got older. I really miss her." He put his elbows on the table and pressed his fingertips to his eyes. When he moved his hands away, tears clung to his cheeks.

"Oh. I'm sorry. I didn't know." Celia handed him a napkin from the dispenser on the table.

He wiped his eyes before looking at Celia. "Yes, she died just last year. That part has been hard. Very hard. And there is a lot I wish I could tell her now." He sighed. "But she knew I loved her. Her name was Marjorie." He took a drink of water. "I haven't said much about my mom to anyone, other than my boss, I guess. Sorry about unloading all this when we should be having a good time. I just felt like, I guess, you should know."

Celia touched his hand. "It's fine. Really. I enjoy talking with you. It's all okay. Would you like to tell me more?"

"I was older when she told me anything about my dad. He just wasn't a good man. Knowing my mom, I'd say he never deserved her. And he drank a lot too. Between all that and raising me alone . . ." Paul looked up at Celia. "I saw him a few times as I got older, but mostly he was absent." He fidgeted and ran his hands along his jeans again. "Look, I think this is a mistake and I'm not sure what I was thinking. You seem great." He hesitated and looked at her. "And really beautiful." He smiled but his eyes were teary.

Celia covered her mouth. Nobody had told her she was beautiful before. Not even her mother, at least not that she remembered. She had always accepted she didn't meet beauty queen standards and tried to remind herself that the attributes she had were more important than physical beauty. She was capable, strong, and independent. She smiled but shook her head, embarrassed.

"No, really. But besides that. We don't know each other, but I have this way of knowing people. I know that sounds weird. But I'm . . ." Paul looked as if he was going to cry.

"It's okay. What? Really, it's okay. Whatever." She leaned closer and rested her hand on his arm.

He wiped at his eyes with the cuff of his shirt and shrugged her hand away. "No, I know. I mean I have a lot of stuff." He pointed to his chest with both hands. "Although I've been doing pretty well. It's probably why I've nearly never dated. It's a lot to share with anyone. It's a lot to expect anyone to get or want to be part of." He dropped his hands at his side.

"It's okay. Maybe we should order." *Either that or go home.* Seeing Paul so emotionally distraught wrenched her gut, and she hoped a food break might help them both.

Paul nodded and stood up quickly but waited to follow her to the counter.

After ordering, a salad loaded with beans and cheese for Paul, and a burger for Celia, they returned to their seats. Celia had insisted on paying her own way, and Paul didn't argue.

He laid out his life as if he was telling a story.

Celia bit her tongue when he paused and ignored her impulse to fill uncomfortable gaps in the conversation. She learned about his growing up in Portland, and how he never fit in. He told her how he found help recently with both a therapist and medication, and how much better his life was going, even with his mother having died. He loved his job at the animal hospital, even if it didn't pay great. And he believed in living simply.

Paul looked at her straight on. "I think that's the most important thing." He took a deep breath and audibly exhaled. He repeated it a second time, and Celia could see it calming him.

"What's that?" she asked, worried she had missed something by focusing on his breathing. "I mean, the most important thing?"

"Oh, I believe we each have a responsibility to be good to whatever is left in this earth, you know?" Paul looked at Celia, his voice calm and confident.

Celia nodded but knew she hadn't thought a lot about these things that Paul cared so much about. It made her feel as if it was too complicated to imagine how they might be together, even if it was just a first date.

The server approached with the meal and placed their plates in front of each of them, together with napkins and silverware. "Let me know if you need anything," he said before hurrying back to the counter.

Celia eyed Paul's salad. "Are you a vegetarian?"

"Oh yes. For sure. I try to be vegan too, but I find that hard. Sometimes." He gave a sheepish smile. "I really like ice cream." He looked at her burger. "Oh, but it's okay. It's a personal decision. I try. I try really hard. I mean, not to judge people. I don't know back stories, just like some don't know mine. And I don't want others to judge me for what they see me do or know about me." Paul hesitated and then took a bite of his salad.

"Like what?" Celia bit her tongue. She should stop provoking their conversation with questions but was curious.

Paul looked into her eyes and then wiped his mouth with his napkin. He set it back in his lap, rubbed his hands on his thighs, and looked out the window. Their conversation gaps were becoming less uncomfortable.

"I had a horrible experience a few years ago. Here. I mean, here in town." His eyes filled with tears. "I don't blame anyone. I mean, don't think that I did anything wrong, because I didn't. I just got overwhelmed when I became aware of someone who had been mistreated. Killed . . . and . . . It's just that when I saw it, I overreacted, and the police thought I'd done it. I mean that I had done something horrible. Like murder a stranger." He covered his eyes with his hands before returning them to his lap. He stared at Celia with a new intensity. "I was arrested. It was really awful. For me. And, for my mom, Marjorie. Then." Paul nodded before sipping his water. He looked as if he was swallowing a huge lump along with the water.

Celia nodded, forcing herself to stay quiet and focus on his words.

"But it helped me understand. That's the thing. That none of us really know about each other." Paul drained the water in his glass. "I've never talked with anyone about this. I mean, besides my mom and my therapist."

Celia felt badly that answering her question would ruin his meal.

A memory flashed before her eyes. Of a man screaming on the sidewalk. Flashing ambulance lights. Streetlights. Her hurrying on by.

The cop car streaming down the street. And then the memorial service, and her visits with the old guy. And recently, finding Paul remembering somebody while sitting at the Riverwalk nearly in the same spot as she had seen the police that evening long ago.

"Oh God, Paul." Tears filled her eyes.

Paul gave her a questioning look.

Celia touched his hand. "Let's get this food to go." She swallowed her tears, went to the counter, and returned with containers for their leftovers.

"Come on, let's go." She grabbed Paul's hand.

# Chapter 20
## Celia
### January 13, 2025

THE DAY STARTED out inauspiciously, no premonitions or grand ideas. Celia reheated her morning coffee sometime near noon, doing nearly nothing those morning hours unlike the days of fishing when she rose before dawn. Most weeks she worked Friday through Sunday shifts at the café, leaving gaping holes during the week, hours initially luxurious, but soon weighing on her. Bored, lonely, or lacking meaning? She wasn't certain. Too, her financial reserves would dwindle. When she finally admitted leaving fishing for good to her mom, she had offered to pay for Celia to see a life coach. Celia rolled her eyes. *No thanks.*

After that second cup of coffee, she slid her feet into her leather boots, scavenged around the house for a pen and notepad, and threw them into her bag. She headed out the door but dashed back in for her raincoat before beginning her walk up the sidewalk. Within twenty feet she turned and made a beeline for her car. It had been nearly a week since dinner with Paul, and she wasn't ready for a chance encounter.

A few minutes later she pulled into the library parking lot. As she pushed open the glass door, she was relieved to see the familiar librarian at the desk, although she had lost the card he gave her and couldn't remember his name. The musty smell of books was oddly calming, a signal of new things ahead for her. New things that were old. She fingered the books on the New Fiction shelf near the front door, wondering what it might be like to recognize new book titles and author names. She had loved to read when she was young but somewhere got turned off to it. She took in the quiet of the room, just a few old people sitting in the corner, and a kid with an adult. She felt eyes on her and exchanged looks with the librarian. She felt an imposter, relieved when he smiled at her before attending to the books at his desk.

Be bolder, Celia, she coached herself as she walked to the desk. "Hi. Um, I don't know if you remember me, but I was looking for information . . ."

"Yes, of course. Though I'm not sure I remember your name. Anyway, happy to help however I can. What might you be looking for?" He shrugged and opened his hands. His name was Matthew according to the ID hanging around his neck.

Celia set her bag on the floor. "It was the Camas Mill in the early 1900s." She told him what little she knew and all else she was trying to figure out, stuttering as she put her spilling thoughts into words.

Matthew smiled at her. "That's something. An interesting mystery, I'd say." He gestured to the pod of computers. "Come on over to a workstation."

Celia tensed up, unsure she could perform whatever task she needed to learn more.

"I don't want to take the fun out of the search for you but thought I could help you get started," Matthew said as if reading her mind. He lowered himself into a chair at the nearest computer.

Celia exhaled, removed her coat, and laid it and her bag on a chair. She grabbed her pen and notepad, pretending to be a good student.

"You know the name of the mill, location and date so that's helpful. So, we need to dig into what's out there on websites about early history."

Celia nodded, pushed her things to the back of the chair, and sat on its edge.

"Local universities like Washington State and Portland State University have detailed historical databases," he mumbled, as if to himself. He typed too rapidly for her to take note of anything, impressed at anyone who could quickly get to what they were looking for in the wild virtual universe.

"Wow," she whispered, shaking her head.

Matthew glanced up at her. "I love history." Maybe I said that before. I was a history major in college and volunteer next door too." He stopped typing and gestured at the wall. "The Clatsop County Historical Society. Less helpful for Clark County. You know, for Camas."

Celia was relieved he was in his own world, and again grateful to let him do his thing. She settled back in her chair and watched.

"Hmm." He wrapped his fingers around his chin as he squinted at the screen. Then he went back to clicking things here and there, moving between different websites, even old newspapers. Every so often he'd glance back at his desk, but the library had not attracted any new visitors. "Bingo." He clapped his hands together.

Celia looked up at the folks across the room, but they were oblivious to the two of them.

"Oh," he said, disappointed. "Maybe not."

Matthew invited her to sit at the computer and pointed out a few opened files containing relevant facts including a long research paper and other historical articles. "Have a look at those." He put his finger on the screen. "You might find it useful to take a few notes. I'll be at my desk if you have questions or think of something else." He stood and tucked his shirt into his jeans. He glanced at the desk, and then back at her.

"Oh yes." Celia nodded, not sure how to let him know how much she appreciated his help, although she wished he would stay. "Thank you."

She was surprised how fast the next hour sped by as she moved back and forth between documents while taking a few notes. Some of it confused her, dates from the past, names she had never heard of, processes she didn't understand. Much of it not relevant to her question, even if interesting. But finally, she gathered her things together, disappointed to see a different librarian at the desk. Her neck ached from looking down at the computer screen. She had one final question, so she ripped out a page from her notebook, scribbled a few sentences, and after packing up her things and putting her coat on, headed over to the desk.

"Can you leave this for Matthew? He was helping me with some research." The librarian nodded. Celia was uncomfortable leaving her phone number and told her she'd check back soon.

The misty air outside felt good, and she headed the long way to the Riverwalk. After reading about mills, barges, and steamboats, it seemed a natural thing to do as her mind puzzled together what she had learned. She knew now about the all-woman strike at the bag factory, and about later efforts to organize a union at the mill. Was that what this Emma had worked toward? She walked downriver along the trail, seeing the Columbia River Bar Pilots office and soon after, the Megler Bridge. Boats trafficked along the river, even in the heart of winter. It was no longer misty, and the weak sunlight was fading behind layered dark clouds to the west.

Hunger gnawed at her after another hour or so, and she stopped at a favorite less expensive dining spot. She pulled out her phone to try to find the answer to the question she had scribbled at the library while she forked in bites of rice and curry. Finally, her head stuffed with facts, and chicken curry floating in her belly, she sat back. She wiped her hands on her napkin and rubbed her eyes before taking a sip of water. She looked out at the street, thinking about her first conversation with Paul on the Riverwalk. She peered back at her phone and searched the city website she had viewed weeks ago. She found the agenda for that night's meeting, with a bareboned description for the first item: community climate presentation.

Celia had wondered if Paul might call her, or if she should reach out to him. She knew deep down it was a question of when not if. He had insisted on walking her home that night after dinner, although she figured she was better suited to fend off an attack. Any other night she might have joked about it. He had been quiet after they left the restaurant, as if not knowing how to act after unloading his past. Celia felt badly for encouraging him to do all the talking at dinner, even if it felt right at the time. They shared an awkward hug at her doorstep; both knew they needed time alone to unpack their conversation.

Celia didn't want Paul to feel she was scared off, even if it was how she felt. After all, she was trying to uncomplicate her life. To find more joy and ease. To feel better about herself. To create better and easier paths and ties ahead, not more difficult. Although her time with people had lifted her spirits. She had handed him his dinner leftovers, and they bid their goodbyes.

Celia hadn't originally planned to attend the city council meeting had Paul told her about. In realizing it was that evening, though, she was curious to learn more about him. She hoped she could hide in a crowd and double-checked the time on her phone before heading into the restaurant bathroom. She cupped water into her hand and gargled to try to soften her curried breath.

She passed a group of men bickering on city hall's front steps. She turned her face away from two she recognized from the café as she walked past them. She hadn't wanted to arrive too early, but also didn't want to be late, and walked into the room just as the meeting was about to begin. Five people sat at a front wooden table, and a small cluster of folks of various ages talked quietly near the front in chairs she assumed set up for community members. She spotted Paul facing the front and hustled to an open seat in the back.

Just as she sat down, joining two dozen or so others, the room rang with the hard thump of a gavel hitting the front table, followed by a barely audible voice announcing the meeting coming to order. The handful of men she had seen outside thudded into the room, waterproof jackets swishing as they noisily creaked themselves into open chairs.

"So stupid," one guy muttered as he plopped down two rows in front of her.

The man speaking at the microphone hesitated as someone fixed the PA system. Soon after, attendees rose for the pledge of allegiance, and Paul craned his neck to take in the crowd. He caught her eyes and smiled, before looking back at the flag. Celia moved her lips a bit so not to offend anyone but felt she was back in an assembly in elementary school.

She wished she had seen the agenda posted at the table when she came in and strained to hear the mayor review the evening schedule. She didn't want to make a spectacle of herself by leaving early, nor did she want to stay in the conference room all night. She knew little about city politics, although she had voted, but was surprised the mayor and councilors just looked like normal, everyday people. She'd probably passed them on the street and hadn't thought twice. One councilor, in jeans and a pullover sweater, was younger than her and the mayor seemed low-key.

It was announced that the climate group presentation would be next. And then, before she knew it, the mayor invited Paul to come to the microphone. Paul sat at a small table facing the councilors. She wished she could see his face as he wiped his hands on his jeans. She felt nervous for him, but he spoke in a calm voice, and she realized she had either misread his body language, or he was very good at faking it.

"Thank you, Mayor and Councilors. My name is Paul Stephens, and I represent Astorians Who Care About Climate and Health."

Rough laughter bubbled from the three guys sitting a few rows in front of Celia. "Hell, hippies coming in to tell us what to do." The guy next to the one talking laughed and shook his head.

Celia peeked at Paul's shoes. She'd spent enough time with a few of the locals to guess how some may view him. Good thing they didn't know he was born in Portland. She knew it was still like those early pandemic days with some of the locals. While all hell was breaking loose in Portland, masks required and schools closed, around here like in other smaller towns, some folks asserted it was a ploy by the government to control them all. She knew now that not everyone felt that way, but those folks were loud. These days with politics being what they were, the break between liberals and conservatives in Oregon seemed even bigger, and angrier. She heard more mumbles from the men. "Here we go again, more regulations."

The mayor pounded the gavel on the table. "Please. Allow our speaker to continue." His voice was impatient, and he pounded again for extra measure.

"Not only is climate change the biggest threat facing humans, plants, animals and their habitats, but the livelihoods of fishermen are being forever altered," Paul continued.

Celia wondered if he intentionally didn't say "folks." Some people thought saying "fisherfolk" was a communist ploy or something. Even if there were women, like herself, who fished. Who once fished, she corrected.

"We appreciate your time today and the work you do to improve the lives of Astorians. We ask you adopt this proclamation demonstrating your concern and interest to continue to do what you can to reduce our city's impact of increasing emissions and climate change. Thank you." Paul nodded toward the council.

A few people clapped but stopped as the mayor gestured with his hands to quiet.

Paul stood up.

"Thank you, Mr. Stephens. If you would wait." The mayor looked at the four others at the front table. "Does anyone have a question for our presenter?"

The audience rumbled. One man stood up. "Good God. Don't let these radicals speak for us. It's all a crock, you know." He pushed the chair in front of him causing it to screech against the floor.

"Order, order." The mayor pounded his gavel. "Thank you but you have an opportunity to share comments by email. Or in person prior to our next meeting." The guy stood up, screeched his chair this time, and stormed out of the room. "Give me a break," he grumbled, thumping his hand on the wall as he walked out.

"Mayor, if I may," one councilor said. "While I appreciate these good people coming here"—she nodded at Paul—"we have a lot of things to consider. I mean we have been doing quite a bit in this county, and we need to examine what a resolution might ask of us. All of that needs to be considered."

Celia knew her words were meant to appease Paul, though doubted they would.

"Yeah, look how well this all worked in Portland," another guy in the audience yelled.

"Do I hear a motion to move this discussion to our next work session?" the mayor asked. Someone made the motion, it was seconded and passed. And just like that they moved onto the next agenda item.

Half of the visitors in the small crowd stood up with no intention to stay for the remaining business. Paul returned to his seat, and the folks he was with spoke quietly to each other as they gathered their things. He looked up at Celia, but the person next to him said something, and they talked as they left the room. The mayor hesitated, letting the room quiet, before moving on to the next item.

Celia felt stuck. She was uncomfortable taking one side and was embarrassed around others from the community to claim Paul. Of course, she knew what scientists were saying about climate change, the warming and rising of the oceans. Even big groups like NOAA were onboard, although recent budget cuts were predicted to decimate their staff and gut many of its initiatives. She imagined Paul and his group looked to some like a bunch of yahoos or rabblerousers.

As Celia deliberated what to do, the mayor introduced the City Park Department Manager. She couldn't walk out in the middle of the talk so instead set her bag on her lap and planned to make a break before they moved onto the following item.

"Thank you, Mayor," the woman began. "I'm talking today, as requested by Council, about our needs for improved staffing within our parks department and to support our programming." She cleared her throat. "Astoria today is not the Astoria of the olden days everyone likes to remember. Yes, our parks are beautiful. The river and ocean are gems, and we are fortunate to have them. Yet, times have changed. Our department can't do things the way we have in the past or with the same budget and resources."

Celia was inspired by the women's confidence and passion. She listed the impacts of less affordable housing, homelessness, drug use, and increases in trash. The woman sounded more capable than any of the leaders sitting at the table but did not look like the scripted power-suited executive with her single long blond braid, khakis, and sweater. *She had made such assumptions.* Before Celia knew it, the mayor thanked Ms. Johnson, telling her to put her needs in writing and they would discuss it at a work session. Celia shook her head at what looked like delay tactics;

wait till next meeting, send emails. That would drive her bananas. As the woman returned to her seat near other staff, several people nodded to her, and Celia offered an unseen smile. She had never thought about their city paying people to take care of parks; and work outside in such beauty.

Celia hustled out of the room. Having kept her coat on, she felt sweat in her armpits and was eager to get out of the building. The entrance and sidewalk were vacant, and she was glad her car was parked only a few blocks away near the library. She felt a twinge of disappointment not to see Paul yet had renewed optimism for new possibilities.

# Chapter 21
## Emma
### May 15, 1918

WHEN ANDREW PROPOSED that day, Emma had known it was meant to be. Now, curled up on their bed late in the afternoon, knowing well what it was she was feeling in her belly, she allowed herself to daydream back to those days. Andrew had chummed around with her brother William from the beginning. And it was Andrew who comforted her after the mill accident. In hindsight, even now she recognized the spark she felt that long ago day when the two shared words at the labor organizing oratory after the Rose Festival Parade. It had seemed an impossible coincidence then; to share a private smile with someone miles away from their normal lives. Only later did Emma recognize the shared smile meant more. All of it, not only love.

Then came the day, only a few weeks after the mill accident, when he stopped by the house. Emma was taken aback to hear the knock and carefully opened the front door. Most days they received few visitors.

"Oh, Andrew." Emma had readied herself only minutes before to head out for a solo breath of air, already buttoning up her sweater and putting on her hat.

"Hello, Emma," he said, his face reddening. He stared at her and nervously pulled on the sleeve of his buttoned cotton shirt. His sparkling green eyes and freckles had always made him appear jolly to her, and she was not used to seeing him look uneasy. She wanted to comment about their matching eye colors but felt it would be inappropriate. He removed his cap. "Ahem. Your Father said it would be acceptable for me to call on you." He glanced into her eyes and then looked at his boots and shuffled his feet.

Andrew's face was scrubbed clean, and his short red hair wet on the sides. Emma wondered how he had so quickly cleaned up after clocking out. He was not showing any sign of having spent the day in the mill, even wearing a vest she knew he would not don at work. She first felt delighted but then stung by his comment. Why must Father be the one to know first, or give his approval for a grown woman to choose to see a man?

She shook her head and shoulders, annoyed.

He frowned. "I mean . . . would that be alright with you? To go for a walk?" He shrugged in apology, before returning a gentle smile.

"Of course." She nodded and finished buttoning her sweater. She was thrilled to see him and forced herself to let go of his asking permission. "But do know I am a grown woman and can make my own decisions." She risked sounding rude. "Just one moment?" She raised her eyebrows.

Emma partially closed the front door and turned back to Martha, who still lived in Vancouver but had come for supper. She knew Martha had been eavesdropping, and she nodded before Emma could ask the question.

"I will not be long, and Mother will be home soon. Thank you, Martha. I will see you before supper." Emma was grateful she had prepared their evening meal earlier in the day. She closed the door behind her. "Some days I feel she believes I'm a maid or nanny."

Andrew shrugged into an awkward silence. "Shall we walk toward the river?"

Emma nodded. She wondered if he knew about her special spot, knowing he had seen her enroute before, even though he lived on the mill side of the river.

They walked down the gravel road, arms hanging stiffly at their sides. Emma had never felt less at ease with him. Yet, it was beautiful out, and she was grateful for at least another hour or two of daylight. The smell of cottonwood overwhelmed the sulfurous odor of the mill.

"How are things?" Emma asked, eager to fill in the silence. She had heard bits and pieces about labor unrest, not only at the other mill south of Portland but even within the Camas Mill. It was not something she could talk with him about in their few moments of connecting at work.

"Oh." Andrew shook his head. "There is a lot of pressure on us." He slowed his pace and lowered his voice. "But let's not talk about that. I mean, we do not need to today, in our time together."

"Andrew." Emma stopped walking and looked up into his eyes. He was nearly a foot taller than her. "I may be a woman, but I care about all that. You, of all people should know." She felt hurt but did not want to overreact, so she looked away toward the roofs of the mill buildings as they rose above the treed slough bank, before crossing her arms.

"Emma, Emma." Andrew gently gathered her wrists. His warmth on her bare skin sent tingles up her arms. He moved nearer, his voice soft. "Yes, of course, I know you care. You of all women understand, and I misspoke. I only meant that, well, perhaps?" He sighed. "Perhaps we have other things to talk about. To learn about each other." He looked embarrassed. "You know what I mean?" He looked into her eyes, and then to her lips and away again.

Emma nodded and felt her cheeks warm. Her stomach danced in anticipation. "Yes. Yes."

He released her wrists, although Emma wished he hadn't, and they walked the remaining blocks.

"This way, perhaps?" Emma led him to her usual spot at the riverbank.

"I have a confession." Andrew took her hand and pulled her to him. "I've watched you here. Um, on my way fishing. Honest. Mostly I have left you alone in your privacy. But I would be lying if I didn't tell you I too have sometimes stared longer than was perhaps proper." He looked at her sheepishly. He gently picked off white fibers shed by the cottonwood trees towering above them from her hair.

"Oh." Emma's heart flipflopped in her chest. She was surprised, delighted, and a bit embarrassed. For after all, what other young woman wasted such time staring out at the river?

She pulled him to the edge of the Columbia River. They peered out, ignoring the low din of paper machines still operating into the evening. Opposite them, Mount Hood towered, its white gleaming with the last light of the day, although less snowy than during winter.

Emma felt emboldened. "I like to sit here." She tapped a large boulder with the tip of her boot. "Or perhaps you know that?" She gave a sassy smile.

He shook his head and laughed as they climbed up on the boulder and sat close but not touching.

"I'd like to know more, please. About the mill." Emma moved closer to him, feeling his warmth through their clothing.

Andrew smiled and wiggled his body a bit closer to her. "We have a couple of new workers who are secretly talking about organizing. Really organizing throughout the mill. I would be lying if I did not say it made me nervous. But I am also excited. I mean, imagine what we might do to make things better?" He stroked Emma's wrist. "I know you do understand all that. And, Emma?" He caressed her hand gently. "There is talk about a strike soon. If it happens, I plan to be part of all that. A real part. I need to be." He looked deeply into her eyes.

Emma gripped his hand tightly and held her breath. She knew he was asking her approval to involve himself in controversy. If not now, sometime. "Yes. Of course. Thank you for telling me." She looked at her feet and then back at him. "And I do too. I want to be part of it all. I too need to be part." She inhaled deeply, then slowly released her breath. "Including the strike, if it comes to that." She knew many men would dismiss this request.

"Yes, of course. Yes, dear Emma." He caressed his thumb along the top of her hand.

While Emma remained interested in mill and labor news, she did want to talk about other things. Having a suitor was new to her. She wished she could talk freely with Martha. Yet, one question would not leave her.

"Have you heard where Cassie has moved to? She let me know she was leaving Camas, but I haven't heard anything since?" Elizabeth too had stopped working at the bag factory shortly after marrying. She occasionally saw her at church, although she was busy now with a little one and volunteering with her mother at women's society and aid events.

"I am not sure either," Andrew said. "There are rumors she and her sister moved to Seattle. Someone told me he believed she might be working with the American Federation of Labor, although it might simply be a story." He shrugged.

"Oh my." Emma was surprised. Although she missed this mentor of hers, she hoped it was true and not a rumor. Cassie had a drive that deserved to be part of something bigger.

Emma put her sweater beside her on the rock, having removed it during their walk. She felt emboldened. Downriver the sun dipped behind the mountains, leaving an orange glow on the rippling water.

"Have you watched me on this rock before?" She made a pretend frown, although she was certain her eyes sparkled.

"Uh, what do you mean?" he asked, dropping her hand and fidgeting.

"Oh, nothing." Emma bent to untie her boots. She could not imagine what her mother would say if she knew. She removed her boots and pulled down her stockings, making sure to cover most of her legs with her cotton skirt. Her face felt hot as she stepped off the rock barefooted, holding her skirt above her ankles. She stopped and looked straight into Andrew's eyes.

"Emma," he said, looking astonished and then let out a belly laugh.

Emma giggled. "Shush." She looked toward town, at least half a mile away. "What will they all think?"

"Yes. First a mill worker and now baring your feet with a man in the Columbia River." Andrew laughed softly and Emma joined in. She gingerly stepped over the stones, her feet tender from wearing shoes all winter. Then she waded into the first few inches of water. "It's chilly." She held her skirt a bit higher, looked back and beamed.

"Andrew Brown. Are you sure you are ready for such a wild woman?" She giggled nervously.

He climbed off the rock, and although he kept his boots on, squatted closer to the water's edge. "Oh yes. Oh yes, dear Emma."


AS NAUSEATED AS her stomach felt now as she lay on the bed, Emma giggled at that very first evening together. Although she knew Martha might be eager to know more, she kept it to herself, even the quiet peck of a kiss. She awaited the proper time to share news of their engagement one month later. That memory, like the one of their overnight after the wedding were two recollections she loved to remember in detail when she had time to ponder the joys of her life. These two years later, she smiled in her reminiscing as if a secret, their special times together near the river, beginning with that first evening.

Best of all was how much she loved Andrew. Different than the love she believed others had. Her husband valued her opinion and listened to her ideas as a partner.

She carefully turned to her side to view the clock on her nightstand. She removed a wooden trinket from the table and held it tightly in her hand and closed her eyes as she remembered back.

After their simple church wedding, Andrew surprised her with an overnight steamship voyage to Astoria in celebration, first, making their way to the docks of Portland to catch the ship. Father even encouraged Mother to sew her a special dress, a soft rose fabric with showy bodice ruffles and a gathered skirt. Emma had never shared with anyone about that first time they made love in a simple hotel room in Astoria at the confluence of the Columbia River and Pacific Ocean. And too, she saw the ocean.

The T.J. Potter Steamship was more elegant than anything she might have imagined, her mouth agape as she admired its grand winding stairwells and glass chandelier. Andrew surprised her with a special meal and her first glass of wine in the luxury of the ship's dining room. On their return trip, as she looked out into the current while nestled within Andrew's arm, he placed a wooden steamboat into her hand. She peered at its simplicity, dabs of white paint marking windows, and the black of the sternwheeler. As the steamship headed upriver, she held it tightly between both hands and kissed Andrew deeply. She no longer cared what people might think about their love.

Andrew actively supported the efforts to establish a union at the mill, and she participated in the conversations as often as she could. No longer was it only about pay, as they demanded better working hours and safer conditions. Emma was proud of him.

Emma heard the front door open and softly close. She placed the steamboat gently on the table, knowing she too should arise but awaited his footsteps.

Andrew peeked into their bedroom. "Are you alright?"

"Oh, you are home." Emma forced herself to sit up, smiling broadly. She had to believe this second time would be a charm. For all the nausea she felt, she pulled herself out of bed and padded to him in her stockings. "Yes, I am good. And, I have news. Wonderful news." She dropped her eyes to her stomach and looked up at him shyly.

Andrew smiled and pulled her to him. "Oh, Emma. Oh, my dear, lovely Emma." He gently rocked her into his body.

"Yes. Perhaps after supper we can stroll to our spot."

He kissed her gently on her cheek.

# Chapter 22
## Celia
### February 1, 2025

"HOW ABOUT I walk you home?" Paul asked. "I mean, it's dark and getting late."

Celia knew she couldn't repeat this silly charade. "You know. I appreciate this but I don't need you or anyone else to keep me safe."

Paul winced. "Sorry." He touched her arm.

"I mean I appreciate it. You just must know, I've been around some men who act like . . . well, like asses. In all kinds of ways. I'm jaded, and I do appreciate your kindness." She smiled and shrugged.

She had much to say about herself and to understand about Paul. She had ignored his first text, inviting her to go for a walk. Later she let a call from him go to voicemail, debating whether it was simpler to ignore their future possibilities together. Yet after listening to his message, she felt bad. And here they were.

"Of course." Paul kept his eyes on the ground.

"Well, it's fine." Celia felt exasperated and tugged at the hem of her jacket. "Just so you know, I'm fine alone if you need to get going. But sure, it's okay too if you want to walk with me. I just don't want you to feel like you must."

She had failed in her attempts to stay away, to simplify her life. Now, after two hours of walking together she found him again genuine and kind as she shared her tougher life stories. He didn't laugh or tell her what to do. He raised his eyebrows once as she complained about her mom, and then put his hand on her arm, leaving it there as she continued to talk. Paul excelled at listening. When she described details about the boat accident, he gasped and grabbed her hand. She wasn't sure how to react to his sensitivity. While she was touched at his ability to care so much, his atypical response made her uncomfortable too. Here she was saying she hated macho attitudes of men who didn't always give a shit, and yet why did she react this way?

They arrived at her apartment, and she was glad Sophia was at her girlfriend's place. The walk happened spontaneously when Celia returned his call, and she smiled, knowing Sophia would be disappointed not to have been privy to knowing ahead of time about his visit. They stood at the entrance to the apartment building and Paul looked at her nervously.

"Do you want to come inside? For a cup of tea. Or something. I even have cookies." Celia stopped, wondering if he didn't eat sugar either. "Or just water?"

Paul rocked on his feet. "You know, I like you. I really do." He gave her a slow, sad smile. "But, as I said, I'm not really a guy to get involved. Not now. Or maybe ever." He shoved his hands in his front jean pockets.

*It was easier to let him go.* Yet, Celia felt compassion toward Paul. Too, she wanted more time to talk freely in a way she rarely felt with anyone. She did not feel judged, and was relieved after telling him details and her own fears about the accident and inquiry that she hadn't yet shared with anyone. Paul listened but neither prodded for more nor told her what to do. Sophia had insisted she speak to a counselor, going on about the damage trauma caused. Yes, Celia knew about that but asked her then to leave it alone. They had gotten close, but Sophia exhausted Celia when laying out too many solutions to problems. Celia knew she should deal directly with the pain and anxiety she still held about Ed and the team. But it was her business. Yes, Paul was the only one to make her feel completely heard.

Celia pursed her lips. She didn't want him to leave. "It's okay. We can just be friends. Why don't you come in for tea. I'd like you to. I mean, you need a friend, right? We all do, I guess." She felt dorky. Her, of all people, talking about the power of friendship. She emitted a laugh.

Paul stopped shifting his body. "What's funny?"

"Oh, something just reminded me of my mom. Again." She rolled her eyes. "Will you please come in?"

"Yes. Of course. Yes." He straightened as Celia entered the security code and followed her up to her apartment.

"Do you live in an apartment. Or a house?" Celia asked as she opened the door to her unit. She needed small talk to dig them out of their emotional turmoil.

"Oh, yeah. I rent a tiny place, a house, across town. Well, the upper level. But easy walking distance. Luckily, I'm able to afford my rent . . . it'd be hard for me to have a roommate." Paul's voice was steady but quiet.

Celia led him into the kitchen, filled the tea kettle, and put it on the stove. "I have peppermint or ginger tea. Well, and black too." Sophia was the one who kept tea on hand.

"Ginger, thanks." Paul moved around the kitchen and looked out the window into the half full parking lot. He touched the dishtowel hanging on the oven handle and gently fingered its lace edging. Most of the decorative touches in their apartment were because of Sophia. How stark it might all look if she lived alone? Or might she be challenged to liven things up? Although in nature she seemed to take in all the details, many other times she wasn't very observant.

Celia placed tea bags into the mugs, poured steaming water over them, and carried the mugs to the kitchen table. She grabbed an opened package of Oreos from the cupboard, placed it in the middle of the table, grabbed one first, and dipped it in her tea.

"Interesting combination." Paul laughed and pulled a cookie out of the bag. He twisted it apart and took a bite of the middle filling. "Cheers!" He dipped the half into his tea. "I don't know the last time I had one of these, but they remind me of when I was a kid." He took a bite and chewed contemplatively. "For a while Mom put two in my lunches. Then a couple kids started stealing them in middle school, and I told her I didn't like them anymore, even though I did." He took another bite. "They are good." He looked across the room.

Celia loved how easily they were able to talk about real life stuff, rather than continue only in frivolity. While an intimate relationship might be powerful, it scared her too at how honest you might have to be. Honesty evaded her earlier intimate relationships. As they sipped their tea, it neared ten o'clock, and she was scheduled to open the restaurant in the morning. Yet she was curious about his past and even more attracted to him than before.

"Paul." She bit her lip. "I mean, surely you've had a girlfriend before?" She stopped. "Or a boyfriend? I mean, you're so, well, good to look at." She put her hands to her face. "And kind, of course." What an idiot she was. "Oh, I'm sorry. You didn't want to talk about it."

Paul swallowed. "God. Um, nobody has ever said that to me. I mean outright. Well, besides my mom. She told me all kinds of things about how good I was, some it took me a long time to believe." He placed his cup on the table and rubbed his hands on his jeans.

Celia smiled. "Well?"

"I dated a bit when I was in my early twenties. I felt like I had to. Back then, some people were sure I was gay. Which I'm not." He sat up straighter. "Then I thought maybe I was, you know, asexual, or whatever. But that didn't seem right. I mean I do have feelings." He glanced at her and then at his lap. Celia nodded. "There were two girls. Well, women, really. It was only later I understood they took me on almost as a, well, a project? They didn't work out." He smiled, but his eyes were teary. "I guess you could say I decided the pain of all of that was not worth it, and I'd find other ways to pursue happiness."

He looked as if he had more to say, and she gently touched his arm. The few times they had touched that evening he had not pulled back.

"Celia." Paul's voice was very quiet, and he did not hold her gaze, instead looking down at his cup. "I've only had sex twice. I'm thirty-four years old. And it wasn't a good experience. The woman was mean to me after. And, you know. I'm just different. I'm not like other guys no matter what I may look like. I've never been like them." He put his napkin on the table, stood, and walked to the adjacent living room window. He peered out and rubbed his temples.

Celia let out a deep breath and didn't know what to say or do. She worried he would shrink from her touch. He turned and walked back into the kitchen but remained standing. "No, don't feel bad for me. I have a few friends that get me. Well, they don't know everything but they're good at trying to understand and accept me. And I have a job that makes me feel good. I'm a good caregiver for the animals, my boss supports me, and I believe there's a place for me in trying to make our environment better. I've got all that." He straightened. "And it's enough." He smiled shyly.

Celia looked at her phone and wished she didn't care about the time.

"I should get going, anyway. I know you have an early day tomorrow. And it's been a lot. But nice." Paul tossed his head back and forth, as if knocking something loose, then shrugged. He put out his open hands as question marks.

Celia nodded and carried their cups to the sink.

Paul closed the bag of cookies and handed it to her. "Those were great." He tried to make a goofy smile that only looked sad.

He pulled on his jacket, and Celia followed him to the door. She wanted him to stay but tried to shake it off.

"So, maybe we can go on another walk sometime?" Paul asked.

Celia stared at him. "Don't be upset or frightened. Just one thing."

She leaned in and gave him a gentle kiss on the lips. It was short and sweet, and she restrained herself from offering more. As she pulled away, Paul's initial surprise dissolved into relief. And something more.

"You know. I can open the restaurant in my sleep." Celia took a breath and released it slowly. She reached out her hands, and he clasped them gently. "Why don't you stay? Whatever you want or don't want is fine. We can just be near each other, I promise. If that's what you want."

Paul squirmed but then nodded. He dropped her hands and hugged her gently like a good friend. He held her close, and Celia felt the steady beating of his heart. She gently took his hand and pulled him toward her bedroom. He followed her into the room without pulling back. Paul sat on her bed, watching Celia remove her shoes and socks, jeans and sweatshirt, before standing near him in her t-shirt and panties. She sat back next to him and kissed him, longer this time, but not touching him with her body. She was relieved when he kissed her back and pulled her again, this time close to his chest. They held each other for several minutes.

"I'm going to go in the bathroom and brush my teeth and pee. I'll be right back. Then I'll lie down, and I want you to do whatever feels best to you." Celia avoided his eyes and left the room.

As she sat on the toilet, she wished her first time had been with someone who had treated her as she was trying to do with him. Even if it wasn't his first time.

"There's an extra toothbrush on the counter, if you want," she said upon returning to her bedroom. Paul was still sitting on the bed, although his shoes and socks were arranged neatly near the wall.

Celia set her phone alarm for six a.m., put it on her nightstand, and climbed under her sheets. She heard the toilet flush and then water running and smelled a neighbor's pizza. She watched Paul as he returned to her room and closed the door. Light from outside trickled in through the half-opened blinds, outlining him as he took off his jeans and moved toward her wearing only his t-shirt. Celia moved over in her double bed, and Paul sat up in the open warmed space next to her. He looked down at her and then bent over to kiss her quickly. He traced the features of her face, her lips, and nose, his hands moving to her ears. He followed her neck and touched her braless nipples through the outside of her shirt. As he pulled closer to her, Celia felt he was hard.

"I want to do this, but please help me. I mean, I want it to be right for you. And for me." Paul put his head down on her chest.

She gently rubbed his head; his thick black hair on the pillow. She tucked some behind an ear and traced the lobe. "Yes. Of course." She pulled him up to her and rubbed circles behind his shoulders and lower back. She pulled back and looked at his face, fingering his cheeks through his beard. She kissed him again as his hands gently touched her breasts. He pulled her to him tightly. She knew that together they would find their way into and through the night.

As if afraid to push the other past their comfort level, they lay quietly, their clasps on each other loosening. At first Celia thought Paul had fallen asleep. She quietly kissed him on the cheek. The room was darker, and she saw him in its shadows. Paul opened his eyes. She realized he too had been awake. He kissed her with a new sense of urgency, and his hands explored her hair, back, breasts, and butt, pulling her to him.

"Yes," he said simply. "Yes."

She guided him to her, unconcerned in the moment to her own feelings of pleasure but wanting Paul to feel good.

"Do I need to, you know? I mean, are we okay?" He made an effort to pull back, but his body seemed fused to hers.

"Yes, yes. Yes, yes. We are good." Their previous minutes of gentle caressing rebounded in an urgency they both felt as finally he entered her.

"Oh God, Celia!" Paul called out in a voice louder and more confident than any she had heard him utter before.

"Oh, Paul," Celia whispered into his ear as she pulled him tightly, finding herself fully present in only the moment.

# Chapter 23
## Celia
### February 17, 2025

CELIA DASHED TO grab her phone as it rang in the other room. She normally might have ignored it but was curious about the two missed calls she received from an unrecognized number.

"Hello?" She put the phone on speaker and carried it with her to the bathroom to continue scrubbing black scum out of the sink. She was trying to become a more dependable roommate now that she and Sophia were better friends. She knew she'd slacked off on apartment responsibilities, especially cleaning showers, sinks, and toilets. With more time than Sophia, she was trying to become both a better person and roommate.

"Hello?" she repeated.

"Oh yes, hi, Celia. Thanks for picking up." Celia recognized the voice. "This is Trevor. You know. Trevor?" He laughed. "I would have texted, but I don't know . . . but, well, I wanted to get you on the phone." The words came out in a rush, sounding tentative rather than assertive.

"Hi, Trevor. Sorry, I didn't recognize your number. Um, how are you?" Celia didn't know what to say. It had been two months since the boat accident. She had told herself to move on, but she still occasionally had horrible nightmares about being lost at sea. She had even woken up once wrapped in her covers sweaty and panting, and she had to step out on their deck to breathe normally again. She had only mentioned the nightmares to Paul. Although she hadn't even told Paul, not yet, how this was the first time she'd had nightmares since the ones begun after seeing him and the dead man on the street.

"Yeah, I'm doing fine. I have a decent job on another boat. Fishing for salmon and soon halibut. It's working out." Trevor hesitated. "Of course, we'll see. Hard to tell, you know how it is." She could hear voices in the background and wondered if he was at the wharf.

Celia wanted to know what was on his mind and why he called, but she had to first ask a question that had haunted her. "How is Justin doing?" She sat on the closed toilet and dropped the sponge in the sink, needing her complete focus. She dreaded learning any bad news, even though he had sounded fine when they had last spoken.

"I think he's okay. He seems to be doing good." Trevor appeared to have little more to say, and she wondered if he was talking to someone and holding his hand over the phone. "Oh, sorry. So, hey, we were wondering if you wanted to meet us for a beer tonight? Justin and me. We're planning to hang out and wanted to see what you're doing? It'd be nice, you know? Like old times?" He forced a laugh.

This tentative voice did not sound like the Trevor she knew, and never had they met up for a beer before. The Trevor she knew was full of confident commands and loud jokes, gratefully, funny rather than obnoxious. She was stunned to have the two of them invite her out and knew the old Celia would have made up an excuse.

"Okay," she answered. "What time and where?"


CELIA APPREHENSIVELY ENTERED the pub that evening.

"Hey, Celia!" Trevor called to her from above the hum of the bar, motioning to his table.

She was a few minutes late and glad the two guys were already sipping beer. "It's on me, what do you want?" Justin asked as she neared the table.

"Oh no, that's okay. I'm good. Hey, Justin." He returned her smile, nodded, and put his hand out.

Neither of the two were ones to hug, and shaking hands seemed plain weird so she lightly punched his bicep in response. "Give me a sec," she said, heading to the bar.

When she returned to the table with her pint of Fort George, Trevor and Justin were talking about when halibut season might open. They stopped as she sat on the open stool between them and sipped their beers while eyeing her. She didn't go out for drinks much these days, and she looked around the room. Astoria had become rather hip, although she was glad for the owners to see places like this fill up on a weeknight. Around her were small round tables and stools, about half of them occupied. The cliental were all about her age or younger, and a couple were throwing darts at a target in the corner. The place was louder than her usual café hangouts.

"So, it's great to hear you're doing okay," Trevor began, talking above the noise.

"Yeah, you too," Celia said. The air around them felt tentative and uncomfortable.

They continued to slowly sip their drinks.

"Well, Justin wanted to . . ." Travis began and nodded at Justin.

Justin set his half full beer on the table. "Yeah, I mean I wanted to thank you, really. Like I realize now. I mean, you kind of saved my life. Like, I didn't get it at first really."

Celia looked at him in surprise. She set her glass on the table and put her hands in her lap.

Justin looked near tears. "I didn't get it at first, you know." His voice cracked. "I guess I didn't want to admit that I could have drowned. I might have died. I told myself it just seemed like we did what we should do, no big deal. But, well, Natalie and I have been talking. Oh, we're getting married next summer." He broke into a smile as he threw his arms back as if finishing a big task. "But, really. Thanks for being strong and there and all that."

Celia felt touched in a way she never had before, to be openly recognized for something that was simply the right thing to do. "Wow. Yes. I mean, thanks. Thanks for letting me know." She wiped her eyes on her sleeve and stopped herself before saying it wasn't a big deal. She needed to stop minimizing who she was and what she did. She'd been reading a self-help book Sophia got her for Christmas. Most of it was stupid, but she recognized a couple of things that made her look at herself differently. She had talked about it all with Paul.

The silence grew again.

"Yeah. Um, we two." Trevor pointed at himself and Justin. "We were talking about how sometimes we treated you shitty. We didn't mean it, like it was kind of as if you were our big sister. But even then . . ." He shrugged and took another drink.

"Thanks." Celia looked from one to the other. "So, is everything okay with you?" She focused on Justin. "I mean, you know after being in the water and probably hypothermic?" She had heard about hypothermia leading to kidney or other organ damage, even though she had told herself he was young and tough.

Trevor laughed. "He's a kid, remember?" He put Justin in a brotherly headlock. "He could probably withstand anything."

Trevor let go of Justin but jabbed him in the ribs before taking another draw of his beer. It seemed the two had gotten closer. They did act like brothers, and Celia laughed with relief.

"Yeah, I'm mostly good. I got some money toward the season from Ed. I mean we all did I think?" Justin raised his eyebrows. "And then, well, my medical and even some time off work was covered or paid for by you know that worker comp thing. It was kind of a hassle to figure out as it wasn't with the state, but my mom helped. She knows bureaucratic shit like that." He frowned in disgust and took a drink from his glass.

"Oh, and Celia," Trevor said. "Last week Ed told me he found an owner for the boat. You wouldn't guess it, but he sounded relieved. He actually told me how he and his wife are planning a vacation to visit their grandkids later this month. He also told me to be sure and tell you." He raised his clenched fist as if claiming victory.

Relief flooded Celia, and she sat up straighter. "Wow. I mean, that's great." Apparently, there was a life after, even when what he thought of as his dream exploded. She was glad neither of them asked what she was up to. It was hard to explain.

Two guys across the room were playing pool but the dart players had left, and the bar seemed quieter than before. Even if it was Justin's girlfriend who encouraged they meet up, Celia appreciated it. She felt bolder, sharing what they all had together.

"Hey, this may sound weird. But, well, do you have dreams, nightmares really, about the accident? And, I mean, do you still think about it all?" She felt silly as her words escaped and jammed her hands into her fleece jacket pockets.

"Oh yeah. I think we both do." Trevor looked at Justin who nodded. "I was talking to a buddy's wife who is one of those therapists. I mean I didn't make an appointment or anything. But we were just shooting the shit at their house over the holidays. She said it would be expected but that talking about it might be helpful."

"Yeah." Celia quickly inhaled, then let her breath slowly seep out. "I get these nightmares still sometimes. And I still feel like I could have prevented the whole thing. You know, if I had called Ed out?"

Trevor took a final sip of his beer and quietly belched. "Sorry." He shook his head. "Yeah, I feel that too. I wished I hadn't told you to leave Ed alone. But, I mean, what's done is done. I guess we both have to forgive ourselves, at least that's what my mom said. And bigger than that,

Ed was going to do what he did. I bet had either of us walked off the boat he still would have gone out, he could be such a stubborn ass. But a good stubborn ass."

Trevor and Justin drained their glasses, and while she knew they'd normally grab another pint, this conversation seemed to be enough. Just enough. She took another sip of hers and pushed the not yet finished pint away and stood up.

Trevor and Justin also stood.

"Thanks for calling," she said to Trevor. "So good to see you both."

Justin nodded, and Trevor said, "Yeah."

He punched her arm, and she grabbed him in a hug before heading out the door into a brighter evening.

# Chapter 24
## Emma
### January 8, 1919

EMMA'S EYE SOCKETS felt permanently deformed, red, and swollen. The funeral made it real, even if she felt she was living in a haze. She knew she had to pretend to be strong for her father and the children. Nearly as great as her sadness in Mother's absence, were the regrets she held. Regrets she knew it was too late to ever do anything about. Too late to let Mother know she was sorry she had disappointed her. Greatest of all was the inability for her mother to accept Emma for who she was. All of that, now an impossibility.

"The children are in bed," she said to her father. "They have said their prayers and should be falling asleep."

Father sat in his worn leather chair, staring into the fire in the front room. He nodded slightly but did not look at her. He had aged years in the past month. She knew he was trying to be strong for the children, and he was worn out by the end of the day. Only sleep would recover him enough to repeat the process, over and over. Emma wondered if he dreamt about Mother.

It was past time for Emma to return to her own home and away from her father's quiet sadness, but she had to help him mind her siblings and manage the home. He had to continue to work, or they would have no hope for a future. Earlier that evening when Mary was asleep, Helen softly called to her.

Emma sat on Helen's bed, careful not to disrupt the cozy nest of quilts surrounding her. Helen was now seventeen and old enough to understand the permanency of their loss. Like Emma, she needed to be both sister and mother now. John slept in a hastily built added-on room to create more space for the growing children.

"Yes." She stroked Helen's forehead and pushed back locks of hair away from her eyes. "I am here. Even when I am at my house, my heart is with you."

"Emma," Helen said, pulling back her sobs. "How can . . . ? How can God who is so great allow this to happen?"

Emma sighed and took Helen's hand in both of hers. How could she answer this question when she asked the same thing over and over? She had prayed about it, trying to find her own way to move past the grief she felt.

"I guess it is something bigger than we can understand." Emma had begun to question what merciful god would allow children to be motherless, ever. Little Mary had only just turned ten. She knew she could not say this aloud. "Perhaps we should recite the Lord's Prayer together." Helen curled into her, as if a small girl, and they recited the words they had repeated for as long as they could speak. After, Emma caressed Helen's forehead until she heard the sweet breaths of sleep overtake her.

And now after getting her sister to sleep, she could finally head home. Father had nodded off in his chair, and she knew any moment he'd slip off to bed. If she did not have her life with Andrew, she did not know how she would move on. So much that might have before excited her melted away, unimportant now. And worse, Father was plagued by others knowing someone had suffered a death from influenza within the walls of his home.

At first, as news of the Spanish Flu grabbed headlines in the *Oregonian* and other papers delivered to Camas, her town ignored it as something that could not touch them. Safe in their small town away from hordes of city dwellers. Men at the mill joked about how they heard Portland and Vancouver health officials overreact, mandating school and public meeting closures for several weeks. City businesses even had to follow rules to relieve crowding and improve ventilation. Worse was news that red and white placards were posted outside homes where residents suffered from the sickness.

The Camas Mill continued production to meet wartime demands, workers believing they would escape the illness. Financial fears escalated, not enough men to do essential work with many drafted to serve in the war across the ocean. It was all worrisome enough. Emma continued to devote her time to running their home but also doing what she could to support Andrew's efforts to organize. On top of the grief and fear about the flu, she and Andrew were all too aware of the strikes and violent raids against labor radicals. She didn't know what she felt about it all. She believed in making work better but the violence frightened her. Andrew had told her about the six people killed in Centralia, not even that far away, when the American Legion and Workers of the World confronted each other. She shuddered to think about any of that coming to Camas.

Then Mother had taken ill. Emma tried to figure out how she had gotten the influenza, but Father shushed her. He warned her not to let anyone know. "She is strong and will be well soon." He didn't seem convinced by his own words. "Yes, before you know it." Emma knew Mother had not been strong before the illness, seeming tired for years. Father also insisted the children stay away from her, spending time in Emma's home when not in school. "She'll be better before you know it," he repeated, although new worry lines were visible on his face, and he wore his lips tightly pursed. Even then, none of them believed Mother would die, and it was miraculous no other family members became ill. Later, Emma recognized Father had symptoms early on, but they moved through him quickly. Too, he likely felt he had no option to complain or rest.

Emma quietly put on her jacket and gathered her things into her bag. Father stirred in his chair, opened his eyes, and stared into the dying fire.

"Can I get you anything? Before I go?" Emma asked.

She had made supper earlier, but she doubted he ate much. She did not know what to say anymore.

Stoically, he shook his head. She knew he wanted to be helpful, not wanting her to carry a heavy load. But it was as if a new person had invaded his body. She was grateful neighbors and friends from church continued to drop off meals, though she knew Mother's death left a stigma. She wondered if some felt those infected with the influenza had done something wrong, or maybe even that God felt they deserved it.

Emma hoped Martha might stop by, but her sister was fearful about contracting the illness, insisting on keeping her family away. Their last conversation upset Emma.

"Emma. You must move back in for now with Father and the children. It would be easy for you, just across town. Besides, Andrew would be at work all those days."

"Martha. I too am a married woman with a life of my own. I am committed to my husband, and to things at the mill." Emma had clenched her fists and raised her voice.

Martha continued prattling on, pointing at her and reminding her how she had no children of her own to tend to. "You owe it to the family.

Think of all those years you gave your time to the mill rather than to Mother." She glowered at her, shaking her head.

Emma had never felt so alone after that. She turned her face away, drying her eyes with her sleeve. She could not believe even Martha could be so thoughtless. Soon after the argument, Martha left to return home, and Emma never again brought up her hope for Martha to help go through Mother's things. The next time she saw Martha, it was as if their disagreement never happened, although Martha primarily paid attention to Father and the children.

Now, Emma took a deep breath. "Then, with the children down, I'll be leaving. I will not be over tomorrow, but of course the children are welcome to visit after school. They are always invited to our home, Father."

She stifled a yawn. Father glanced at her and nodded. She was certain he would never disagree again with anything she asked. Back before, Mother would have protested Emma going out alone at night but lost that battle long ago. Now, Father showed up each day to go to work because he must and pretended to be alright so the community would not feel sorry for him. He had not even sent word by post to William, instead, waiting until the day he returned from war to learn the sad news.

Emma slipped out into the early evening where bits of dappled daylight hugged the western sky. The air emanated the musky smell of decomposing leaves and woodsmoke. She might have left her heavy coat at home as the winter evening was milder than normal. It seemed wrong for the night to be beautiful when all else was tragic.

She walked along the gravel to the home she shared with Andrew. Although still in Oak Park, it was a bit closer to the Columbia River than her childhood home. Even tonight she craved this powerful Columbia; it kept going—even when pelted by wind and rain, or storms that knocked out ships and drowned people. It was the only thing that always brought her hope.

Emma arrived at her special place. She thought about the number of times she had come here with Martha or the children, watching rafts loaded with mounds of logs headed to a mill, or steamships moving onward to Hood River or Vancouver. It saddened her to have never stood on the shore with Mother. She looked out, straining to peer as far west as she could. She tried to pray. Where was the goodness of the benevolent

God? She felt she had hit a fork in a road, unless it was simply the road's end.

She crouched by the water's edge, her skirt billowing around her. She had unbuttoned her coat and let it hang loosely. She could see lights of a ship passing and wondered where it was going and who was on board, or if it carried only freight. Back on land she saw a figure nearing her. She smiled and waved; only one person would be out on a January evening at this spot.

Andrew approached and pulled her into his arms. "My darling. My strong one. It is alright to mourn."

Emma looked up at him, nodded, and leaned into his chest. He released his grip and wiped the tears from her cheek before pulling her closer. They stood there together for several minutes, as the bits of twilight faded.

Then he grabbed her hand. "Let us go home, my love."

# Chapter 25
## Celia
### March 21, 2025

CELIA HAD TO learn more. It was a Saturday morning and three months since she had spoken with the old woman, Alice.

"Hi, Barbara?" Celia was grateful she remembered Alice's daughter's name. "This is Celia, uh, I met you when I came to visit your mother. Just before Christmas?" She wasn't sure if a call would work. Alice had fiddled with her hearing aid during their visit, and it had been essential for Celia to speak loudly even in person.

"Are you kidding?" Barbara laughed. "My mother lives for the phone. Seriously. I guess we're lucky she can talk and hear okay, or I'd don't know what I'd do. I did amplify her receiver, one of those gadgets she can press, if she remembers."

Celia relaxed into her chair.

"Anyway, I warn you," Barbara continued, surprising Celia with sudden chattiness. "Before you know it, you'll be her best friend. To protect everyone, I've refused to put phone numbers on speed dial." She laughed, then sighed. "I know it's mean but that way she can't call any time day or night." She sounded like a different woman than the harried one she had met weeks before.

Celia clicked on her phone speaker and stood up to rummage in the fridge for yogurt. She hadn't timed the call as well as she thought and needed to eat something before work.

"So, did you want to talk to her, or did you need something else?" Barbara asked, now impatient.

"Yeah, if that's okay?" Celia moved closer to her phone. "That'd be super." *Super? When did she ever use that silly word?* She grabbed a spoon from the dish rack.

"Hang on, you're in luck. She's doing her morning crossword puzzle. Well, between you and me, her attempt. She doesn't seem to ever get very far but she seems to enjoy it. Hang on."

Celia could hear Barbara telling her mom to pick up the phone, a handset she remembered seeing next to Alice's chair. She sat at her kitchen table and took advantage of the delay by shoving a few bites of blueberry yogurt into her mouth.

"Hello?" Celia heard Alice's voice followed by a click on the line.

Celia swallowed her mouthful. She re-introduced herself and asked Alice if she had a few minutes to chat. "I don't know if you remember me?" She put her mouth close to her speaker and eyed the time.

"Of course I remember you, darling." Alice giggled, sounding pleased. "And you must have outlandish ideas if you think you'd ever be interrupting anything. These days. How are you darling?"

Celia preferred texting to frivolous chatty calls. As awkward as it felt, though, it beat driving back to Salem. She turned off her speaker and held the phone to her ear. "Do you remember what we were talking about the time I visited you? About that woman, named Emma? Uh, the one you said was related to my grandmother?"

The phone line was silent for what felt like a long time. Celia tapped her fingers on the table.

"Of course, I remember," Alice exclaimed. "Trust me, darling. That was about the most exciting thing that happened to me. I mean your visit. Maybe you can come again?"

Celia felt guilty and shifted in her chair.

"Far better than the doctor visit my daughter shuttles me off to. Even if the young man is handsome, merely a boy really," she continued. "Still doesn't make any of that prodding worth it. Oh, I think I have another visit soon. The things they tell us to do as if they think we should live to a hundred."

Celia closed her eyes and sighed, knowing she should have prepared herself for this disorganized stream of words. "Alice. Can you tell me something more? About Emma, I mean?"

"Oh, Emma. Yes, Emma. Hmm."

Celia put her spoon on the table and clasped her hands, trying to become comfortable with the silence. Between Alice and Paul, her lesson plan from the universe must target patience. Was Alice paying attention to her, daydreaming, or fidgeting with her crossword puzzle?

"Oh yes." Alice stretched out the two words. "Emma and her family lived in that tiny town on the Columbia. I can't remember the name. Yes, her name was Emma. You know, when you get old there's so much that gets stored in this thing."

Celia could see Alice tap her head. If she tried to visualize Alice's gestures the silences were easier.

"Who knows why some things stick and others don't? Trust me, it is mighty frustrating sometimes. Like these things my doctor says, as if I could care to remember. Or when he asks me to count backward or what month it is."

Celia was losing her patience. "So, the town was Camas . . ."

"Oh yes," Alice exclaimed, delighted. "My mother, rest her soul, was friends with your great grandmother. Or maybe great-great? I get confused on all those greats." Celia imagined Alice touching her fingers with each "great." "I think that's why I became friends with your grandmother. Sorry. darling, some of that is fuzzy. How is your grandmother?"

Celia looked at her watch, sighed, and waited. "So, tell me about your mother. And more about Emma." She hated nagging her to get back on track.

"Oh, my mother loved a good story. Like me. I inherited that part of her. Not my father. Such a boring man. Yes, she told the best fairy tales too."

Celia let out an audible sigh and rolled her head back onto her tight shoulders. She put her cell back on speaker and stood up to throw away her yogurt container.

"And she told you stories about Emma?" Celia asked directly into the phone.

"Oh yes. She told me Emma stood up to folks, her and some others. Something like that. Sorry, darling. I don't remember the details I guess." Alice blew her nose. "She was brave, though. That was the important part. I was young and frustrated at what everyone expected of me. Oh, my mother liked that too I think. All until that silly husband I chose." More silence.

How much of this was about Alice's mother rather than Emma, Celia wondered? She headed into her bedroom to get dressed.

"So, do you remember what it was that Emma did? That you admired?" She put her phone back on speaker and replaced her sweatpants with a pair of jeans.

"Oh, my mother, let me tell you. She loved to tell stories. You know, I do really miss her. Sometimes she visits me, late at night." Alice blew her nose again.

"And Emma? What did she do that was so great?" Celia tried again, feeling bad not to comfort Alice about missing her mother.

"Emma? Oh yes, Emma. It was something big, that's all I remember. She probably won some big award, I bet. That would have been something, don't you think?" Celia pictured Alice smiling, but they had reached the end of the line. She finished tying her shoes and sat on her bed, straining to listen.

"Thank you for calling, darling," Alice said abruptly.

Celia stared at the phone, surprised to be dismissed.

"We can chat again sometime. Maybe you could come visit and I'll make cookies. I make the best spice cookies that I'd love to share with you."

After saying goodbye, Celia hurried herself into the bathroom, brushed her hair, and tied it back with a simple hair tie, long enough now without a recent haircut. Her energy dropped, and she wondered how she'd get through working her shift. Sad for the loss of stories, whatever they may have been.


IT WAS A busy day at the café, and Celia did not have a spare moment to regret her morning conversation. The dining room hummed with energy as folks ordered the special—fried eggs, hashbrowns, crisp bacon, and toast—before setting out to the docks and boats. The fewer seasonal out-of-towners tended to tip and were in a good mood. A couple of down and outers sat hovering over their expected bottomless cups of coffee, bags near their feet. They didn't cause problems and always found room at the counter. Occasionally when business was good, Kate gave them a special to accompany the coffee they paid for.

Hours later, Celia reversed the sign in the window from open to closed and turned off the brightest lights before wiping the tables with the bleach mix. Kate had refused bleach products before the pandemic, but now they seemed to be part of the café forever. Celia was grateful for the seasonal reduced hours. Days were lengthening, but darkness still seemed to come earlier than she expected. Kate had learned through the years how to make her restaurant work, and winter dinners were not part of a winning plan.

"Well, that's kind of cool," Kate said as she swept the floor. Her popularity as a boss was bolstered by her completing the same chores as her staff, always taking on more.

Celia raised her eyebrows. "You think? How so?" Over the past few weeks, she had told Kate bits about her information quest. When she had arrived that morning, Kate could tell something was up and wheedled out details of her call with Alice.

"Just that this woman knew of your great-great something. Maybe she did, I guess. I just think stories are cool, and this old lady sounds like a kick. It's cool you even got to meet her, don't you think?"

Kate continued sweeping but Celia stopped wiping a table and sighed. Sometimes Kate was too optimistic for her likes.

"I mean, you already learned about the strike, and so what if someone related to you was part of it or not? It still seemed to make a difference to this woman. This, Alice." Kate set down the broom, marched to Celia, and put her arm around her. "You know, my friend. Not everything in life has to be big news or the big deal."

Celia shrugged, set down the rag, and folded her arms, embarrassed to admit she hadn't thought as much about the limitations women faced back then. She was angry enough about all the crap now pushing women back to ancient times.

"The thing is, I would think even just the story about the all-female strike would resonate with you." Kate leaned on a stool and rested her foot on its rung. "Before I was born, my dad worked in a paper mill. That work is kind of like the fishing industry, don't you think?" Celia stared blankly at her. "You know, most people thinking it to be a manly kind of job, even though women do it. Of course, now, it seems most all of them have been laid off." She shook her head and frowned.

Celia didn't understand where Kate was going with this. She only wanted answers about this Emma but was losing interest in all the homework to figure it out. Her brain didn't work like the librarian Matthew's, challenged to tease facts together. She wanted a simple answer. Matthew told her he would look for Emma's obituary. Celia did not want to admit she was procrastinating asking the most obvious person, her grandmother. She felt Kate's stare and put the rag in the bucket.

"You are somewhere far away," Kate said gently.

Celia nodded and carried the cleaning supplies to the back utility sink behind the kitchen. In the darkened closet she rinsed out the rags and hung them up, put the spray bottle and bucket back on the shelf, and washed her hands. She arched her back and stretched her arms toward the ceiling as she massaged her tight neck muscles. All this seeking was getting her nowhere on her journey to whatever was next for her.

"Hey!" Kate called, appearing with the broom and dustbin. She wiggled her eyebrows up and down, with a mischievous smile. "How about a glass of wine?" She danced a quick two step, flapping her hands to the side like a dork.

"What?" Celia asked, screwing up her face.

The café didn't serve alcohol, not even when they expanded to dinner in the summer. Besides, it was only a few minutes after three in the afternoon. She was raised by a mother who claimed you had to officially wait until at least five in the late afternoon to begin any form of happy hour. But then it was nearly on the dot. She knew her mother's generation epitomized the meme, "Is it five o'clock yet?" "Since when do you have wine? Here?"

"Oh, a customer gave me a bottle for Christmas, and I keep forgetting to take it home. Hang on and I'll get it. Besides I have a favor to ask." She turned away quickly.

"Buttering me up?" Celia faked a laugh and rolled her eyes. She was determined to put the Emma business out of her head. Nonetheless, she sat at the clean counter. A clatter in the kitchen startled her, and she watched Kate reenter with two small juice glasses, a corkscrew, and a bottle of red wine. She set them on the counter and climbed onto the stool next to Celia.

Celia picked up the corkscrew and raised an eyebrow.

"Well, you never know?" Kate shook her head and smiled wryly. "Before you began, I applied for an alcohol license. A money maker for sure, but it became a hassle." She tore off the plastic at the bottle's top and laughed. "Twist off." She unscrewed the top and half-filled the glasses. "So . . ." She handed Celia a glass. "Cheers." She took a sip. "By the way, how's your friend Paul?"

Celia made a disgusted look and shook her head. "Really?" She scowled. "You're going to get me drunk and hope I talk when I never wanted to tell you in the first place?" She had reluctantly mentioned her overnight with Paul to Kate back when she was late to work the morning after their first night together. "He's good. I mean, he is a good guy. Hard to always figure out, but. Well, I am beginning to get him."

Kate waved her hand, asking for more.

"No, but I mean that's kind of all. I think we'll just be friends." She didn't feel like talking about this private relationship, and the several special nights they'd already spent together. She took a sip, although she wasn't much of a wine drinker. "You said you had a favor. Is it about Paul?"

Kate laughed and shook her head. "No. It's about the kids. Well, Addie. Her third-grade class has a field trip to the Astoria Column coming up. I guess it's an annual trip for that grade, connected to a history lesson or something. Anyway, we need to better support her school and neither of her other parents can be there. She likes you. And, well, since you've got time?" She looked at Celia with fake puppy dog eyes. "I'm not trying to take advantage of you, I promise. It'd be a huge help." She dropped her stare to look at her phone.

"Oh God." Celia sighed and exaggerated shaking her head. "You know, I'm not at my best with kids, especially gangs of them." She knew she owed Kate, given how much she had accommodated her schedule before, and now giving her extra shifts. She took a deep breath, let it out, and then thumped her feet on the floor. "Okay. But just this once."

"Great," Kate said. "I'll text you the details. Oh, and Addie will be thrilled. Really. You were her first pick."

"Whatever." Celia was unable to hide her surprise, and her irritation dissipated. She knew she and Addie had fun together the times she had been invited to their house but never expected an invitation like this.

"Ahem. But, since you were late to work, I guess it should be fair to ask what kept you that morning? Sex on a first date, Celia?" Kate held the bottle to pour more wine, but Celia put her hand over her glass.

"No, that's enough. But thanks. You don't stop, do you?" She pretended to be irritated, but was now touched by Kate taking time out of her busy life to check in. She couldn't figure out their kids' custody schedule and knew that responsibility alone must take up an entire calendar. "Let's just say, Paul hasn't had much experience. I mean on the dating front." She took a sip, wondering how much was fair to Paul to share. After all, everyone seemed to know each other in this town.

"Is that why you say you are only friends? I mean . . . he isn't into a relationship? Or . . ."

"No. I mean, well, him staying over was nice. Really nice." Celia had no intention to talk details about sex with Kate, no matter how good she was to her. She sighed and massaged the back of her neck muscles. "Paul is very different. Perhaps the most sensitive person I've ever met. And that is wonderful. But somehow it feels like a lot of pressure too. We are . . . well. We are very attracted to each other. That's not the thing. We might just be better as friends. For now." She could tell Kate was restraining herself from asking more. "Thanks for asking. Truly." Celia smiled but was relieved both glasses were empty. "I just need to think it through."

Kate nodded. "Just don't overthink it." She clinked her empty glass against Celia's. "Take it from an expert." Then she changed topics, and Celia nodded along. She knew there was more for her and Paul. She just wasn't ready to talk about it.

# Chapter 26
## Celia
### April 10, 2025

AGAINST HER BETTER judgement, Celia agreed to ride the bus with the class and other willing volunteers to the Astoria Column. While she liked Kate's kids, she was oddly intimidated by large groups of children. Her mother would probably tease her, if she knew, about carrying childhood anxiety around cliques of girls all the way into adulthood.

Celia arrived as instructed on time at the school meeting spot. The bus hadn't arrived yet, and most of the backpacked clad kids wore hats and coats although a few hung around in t-shirts even though it was a chilly April. The group seemed to be at that age where many of the boys were smaller than the girls, and a few of the girls looked much more grown up than third graders.

"Hi, Celia. I'm so excited to go up there." Addie's eyes were bright and her cheeks red. Her long sandy brown hair was contained by a brick red knit cap.

She pointed at the top of the hill, although Celia couldn't see the column from where they were. The morning was cool, but luckily clearer than a normal coastal spring morning.

"We get to fly airplanes off the top our teacher says. As long as we walk all the way up." Addie nearly shook with excitement. "I'm a good walker."

Celia was relieved. She'd hate to be stuck with a kid who refused to climb the dozens of steps. She thought of the column as a tourist thing, having climbed up only once when visiting Astoria the first time with her mom. She didn't remember ever doing cool things like this field trip when she was in school, though she may have forgotten happenings from those long-ago days.

"Okay, line up everyone. And remember our agreements," the teacher instructed through a silly looking megaphone. She was young and full of energy, dressed like some of the kids in jeans and tennis shoes, but hatless so her curly dark hair streamed over the shoulders of her rain parka. The kids seemed to listen, although a few bubbled excited words to one another. Celia wasn't sure if the enthusiastic aura was about going to the column, the anticipation of flying airplanes from the top into the whirling breeze, or just escaping school.

Addie grabbed Celia's arm and pulled her close to her small body. "This is my adult," she bragged to another kid.

Celia smiled. She had never been claimed as someone's adult before. "Okay, Addie. Thanks." She bent down and whispered in Addie's ear, "You have to tell me what to do. I don't know about stuff like this."

Addie laughed. "Oh. You're so funny." She pulled Celia's arm as she walked to the just arriving bus.

Celia could not remember the last time she had ridden a school bus. As they waited in a short line to board, a different woman with a clipboard paused next to them.

"And your name?"

Celia felt like an imposter as she nervously gave her name.

The woman smiled. "Just checking. You never can be too careful these days." She rolled her eyes. "Even here."

Celia nodded.

After the kids and adults boarded, the bus climbed the steep hill, its engine laboring and whining louder than any vehicle Celia remembered riding in before. She loved how neatly downtown Astoria was positioned adjacent to the Columbia River, and yet the steep Coxcomb Hill behind it offered a premier viewing spot of the river, ocean, nearby Youngs Bay, and coast mountain range. When she had first moved to town, she would frequently drive up, park, and sit on a bench to look down on all of it, even the days it was mostly socked in. Now, the driver warned the kids to stay in their seats as the bus puffed its way up the windy streets. Many had a hard time containing their excitement and continued to fidget up and down on the bus benches, with only a few quietly looking out a window. One of the older chaperones, perhaps a grandfather, raised his eyebrows at Celia and made a brave face as if they were about to go to battle.

Before Celia knew it, the bus hissed into a pullout at the top of the hill. She was grateful the ride wasn't any longer. While they continued to sit, the teacher with the curly hair reminded them of the agreements they'd made to stay with their group and listen to the adults. Celia's stomach dropped; she hadn't realized she would be responsible for a group. She took a breath to gather her confidence, before standing and following Addie and the kids off the bus.

"Okay everyone," Addie said as their group of five plus Celia stepped off the bus and clustered on the nearby grass. She gestured for them to come close. Just then the teacher approached Celia and handed her a folder.

"Here's some things to share," she said simply.

*Oh Kate, what have I agreed to? You owe me big.*

The teacher walked away from the bus. "Kids, gather." Miraculously, all the kids went to her. "We will be here for ninety minutes—that is one hour and a half. Then we will reload the bus to return to school. Do you all have your snack?"

The passel of kids nodded. Words like banana and cookies and juice passed through the group. The teacher pointed to the air and like magic, most of the kids stopped talking. Celia's mouth dropped open.

"In a minute your team leader will give you directions. Then when they have finished, they will instruct you to gather over there." She nodded at a monument where a woman stood waving at them.

"Okay, everyone." Addie gestured to her group to come close. "This is my friend Celia. And she's great. And you need to listen to her so we all have a good time and maybe she can come with us again." She grabbed Celia's arm and nestled into her. "Celia, this is Henry and Isabelle and David and Georgia. Oh, and you know me." She laughed.

Celia was speechless. How did this child find such self-confidence? "Um, hi, everyone." She pulled a sheet of paper from the folder and shared the three points with the kids, including about letting her know if they had to go to the bathroom.

As Celia put the checklist back into the folder, Addie pointed to the monument. "Okay, kids, over there."

Celia was grateful to have Addie as a co-captain. "Yes, let's stay together and head over to where your teacher told you to gather."

"Hi, everyone," the woman in front of the column said. "My name is Joy, and I work for the City of Astoria Parks Department. I'm excited to have you here today at the famous Astoria Column. Have any of you been here before?"

Some of the kids nodded, and several yelled, "Yes!"

"When do we fly airplanes?" one boy yelled.

Celia noticed how Joy took everything in stride, reminding them gliders would happen, but after they learned more about this spot. "First, does anybody know what this Astoria Column honors?" She pointed to the tall metal column , moving her hand up and down as if tracing its height from the ground to the sky. Muted yellow, blue, and maroon pictures representing people and historical events circled above the gray cement base.

"The ocean and all the ships," one boy with a jacket tied around his waist yelled.

Other kids called out ideas. "Lewis and Clark! Astoria! Salmon!"

Joy nodded. "Yes." She smiled and told them it was to honor all the people who first settled in the area, and the resources provided by the land.

"And the Indians," a girl with two blond ponytails said.

Joy smiled and nodded. "Yes, especially the First Peoples. Make sure you look at the pictures on the outside of the column when you get closer."

Celia frowned, wondering what Indigenous Peoples would really have thought about all this. She knew not everyone shared the same patriotic feelings about development of white settlements in the Pacific Northwest.

Joy pointed out the view of the Pacific Ocean and the Columbia River, and then the mouth of the Columbia River. "Sometimes people call that part of the river the Graveyard of the Pacific. It's why the very biggest boats and barges use river and bar pilots to help them move between the ocean and the river."

A couple of kids repeated the word graveyard and made a silly face, and she smiled.

One kid laughed, and two kids called out. "Like on airplanes?"

Joy laughed softly. "Oh no, these pilots don't dress or work like airplane pilots, but they are among the best mariners—well, boat captains. Maybe later your teacher can share a video in class about how they do their jobs. Have any of you seen the exhibit of the pilot boat just down the street from your school?" A few kids nodded and some started talking loudly. Celia felt her phone buzz. glanced at it, and put it back in her bag. Kate had texted, *Doing okay?* She smirked. *Well, Kate can wonder.*

The kids' attention span was used up, and the teacher thanked the guide and signaled to the kids to clap five times, which they seemed happy to do, even if they couldn't keep their hands off each other in between claps.

The teacher reminded them what would happen next: groups would take turns having their snack and beginning the climb of the 164 steps in the column. She handed each adult a bundled bag of balsa gliders, quietly instructing them to hold the gliders until they reached the top. Celia was grateful to have only five kids in her group.

As they walked to a bench looking down over town and the river, Addie snuggled into her side again and grabbed her arm. "I'm so happy you are here." She nuzzled closer. "I love Kate and Dad, and of course Mom and my stepdad. But you are cooler. Way cooler." Addie grinned at her and pulled her near the bench, before dropping her arm to squeeze in next to her three friends. *Cool? Never had she been referred to as cool. She couldn't wait to tell Kate.*

The kid named David stood to one side of the bench, quietly eating a granola bar. Celia identified more with him than the chattering pod of kids on the bench. "Hey, David," she forced herself to say, moving closer to him. "What do you think of all this?" She pointed to the column and then back to the ocean and river.

"Good," David said, staring at the ground.

"Have you been here before?" Celia asked.

"No." David avoided eye contact. "My parents . . . work a lot. And Grandma doesn't drive." He shifted his feet and took another bite. Then he glanced at her. "But I've seen it from far away. You know, from below." He pulled a water bottle from his backpack.

"Well, it's nice you are here," Celia said simply.

He looked back at her and smiled shyly.

"David, take a deep breath and tell me what you smell?"

David took a big breath, let it out, and then shrugged. "I smell trees, like a bunch of Christmas trees. And that beach smell."

Celia nodded and smiled at him. "I love that smell."

David smiled.

The kids were beyond excitement when it was finally time for her group to climb the stairs. As they stomped up the spiral stairs, Celia was glad none seemed to be claustrophobic.

Isabelle, stopped. "How high are we going?" Her shoulders slumped and she set her backpack on a stair.

"The sign said the column is 125 feet and 164 stairs." Celia was glad to pause and catch her breath, thinking she should feel in better shape than she did. Addie and the other kids were approaching the top. "Just a bit more. Can you make it?"

Isabelle nodded, put her pack back on, and grabbed the handrail. She took another breath and climbed. Finally, they joined the others on the observatory deck, just as another group headed down.

Celia looked around, eager to walk the circle of the deck and admire the 360-degree view. She was surprised she had forgotten how stunning it all was from the top. The children were eager to receive their gliders.

"Okay, everyone," Addie yelled as they held their planes. "Wait!"

Celia had no idea Addie was such a leader, and hoped she wasn't also a bully.

"I've done this before," Addie continued, "and I don't want you to crash your plane."

The kids looked at her, their eyes wide. Addie gave them tips about how to launch the planes out further from the tower to better catch a breeze.

Celia was relieved by Addie's leadership. She could learn from her, she guessed. Two of the kids threw their glider quickly, and one took a nosedive to the grass. Addie hesitated, carefully watching the wind direction and threw hers into an upward arc, yelling gleefully as it circled its way down. David finally launched his plane, and watched it dive, nose down before catching a breeze and circling part way around the platform. He smiled broadly.

Celia pointed at his plane. "Wow, look at that," she said quietly.

"I know," he said, his smile still wide.

The four other kids jogged around the deck, trying to spot their planes. Celia wondered if she should tell them to quiet down or not circle the deck but let them be. She strained her neck to look upriver, wishing she could see past the furthest bend. Imagining a time long ago when folks would choose water travel over the then more difficult travel by land.

"Um, Mrs. Addie's friend?" David asked.

"Yes, David?"

"Where does the bridge go?" He pointed to the Megler Bridge as it spanned the width of the Columbia River.

"It goes across the river to a whole other state, Washington. That big river, the Columbia River, separates our Oregon from Washington." Celia pointed further to the left of the end of the bridge. "And out there is a place called the Long Beach Peninsula, with two cool light houses and a museum about Lewis and Clark." She hesitated. "Maybe some time you can drive across with your family?"

He smiled and nodded. *This is fun.*

"Celia, our teacher is signaling below," Addie called.

Celia nodded, again glad to have someone keep them on track. Even if she was only nine years old.

As they reached the bottom of the column the teacher shepherded the last two groups to the bus to join those already boarded. Sitting in the bus, Celia watched the park employee pick up gliders still littering the grass at the base of the column, as if souvenirs from imaginary pilot training. She wondered what happened to all the other gliders, the ones that caught the breeze and circled off into nearby trees and neighborhood.

The kids chattered with each other about how their flights went. One boy was crying, and an adult was trying to comfort him. Finally, the driver reminded the kids to stay in their seats, and the bus bumped along, circling the swath of green around the column, past the gift shop, and groaning its way downhill to school.

Celia felt a strange calming sense of joy. None of these kids were probably thinking about what big thing they were going to do in their life, or about the world ending or the doom of womanhood and reproductive rights. She knew one couldn't always put their head in the sand but realized sometimes it was okay. At least in this moment, and maybe during some of the moments she had left. She let out a long breath, closed her eyes, and smiled.

"Thank you, Addie," she said softly.

# Chapter 27
## Celia
### April 13, 2025

"HI, GRANDMA." CELIA'S grandmother peeked through her front door and gave Celia a gentle hug.

"Come in. Is everything okay? You didn't sound like yourself on the phone?" Her grandmother frowned and her face looked tired and old.

"Yes, Grandma." Celia was tempted to ask her not to mention this visit to her mom but knew saying that would be like sending off a SOS flare. "I promise." She forced herself to sound reassuring. "But to be honest, my winter was a lot." Putting it mildly, she knew. She pulled off her boots and set them to the side of the door on the outside porch.

Her grandmother patted her hand before motioning her into the house. Once inside, Celia inhaled that old people smell, unsure whether it was comforting or not. A mix of synthetic scented detergent and persisting stale smells from last night's dinner. She knew deep down her grandparents had always been present for her, even if she saw them infrequently these last few years.

"I'm sorry you can't stay for dinner, but are you hungry?"

Celia shook her head.

"Then how about coffee, there's still some left from this morning. Or tea. Or a soft drink? I have the ginger ale your grandad drinks."

Her grandma was dressed in corduroy stretch pants and flowered blouse and rested her hand on a nearby table. She examined Celia from head to toe. She looked older, her body frailer and thinner than the last time Celia had seen her the previous summer. She must be at least eighty, Celia thought, embarrassed not to know her birth year.

"A cup of coffee is fine. Black. Thank you." She felt awkward and her arms hung helplessly to her side. "But I'm fine without it too. Here let me help."

"Nonsense." Her grandmother gently pushed back her hand and prodded her toward the couch in the living room. "I'm sure you had a long drive. I'll be right back." She waved her off.

Instead of sitting, Celia wandered to the far wall, stark white except for a dozen photos. Her grandparents at their church wedding, looking so young. Her mother smiling as a kid, both upper front teeth missing. Her uncle dressed in a baseball uniform, holding a mitt. Celia at her high school graduation. The photos were decades old.

"So," her grandmother said as she returned, "here we are." She set two cups of coffee on coasters on the dark wood table between the plaid couch and a soft chair. They lived in a quiet neighborhood not far from her mom, and Celia couldn't hear any sounds from outside.

Looking expectantly, her grandmother lowered herself down into the chair as Celia sat on the couch and pulled her hands tightly together in her lap.

Celia wasn't sure how to begin the conversation. She picked up the cup by its handle and blew on the coffee out of habit, knowing it would be lukewarm at best. "Thank you." She hesitated, fidgeting to get comfortable. She loved her grandma, confiding in her when she had been a girl and regularly going to her house after school. Yet, mid-way through high school she had been unable to separate her frustration with her mom with her feelings toward her grandmother and distanced herself from sharing her heart.

"I missed not seeing you at Christmas," Grandma began. "Did you celebrate it with friends?" The wrinkles on her forehead deepened.

"Yes, I did. It was fine," Celia said, partly true. She took a deep breath and set the coffee down. "I have a question for you. And it'll probably seem silly or maybe you don't know anything about it."

Her grandmother raised her eyebrows and looked sideways at her. Celia recognized the look from her childhood. She brought her hands together, massaging her fingers as she told her about Ruth connecting her with Alice.

Her grandmother's eyes widened, and she looked upset. Finally, a relaxed expression spread from her wrinkled forehead to her narrow lipstick-free lips. "My friend Ruth in Astoria? And old Alice? You mean, nothing bad is going on with you?" She let out a breath, making a whistling noise as the air left her mouth. "I was worried when I heard from your mother how you were done fishing, and she was certain something awful was going on. She's been quite worried, but you know." She hesitated. "She doesn't want to nag you. With her worries. She knows you don't like it when she nags."

Celia caught her breath. She had no idea her mom was any more worried than normal about her. More surprising to her was learning of her not wanting to be a nag. She set that bit away to unravel later. "Yes, I met with Alice, in Salem. Your friend? At least once a long time ago?"

Grandma gave her a questioning look.

"She told me about Emma. Long ago Emma. But I needed to learn more. About what was true, and I don't think she really knows? Or if she once knew she has forgotten."

Her grandmother gasped. Then she frowned and shook her head. "Emma? Our Emma? Celia, my dear, how in the world are you talking about such a long-ago story? And why? Why in the world would this matter to you?" She glanced toward her husband's bedroom. She put her coffee cup on the side table and took a deep breath. "Well, first, you should know that Alice always loved to tell a good story. I haven't thought of her in years. Even back then she stretched the truth." She muttered something Celia couldn't hear. Celia wondered if something happened to break their friendship. "But Emma? Why in heaven's sake would Alice bring this up to you?" Her expression darkened.

Celia was confused by her grandmother's sudden anger. She only wanted answers, not to upset her. "No, no, don't be upset. It's not like you think."

She told her about learning about the bag factory strike and her curiosity. About how the librarian had recently found Emma's obituary.

Her grandma looked at her befuddled.

"Grandma," Celia could no longer contain her tears. "I guess I just wanted to know more about family. You know, our stories—especially someone who did something. I only wanted to know for sure. To know more. I mean . . ."

She hadn't cried in front of her grandma since she was a little girl. She didn't even understand why she was so weirdly invested in a story from long ago. She wiped her face with her sleeve and returned her hands to her lap, trying to appear calm.

"Why didn't we ever talk about family?" She didn't know what else to say. "Here, read this."

Celia pulled a printout from her pocket and unfolded it. She handed it across the coffee table to her grandmother.

Her grandmother set the printout on her lap and picked up her glasses from the table. She looked at Celia as she pushed them up her nose and then stared at the paper for what seemed a long time. She set her glasses back on the table and wiped her eyes.

"Can you read it aloud to me?" She handed the paper back to Celia. Then she closed her eyes and rested back on the chair.

Celia swallowed and nodded.

"June 15, 1930. Mrs. Emma Brown passed away at her home in Camas, Washington after a brief illness. Private services were held at Camas First Christian Church followed by cremation. Mrs. Brown was employed as a young woman by the Camas Bag Factory. She volunteered with the Camas Women's Club and Portland Women's Union. Mrs. Brown is survived by her husband (Andrew), sisters (Martha, Helen and Mary), a brother (Jonathan), and three nieces and nephews. She was preceded in death by three unborn infants, her parents, and a brother (William)."

Her grandma sat for a while, staring into space. Then she straightened and began to push herself to her feet but fell back into the chair. She took a deep breath and pushed down on the chair arms to hoist her body up.

She went to the couch and eased herself down next to Celia, using the armrest to steady her. She grabbed Celia's clasped fists and held on tight with her thin veiny claw-like hands.

Celia wondered if she would live long enough to have hands like that one day.

She petted Celia's hands. "What is it, Celia. Dear?"

Celia was embarrassed and felt childish. She blinked back her tears. "It's just that . . . It's just that I thought if someone else I was related to, a woman, had done something amazing. Like, for a woman, I mean. That maybe it would be a sign. Telling me there might be something out there, special, for me. And now, to try to learn about Emma but find nobody in our family seems to know or care?" *This was not the Celia she wanted to embody.*

She was at least thirty pounds heavier and six inches taller than her grandma yet felt oddly calmed by this wrinkled old woman who continued to pet her hand, clucking, "Oh Celia, Celia. My dear. It's all okay."

Celia sobbed, leaning into to her, trying to focus on stabilizing her breath. In and out. In and out. She could hear the clock ticking on the wall, and then a car as it drove by outside. She wondered if her grandfather was sleeping. Finally, her grandma let go of her hand and pushed back further into the couch. She sighed and looked as if she was debating what to say. "Emma would have been your great-great aunt."

Celia's eyes widened and she caught her breath. "What?"

"Emma was five years younger than your great-great-grandmother, or my grandmother, Martha," Grandma continued, looking across the room. "Times were different. Back then." She hesitated, confirming to Celia this was not often repeated family lore. "Yes, as I understand it, Emma did work at the mill's bag factory. But it sounds like you know that part of the story. It was a different time, and she felt she needed to help the family, I think especially after her brother joined the armed forces." She tried to sit up straighter but slid back into the cushions. "He died in the war."

"Yes. I do know some of this. I mean, about the bag factory at the mill, and the strike. But nobody even celebrates that, or anything she may have done after. Why have I never heard about her? Or any of this? Why am I left so in the dark about my own family?" Celia threw up her hands. She concentrated on pushing her tears back. It was silly to feel emotionally tied to this story, as if figuring out the puzzle would heal her hidden wounds from the accident and worries about what she might do next.

"Celia, Celia." Her grandmother pushed back Celia's hair. "Sometimes family stories get disrupted or lost. And I'm sorry if I didn't do better in sharing what I knew. It's just . . ." She touched the tip of Celia's nose. "Emma was unusual and a strong woman. Maybe a bit like you?" She placed her hands gently on either side of Celia's face. "She never had children and maybe she didn't get to do everything she hoped to, but maybe she did get to do some of what she wanted? Maybe she did find love." She took a deep breath, and Celia could tell she was trying to collect herself. "Martha's husband was worried about Emma. Or I suppose, it was more about Emma's husband's involvement with the union. Martha and her husband felt like he was some kind of rabble rouser and didn't want their family connected with that. I guess Martha's husband was a lumber trader or something like that."

Celia was grateful to learn more but also felt guilty upsetting her grandma. She gently nestled into her grandma's shoulder, feeling protected for a moment as she had as a young girl. Only then did she imagine the sadness hidden deep inside her grandma.

"My grandmother Martha, Emma's sister, never recovered from her guilt. And I think she blamed herself for not being there for her sister. I don't know most of the details other than her sadness and then never wanting to speak about those early years. Maybe she always thought she had time to recover their relationship but Emma ended up dying young." Grandma looked out across the room, as if through the opposite wall. "Their mother, I mean Martha and Emma's mother, died early. Martha had already married my grandfather who made a good living, and they eventually moved from Vancouver to Portland to finish raising their family. But I never remember her speaking about Emma. After my grandmother Martha died, my mother shared tiny bits of story. She always thought their problems were because of regrets her mother Martha had after Emma died. But even my mother didn't know much. She was very young when Emma died and only her older sister Nina had any real memories of this aunt of theirs." Her grandmother touched her arm and looked into Celia's eyes. "It seems every family has secrets, and some carry regrets to the grave."

Celia picked up her cold cup of coffee and took a sip as if it might break the heavy cloud hanging over the room. Out of the corner of her eye she saw her grandmother first dab at her nose with a tissue, before blowing it with more force as she straightened up on the couch again.

"Celia," her grandmother said in a stern voice. "I may not understand what you are going through, but you need to remember a few things. It is hard to be a woman. Then. Now. Maybe always, even though each generation tries to make it better."

She took Celia's hand again and peered deep into her eyes. Her gentle expression hardened.

"But speaking of regrets. I don't think you give your own mother enough credit."

Celia stared at her surprised.

"Yes, your mother."

Celia wasn't prepared to be lectured, and she squirmed in the couch cushions.

"I know you think your mother was hard on you. At least that's what she thinks you think." Her grandmother rolled her eyes. "I promised myself I'd never get in the middle and here I am." She sighed. "I don't know why you two can't simply talk. She's afraid to bring it up but she's so proud of you. She may not always know how to express it." She sounded exacerbated and threw her hands up.

Celia could only stare at her.

Her grandmother shook her finger at her. "You remember what she has had, and just maybe there's a few things she never told you."

"Like what?" Celia squeaked out.

"Your mother cared so much about raising you the best she could. Better than she thought we raised her, I'm sure. Even though we thought we had reared her the best we could. She knew you were smart. Talented. Strong. All those things you quest to be. She didn't want to push you, but she didn't want you to end up like your father either."

Celia was stunned. Her grandmother had never mentioned her father to her. It had been as if her mother had gotten pregnant from an anonymous donor, although Celia knew they had at first been a couple of some sort.

"Your mother at first thought he could be a good enough man to be a dad to you. It lasted not quite a year. But he was often mean and couldn't hold down a job, and, well . . . the stress of a family broke him further. They were so young and not ready for the responsibilities of being a family. Your mother would never want you to know this, his frustrations verged on violence. At least back then. More than anything your mother wanted to protect you."

Celia sat numb with shock.

"I shouldn't have told you all this. It is not my place. But I can't have you on this strange pursuit of finding meaning or importance when all you need to do is look at what your mother has done." Her grandmother dropped Celia's hand and pushed both hands on the couch as she attempted to stand.

Celia supported her as she made her way to her feet. She felt as if all the air had been taken out of her lungs, and she couldn't think straight. Nor had she learned what she hoped she might, but at the same time, much more.

Her grandma stood across from her and wiped her eyes with her tissue. Then she walked across the room and took an item down from a shelf. "Here. I'd like you to have this." She placed a small wooden steamboat into Celia's outstretched hand. "It had been my mother's, and I think it should be yours now. I don't know where it came from, but I remember her saying Emma and Martha loved to watch steamboats on the river when they were young."

Celia circled her hand around the small roughly carved boat she vaguely remembered noticing before. She could just make out a paddlewheel, and her eyes filled with tears. "Oh Grandma. Yes. Thank you."

Her grandmother picked up her coffee cup and smiled gently at Celia. "And perhaps you should pop in and say hello to your grandfather." She hesitated. "You understand he won't be with us forever. I'd hate for you not to get to see him. You know, another time."

"Yes, Grandma. Of course," she answered meekly.

"Oh, and Celia," her grandmother said. "One more thing. Do give your mother a chance. She might surprise you. Lord knows, you don't want any regrets whenever that time comes."

Celia peered up at her grandmother and nodded, forcing a smile through her tears.

"Give me a minute first," her grandmother said before shuffling toward the bedroom.

Celia sat back in the couch and closed her eyes. She tried to take in all she had heard. How many family stories were lost because people were afraid to talk about them? She thought about the years that had passed without knowing much, not just about Emma, but about her grandmother and her own mother.

"Celia?" Her grandmother peeked out from the bedroom. "He would love to see you."

Celia stood and followed her grandmother to visit with her grandfather and begin mending scars of her family's past.

# Chapter 28
## Emma
### May 2, 1925

"GOODBYE, EMMA," ANDREW said after kissing her goodbye. "I will see you upon your return day after tomorrow at the steamboat landing. I love you, my darling. Travel safely." He stole a final look before closing their front door as he headed to his morning shift as lead millwright.

Andrew continued to seek avenues to unionize the mill. Every year he felt they were getting closer, although Emma could not believe how long it seemed to take. She knew it wasn't only about pay but that agreements would better even the playing field between workers and management. It would improve the lives of workers and their families. Andrew's name had even been inscribed onto Camas's Pillar of Shame on Columbia Street outside the mill as one of several who defied management. Or, as some would say, rebelled against the company that took care of the community. Mother would have been embarrassed to know her son-in-law might be forever remembered on the same pillar that once listed the names of men who refused to go to war. But not Emma.

Emma was grateful Elizabeth helped her arrange a ride to catch the Harkin Line steamboat in Washougal for her trip to Portland. She was pleased to have the skies clear with both ice cream cone topped Mount Saint Helens and craggier Mount Hood visible. Although nervous the first time, she loved occasional invites to assist with events at the Portland Women's Union. She knew if she and Andrew lived in Portland, she would try more actively to support the night school and help at the women's hotel. But she had to be satisfied with this bit of volunteer work. Besides, she was busy as she led other volunteers with their newly built Camas Public Library. While she still supported Andrew as he and others worked so far unsuccessfully to organize workers at the mill, she had known she needed to find something that was just hers.

"Hello, Emma," Elizabeth called out as the car picked her up near her father's store.

Emma carried a small satchel for the two nights away and pushed her fedora firmly onto her head before climbing into the back seat of the Ford sedan. "Thank you so much, Mr. Miller, for the ride into town." She reached over the front seat to clasp Elizabeth's outstretched hand.

"Of course, Emma. It is important work you are doing. Besides, both Elizabeth and I have appointments in Washougal today, so it works out grandly. Tell us, what can you expect to be doing during your time in Portland?" He kept his eye on the road, but she could see his smile in the rearview mirror.

Emma rested her bag on the seat next to her. She still was not used to how quickly one could travel to places she rarely even visited before. "I'm not certain, honestly. But the Women's Union is hosting an event tomorrow evening that they hope will gain supporters and donors for both the women's hotel and school." She sighed and clasped her hands together, wishing she might help directly with the night school. "I am very appreciative of the overnight accommodations they provide for me."

Elizabeth sighed. "Oh, Emma. I am so proud of you. Sometimes I think I should have done more."

"Now, now, Lizzie." Elizabeth's father glanced at her. "Look at those fine children you are raising. It takes well educated and thoughtful children to make our country great, you know."

Elizabeth frowned, her eyes darting back to Emma.

"There will be more time for further involvements as they get older, my darling," he added.

The few miles sped by quickly in Mr. Miller's new automobile.

"Thank you both again." Emma opened the door, gathered her skirt, and stepped carefully out of the car. "Andrew will be arranging my pickup."

Elizabeth blew her a kiss as she reached across the seat to grab her satchel.

She walked toward the dock, knowing she had several minutes before it was time to board the steamship. As she neared the Columbia River, white fibers released by nearby cottonwood trees onto the ground reminded her of her first visit at the river with Andrew. She walked by the hotel and grocery store, both echoing sounds of a bustling community. So many things her mother had missed. She was grateful her siblings had been able to continue their schooling, and that John seemed happy with his work at the mill. He and Andrew had become close brothers as well as coworkers. Although she knew Father would never remarry, he seemed content these days with friends and staying on top of local news. He adored spending much of his free time with books from the library; it had added a new dimension to his life. She was grateful they could share that love in the small amount of time they got together, even if she knew he was sad to infrequently hear from Martha and her family, now in Portland.

The whistle from the steamboat pulled her from her thoughts, and she picked up her pace to the dock. Yes, the times had certainly changed. She walked excitedly into her day.

# Chapter 28
## Celia
### May 2, 2025

CELIA INHALED THE smell of late spring. Unlike Portland where the pungency of freshly cut grass mix with budding cottonwood resin, the coast lent an earthier tang. It was as if warming salt air was reawakening seaweed and kelp. Whatever it was, Celia loved its refreshing welcome. As much as she walked the Riverwalk, somedays exploring the beach south of town, she did not miss fishing. Yes, these five months later, she knew she had made the right decision.

Now as she walked around the block twice to kill ten minutes, she hoped to extricate her nervous energy. Paul had given her a pep talk the evening before—she hadn't told anyone else about the job interview. She was certain she would not have applied if she hadn't recognized the woman's name as the point of contact.

"I haven't interviewed in years," she told Paul over dinner. "And even that was not this kind of gig, trust me." She laughed as she remembered Kate's desperate table waiting ad.

"Take a deep breath. Remember how capable you are."

Celia made a face.

"Really." Paul dropped his chin and stared at her for full attention, and then gently put his two hands on either side of her face and nodded her head up and down.

Celia laughed. She loved how they had become honest yet heartfelt supporters of each other.

But now her heart was beating faster than she thought healthy. Outside the building's front door, she stopped and reached into her bag and held the wooden steamboat tightly in her fist. She blew on it, as if to extract good to carry forward into the building with her. The possession felt like a good luck charm. She returned it to the bag and opened the front door, taking one final deep breath as she stepped into Astoria City Hall.

"Celia Roberts for an interview," she told the middle-aged woman who moved a stack of papers across her desk before looking up at Celia.

"Yes, they'll be right here. You can have a seat." The woman nodded toward chairs across the room, her hands grasping a stack of paper.

Celia sat in one of the four chairs across from the window, next to the restrooms and drinking fountain. She glanced at the bare walls. Ugh. How could anyone spend all day inside this building she wondered, worried she wasn't cut out for any of it.

"You'll do great," Paul's voice repeated in her ear. "Just be yourself." Although she and Paul had spent many nights together, they too decided to spend time focusing on their friendship. She knew they both felt something grander growing between them, creating euphoria laced with dabs of fear.

A familiar-looking woman entered the lobby and hesitated. "Celia?"

Celia nodded and the woman smiled and delivered a firmly gripped shake. "I'm Rita Johnson, Park Director. Just call me Rita if you wish."

Celia nodded again, feeling shy as she followed her into a small conference room down the hall but wanting to tell her how she'd seen her before. She was relieved the room had a small window. She had taken her coat off in the waiting area and lay it in her lap, and her new khakis felt foreign and stiff. She pulled at the collar of her sweater to try to feel less disheveled. The woman was casually dressed in gray cords and a light blue collared shirt, and Celia breathed a sigh of relief.

"I'm glad you were able to make this time, thanks for being flexible," Rita said.

Celia had originally had an earlier interview date booked, but there had been a city emergency. She was glad to have seen Rita at the council meeting, giving her some sense of the kind of person to expect. She was certain she wouldn't have had the nerve to apply otherwise.

"Uh, yes. Thank you for the interview." She felt silly and yet hadn't even begun to answer questions.

"Of course. I was pleased to receive your application." Rita looked steadily at Celia with a hint of a smile. "I mean, to be honest, I'm happy to receive applications these days. I mean especially from someone used to hard work." The smile disappeared and she shook her head. "You don't need to be nervous, just take a breath. And it's not like it sounds. So, I've reviewed your application, and your answers to the questions, and it was helpful to learn a bit about your skill sets."

She fingered Celia's printed application and turned to its final page. "How do you know John Lewis?"

She had listed Dr. Lewis as a reference, only after Paul had helped her brainstorm possibilities. "Uh, he's a friend, well he was a teacher at Clatsop. Clatsop Community College. He was a favorite teacher of a class I liked a lot, and I got involved in some special projects. Back then. But it was a number of years ago." She clasped her sweaty hands in her lap.

Rita asked her about her studies at college before moving on to how she felt about working outside, her comfort with heavy lifting, taking on tasks like mowing grass or hauling trash. Rita explained they currently had a small staff, "small but mighty. It's not ideal but it seems everyone is being asked to do a bit more and sometimes things beyond the job description."

Celia stifled a laugh.

Rita raised her eyebrows and put her pen on the table.

"I'm sorry. First, I'm very nervous," Celia admitted.

Rita smiled.

"The thing is, being cold and lifting heavy things? Using equipment like mowers? Those are some of my top skills to be perfectly honest." Celia shrugged.

"I see. Well, good. Again, no need to be nervous." Rita looked at the door, and then back to Celia. "You may not believe it, but there are worse people to interview with than me." She raised her eyebrows and turned to another page of the application. "Can you tell me a bit about the carpenter's apprentice work you listed?" She closed the application and looked up at Celia expectantly.

Celia could not hide her surprise. It had seemed a stretch to list that experience. She ignored telling the part that she had made the decision to apply to the program then mostly to upset her mom and push back on college.

"Uh, yeah. That was in Portland. Well, I guess you can see that. And I think it was twelve weeks long? I had been good at math in high school, and my mom thought I should be an engineer." Truthfully, her mom had rambled on and on about how there were good jobs for women in engineering; about how she could stand out and make a good living. Back then Celia had argued with her mom, telling her just because she was good at something didn't mean she wanted to spend her life doing it. It was only since talking with her grandmother that she better understood why her mom had acted the way she did. "I just wanted to do something different, and someone at my high school lined it up. When I finished the apprenticeship, I had already decided to move here. Well, the rest is history. I mean, then I took classes here and eventually got into fishing." The cannery and café work seemed incidental to mention, even though she had listed them on the application.

"Thanks for sharing." Rita sat back in her chair and pushed the closed folder away from her. "The thing is, you don't quite have all the qualifications for this job, at least not how it is written."

Celia let out a sigh and nodded. *She knew it. Now what?*

"But, that doesn't mean everything. I just want you to know we have a couple of other candidates to interview for this coordinator position. But we've done it before with motivated people who can learn on the job, sometimes even acquiring needed credentials later, if you're open to that. So, just keep all that in mind." Rita brought her hands together and set them on top of the folder. "Do you have any questions?"

Paul had advised her to make sure she had some, but her brain was empty, and she hadn't written any to bring. "Uh, no thank you. I mean, not at this time?" She hesitated, not knowing if this would be inappropriate. "I would love to work for you. I mean, learn from you."

"Well, thank you, Celia," Rita added. "Also, to be clear, there is other work, like I alluded to. Even things like occasionally pitching in to help with some of the kid educational programs. I'm not sure how you feel about that."

The image of the woman at the column flashed back to Celia. "That would be fine." She meant it too, even if she had to ask Addie for tips.

Rita shared a few more details about the position, before asking Celia if she had any questions about the benefits package.

"Benefits?" Celia was embarrassed to admit how at her age she had never had a job that came with benefits.

"Oh, you know, healthcare and sick leave, vacation. Normal stuff like that. Some don't kick in until after a probation period."

Celia shook her head.

"Any details about that will be shared later. I mean, if we offer the job." Rita smiled, and Celia felt they shared a secret. Rita looked at her watch. "Oh my, I lost track of the time. Thank you for coming in and for applying. You should hear something early next week."

Rita stood and grabbed her folder. Celia nodded, picked up her coat and bag, and followed her out of the room.

After saying goodbye and thanking Rita, Celia opened the front door. A gentle spring shower wetted her face. She would choose to work for that woman without any so-called benefits, although she wondered what her mom might say if she got the job. A real job. It bothered her less than it would have a few months ago that her mom's approval was also on her mind. Yes, her grandmother's voice echoed in her ears. Her reminders about what it meant to be a strong woman. About living life without regrets. She smiled. Despite all she worried about in the world. In spite of her past. One step at a time.

She slowed to peek at her phone inside her bag and pulled out the steamboat, before picking up her pace to meet Paul at the cafe. She held the boat in her hand, rubbing her fingers along its paddlewheel. She was eager to share it with her mother. Their weekly phone calls had slowly changed, and recently Celia looked forward to them. Maybe she would ask Paul to meet her when she arrived for her visit in Astoria that weekend.

As she neared the river, she looked out toward the ocean. She stopped before turning to the cafe and looked eastward, promising herself one day she would follow the river all the way past that mill where her relative once worked.

"Thank you, Emma," she whispered, before waving to Paul as he waited nearby on a bench in the mist.

# Acknowledgements

I feel grateful as I publish this sixth book placed in the Pacific Northwest. Thanks to family who have long shared the power of story and instilled the gift of writing. I thank Bedazzled Ink Publishing for helping to get my stories out, and especially to Casey for her patience with me. Beta and development readers have been critical to me on this writing journey. Thank you to my writing group, Shelly Parini, Leigh Manning, Michael Wood, and Maura Doherty. Too, I know this work would not be what it is without reviews by Gregg Townsley, Karen Lennon, and Gorgon Gregory.

It was serendipitous to come across Bradley Richardson's thesis (*The Forgotten Front: Gender, Labor, and Politics in Camas, Washington, and the Northwest Paper Industry, 1913-1918*) which inspired me to create Emma's character. I thank Bradley and Jeffrey Hunt for helping me better understand Camas history. Huge thanks to Ron Hawkins for sharing mill history and reviewing parts of an early draft. Thank you to my friends Marcus Widenor for reviewing my final draft for accuracy and authenticity about all things Northwest union and labor, Kay Demlow for authentic fashion advice, Michael Selvagio regarding union negotiations, Sandy Carter for stories from the Crown Willamette Pulp and Paper Mill, and Rick Quashnick for crab fishing insights.

Thank you to my daughters for their support and offering windows into what it is to be a "thirty-something" woman in today's world. Finally, to Russell, for being my constant source of creative support on this writing and life journey

Dede Montgomery is the author of From *First Breath to Last: A Story About Love, Womanhood and Aging*, *Humanity's Grace*, *Then, Now and In-Between: Place, Memories, and Loss in Oregon*, *Beyond the Ripples*, and *My Music Man*. She is a thoughtful and introspective author and blogger whose work blends personal narrative, historical reflection, and social awareness. Dede often writes with a deep connection to place, particularly the Pacific Northwest. She lives near Portland, Oregon.

Learn more at https://dedemontgomery.com